"Toss your gun down real slow," Lily said.

Nate was faster, but in the struggle he soon had his arms wrapped around her as he fought to keep her from shooting. In moments he'd taken the gun away.

The next thing his brain registered was that he was holding her near-naked body pressed against him. She was soft, warm and feminine.

"Sheriff?" The question came out as a breathless discovery. "Did you follow me?"

"Had to see what you were up to."

"And what business is that of yours?"

"It's my business if you're in trouble—or if you're not safe."

"It's a hot night, and I came to swim. And if you've seen enough, I intend to do just that."

The bushes rustled as she headed to the stream. His imagination went wild.

Lily Divine naked in the moonlight.

Nate realized he still held her Colt in his hand. Against his better judgment he followed the path she'd taken

A peacemaker, a romantic, an idealist and a discouraged perfectionist are the words that **Cheryl** uses to describe herself. The author of both historical and contemporary novels says she's been told that she is painfully honest.

Cheryl admits to being an avid collector who collects everything from teapots, cups and saucers and pitchers, to Depression glass, dolls and tin advertising signs. She and her husband love to browse antiques and collectibles shops.

She says that knowing her stories bring hope and pleasure to readers is one of the best parts of being a writer. The other wonderful part is being able to set her own schedule and work around her family and church. Working in her jammies ain't half bad, either!

Cheryl loves to hear from readers. You can write her at P.O. Box 24732, Omaha, NE 68124, or e-mail CherylStJohn@aol.com.

THE BOUNTY HUNTER
CHERYL ST. JOHN

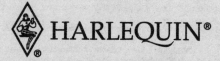

HARLEQUIN®

TORONTO • NEW YORK • LONDON
AMSTERDAM • PARIS • SYDNEY • HAMBURG
STOCKHOLM • ATHENS • TOKYO • MILAN • MADRID
PRAGUE • WARSAW • BUDAPEST • AUCKLAND

Special thanks and acknowledgment are given
to Cheryl St.John for her contribution
to the MONTANA MAVERICKS series.

ISBN 0-373-81121-7

THE BOUNTY HUNTER

CHAPTER ONE

Montana, Spring 1890

"*'ONWARD CHRISTIAN SOLDIERS, marching as to war! With the cross of Je-e-sus going on before'!*"

"It's the Bible thumpers again." Annoyance tapped a cadence along Lily Divine's nerve endings and raised her temperature a degree. She set aside the freshly washed and dried glasses she'd been stacking behind the bar and stepped around Old Jess to plant herself in the open doorway of her half-filled saloon. The light from the interior spilled out and, aided by the hissing gas lamps on the boardwalk, lit half a dozen women wearing prim dresses and bonnets. Standing in the street, they held signs lettered in charcoal on brown paper.

The Dens of Vice are Stealing from Us, one sign read. Another spelled out, Wicked Women Repent.

"Move along!" she called. "There's nothing illegal going on here."

"*'Christ the Royal Master, leads against the foe'!*" they sang at the tops of their voices with tambourine accompaniment. "*'Forward into ba-at-tle, see His banners go'!*"

At the very front of the gathering was Meriel Reed,

wife of Thunder Canyon's livery owner and the leader of the newly formed Women's Temperance Prayer League. Lily narrowed her eyes at Wade's wife of one and a half years. Tall and slender, with every mousy-brown hair in place, Meriel seemed to have honed in on Lily as the personified harbinger of evil and used every opportunity to get under her skin.

These women had taken to praying and singing in front of the town's three saloons in hopes of discouraging customers. At first their unwelcome visits had been only on Friday and Saturday nights, but lately their zeal had extended to the weeknights, as well. So far, their behavior had been merely a nuisance, but Lily resented their holier-than-thou attitudes—and their assumption that something wicked was going on in her establishment.

The song wound down, and Lily got a word in before they caught their second self-righteous wind. "There's no law against selling whiskey and playing cards," she called. "You're wasting your breath here."

"There are moral laws," Beatrice Gibbs returned. "God's laws." As the mayor's wife, Beatrice was a visible and vocal presence in this new protest. She was as buxom and sturdy as Meriel was thin.

"Nothing immoral goes on in the Shady Lady," Lily assured her, with a sweep of her arm. "Come in and see for yourself."

As a whole, the women sucked in a shocked breath and drew back as though Lily had suggested they step into the flames of hell and dance a jig with the devil. Blythe Shaw, the mercantile owner's new wife, bristled and spoke up. "No self-respecting Christian woman would set foot within the walls of that den of wickedness. And no one believes you aren't dispensing more than whiskey in those rooms next door. We're not fools."

Disgusted, Lily turned back inside and closed the interior doors, which were normally open on warm May Montana evenings such as this. She called to Isaac Worthy, "Play that piano louder! We have competition outside."

Isaac, with hair to his shoulders from the sides of his head and none at all on top, stepped up the tempo and volume of "Buffalo Gals."

Granted, the connecting house had been a bordello until seven years ago, but when Lily had inherited the house from her friend, Madame Antoinette Powell, she'd added on the dance hall and given the last two remaining working girls different jobs.

"It's them again?" Mollie asked. Mollie was an Omaha-Ponca Indian who had worked for Antoinette.

"Seems we're the only ones who believe there's no sinning going on here," Lily told her.

"What about all the men who drink and play cards here of a night?" Mollie asked. "They can make it plain that this isn't where they come for a poke."

There had been many a misunderstanding when newcomers expecting to take their ease with one of Lily's girls had been told to look elsewhere. After seven years, the regulars knew they could buy good whiskey, play a fair hand of cards, and buy a dance with a pretty lady. But anyone treating a female disrespectfully was promptly ushered out.

Lily smiled. "And so they tell their wives the same about us as they do about the Three Moon Palace and the Big Nugget—that there's no whoring going on?"

"I suppose you're right," Mollie conceded. "What's a wife to believe?"

"I bet some of those women are nice ladies," Lily said affably.

Molly's black eyes took on a sparkle. "I'm sure they are. We'd probably be their best friends if we closed the place down and married town big shots. They'd be gracious and have us over for tea."

They leaned in close for a shared chuckle at the image.

"Well, I'm not closing the place down." Lily's dance hall was a flourishing enterprise. Early on she'd learned that there was plenty of money to be made from the miners.

Ten years ago she'd begun a laundry business, tucking away her earnings while living under the protection her friend offered. Upon Antoinette's death and Lily's inheritance of the bordello, she'd used part of her savings to build and appoint the saloon.

She had ordered the gigantic curving cherrywood bar all the way from Pennsylvania. The huge expanse of mirror behind it had cost fifteen hundred dollars. She was especially proud of that mirror. It reflected light and sparkling glassware and the faces of the patrons and those who worked within these walls. It spoke of Lily's enterprising success and independence. She was never ashamed to look into it and see the reflection of a hardworking woman.

"Miss Lily, may I speak with you?"

"Excuse me, Mollie." Lily turned to the man who'd spoken. He was middle-aged and slender, wearing a black suit with a white shirt and string tie. "Good evening, Edward."

"I wanted to thank you for putting me up for a few nights. I'd have camped outside town, but I really wanted to stay nearby so I wouldn't miss any arriving trains or stages. I've been watching for a friend who will be accompanying me on to the coast."

"You earned your keep, Mr. Mulvaney. Old Jess is a fine barkeep, but his bones are a might creaky from his years of prospecting, and he can't stack and clean the way you did. That storeroom fairly sparkles."

"I was wondering, Miss, if you would grant me a few hours of your time tomorrow."

Lily gave him a curious look.

"I'd like to paint you."

Lily had seen the paint under Mulvaney's nails and the wrapped canvases he'd carried with him upon his arrival. "You do portraits?"

He nodded. "That's why I'm traveling to the coast. To study under a gifted teacher. I've sketched something out, but I'd like to capture your countenance to my liking…if you please."

Lily considered his request for a moment. "I can't see any harm. Tomorrow, midmorning, right here?"

"That would be perfect. Thank you very much, Miss Lily."

He took his leave at the same time one of the double front doors opened and Thunder Canyon's aging sheriff, Randall Parson, entered the dance hall. A few nods were directed toward him as he made his way to the bar, but his presence wasn't anything unusual. With a wince, he settled himself on a squeaky stool.

"Evenin', Lily."

"Evenin', Sheriff."

Old Jess poured a shot of whiskey and slid the heavy glass toward the lawman.

Like clockwork every evening, he got his two shots on the house; in seven years he'd never missed his drinks. Sheriff Parson going much of anywhere beyond Main Street would have been remarkable.

"Choir still practicing in the street?" Lily asked.

She knew the answer. He'd waited for his whiskey until they were gone. Sheriff Parson didn't like confrontations.

"They've moved on up to the Big Nugget," he replied.

"Glad the ladies are getting their exercise," she said. "Nice night for it."

He didn't meet her eyes. "They're causing more of a stink than you know, Lily."

"What do you mean?"

"They've called meetings with the councilmen over the past couple of months."

Lily had caught wind of meetings after the fact; she and the other saloon owners hadn't been informed ahead of time. "There's no law in Montana against running a gambling establishment or selling liquor. There's no law against prostitution, for that matter. They're trying to hurt my business."

"Lily, you know as well as anyone that the Shady Lady is a big part of the economy of Thunder Canyon."

"I remember that every month when I pay my taxes, Randall."

Early on, the town fathers had shrewdly made the dance halls pillars of financial support. Officials loved the saloons, not only for their own pleasure, but also for the steady cash flow. Like the owners of the other two establishments, Lily paid four hundred dollars a year for a license and a hundred dollars a month in taxes. Fines for disturbing the peace were added on top of those costs. It was an arrangement that kept everybody happy—or it had until lately.

Sheriff Parson knocked back his first shot. "These eastern women with their city ideas are more'n a nuisance. The more of 'em there are, the more they band together. The more they make trouble." Finally, he looked directly at her. "They have influence with their menfolk, Lily."

She shook her head and gestured with a hand in the air. "Something needs to be done about them. We were here long before they came to Thunder Canyon."

Sheriff Parson rubbed his chin. "They've complained about the amount of money squandered in the dance halls and…they claim I'm not doin' my job."

"What do they think your job is? You keep the law."

"They're zealous."

"Obviously."

"Won't tolerate drunkenness or prostitution."

"I don't have sportin' women, you know that, and I'm not gonna be run out. My place operates within the law."

"Town officials can influence state laws."

"You know me and my saloon, Randall."

· "I do, Lily. But it looks like it ain't gonna matter anymore."

"What do you mean?"

He threw back his second shot and studied the bottom of the glass. "I'm bein' replaced."

She stared at him. "What? By who?"

"Some man hunter they hired to bring law and order."

Stunned, Lily glanced around the inside of her place. "I'm not changing a thing until they can change the law."

"Good luck, Lily." He stood and picked up his hat from the bar to settle it on his head.

"When?" she asked.

"A month or two, I reckon. Soon as he can tie up his other business and get here."

"What'll you do, Randall?"

· "Got me a sister in St. Louis. Figured I'd go there for a spell. Never met her children, and they're growed already. Evenin'." Lily noticed his pronounced limp as he made his way to the batwings and pushed out into the night.

Isaac was pounding out a melody on the keyboard, and half a dozen men and women danced to the gay tune.

Lily turned to the mirror and found her reflection. Auburn hair in ringlets caught up on her head; blue eyes; a determined jaw; a glimmer of attitude. Nothing had changed.

And she wasn't about to let anything change. She'd been here first.

NATHANIEL HARDING RODE into Thunder Canyon from the east midmorning on a day late in July. He saw a typical mining town that had been built up and prospered over the years because of the railroad coming through. The first building he passed, set apart from the rest and new, was a schoolhouse. It sat in the center of about an acre of land, shaded by a gnarled oak and several piñon trees.

The other buildings showed a wide variation in age and expense and were set along three connecting streets that formed an H. Some were unpainted wood frames, while a few were brick and several were made of logs. The wooden buildings along Main Street stood close together and were joined by boardwalks and awnings. Some shared roofs.

Most were easy to identify. He'd been in a hundred towns that looked just the same. A milliner's, a mercantile, a butcher shop, post office and freight station combined, a town hall, a bank, three saloons and, at the west end of the street, a whitewashed church. This one was called the Congregational Church, and the sign on the fence announced that Reverend James Bacon presided.

A garden plot occupied an entire lot in the midst of the businesses, an oddity to be sure. The flourishing vegetables looked well-tended.

An impressive three-story brick structure on Main Street appeared vacant, which struck him as odd.

The sheriff's office and jail was a building set off by itself at the southwest corner of town. Dirt-streaked windows bracketed the door. There was a hitching post and a wooden porch with a long bench, but no roof to protect whoever sat on the bench from the blazing sun.

His arrival seemed to have caused a stir. The women stared and spoke to each other, and shop owners came out on their boardwalks. He touched the brim of his hat in a silent greeting and rode past.

The telegram tucked in Nate's pocket instructed him to go directly to the town hall when he arrived, so he tied up his horse and entered the brick building. The impressive structure was large, with a foyer and doors that opened from the main area. He rapped on the one that had a placard announcing Peyton Gibbs, Mayor.

The sound of chair legs scraping the floor met his ears, and a moment later the door swung partway open.

A thin, dark-haired man in a suit and wearing gold-rimmed spectacles took a step back, his eyes growing wide as he took in Nate's appearance. Nate wore his .45 in a holster on his hip and carried his Remington rifle. He'd been riding for over a week and hadn't shaved in all that time. No doubt he looked a mite rough around the edges.

"Er. May I help you?"

"The mayor here?"

The man blinked like a mouse confronted with a bobcat. "Er. Who would be asking?"

"Nathaniel Harding."

"Oh. Oh. Yes, Harding. Come in, won't you? Just one moment." He opened the door completely and scurried away to enter another room.

A few minutes later, a portly man with dark hair parted in the center and a handlebar mustache greeted Nate with a handshake. "Pleased to meet you. Your references were impeccable. Very impressive. Your reputation is just what Thunder Canyon needs."

Nate eyed him from beneath the brim of his hat. "Sheriff's job, right?"

"Precisely. We have a sticky situation, and we're trying to handle it."

He ushered Nate into his office and offered him a seat before he outlined the problem with the Women's Temperance Prayer League and the reforms they were insisting upon.

Nate sat and rested his hat on his knee.

"Mind you, these are our wives. Their displeasure makes our lives miserable."

"You hired me to handle a bunch of *women?*"

"No, no. We need you to appease them and clean up the town."

"Get a lot of undesirables, do you? Gunfights and such?"

"Drunken miners mostly, not many outlaws. The problem is in the dance halls."

"There's no law against gambling or drinking."

"There's disturbance of the peace on occasion. What really gets the women riled is the money bein' spent. Just between you and me, those houses support the town, always have. Miner sells some gold dust, he spends his coins on whiskey and women. But there's trouble comin'. These women aren't going to be satisfied until the town is as clean as a whistle and the sportin' women are gone."

"I'll enforce the law, Mr. Gibbs. What more than that do you want?"

The mayor opened his desk drawer, took out an object and leaned across the desk to place it before Nate. "It has to *look* like you're cracking down, Harding. Be vigilant. And be visible."

Nate glanced at the tin star on the desk top. "In other words, impress your wives."

Mayor Gibbs's face reddened. "Just do your job."

"You don't have to worry about that. Just keep the women out of my hair." He picked up the badge and tucked it into his vest pocket. "Your telegram said you'd have a place for me to stay."

"You can take a room at Mrs. Staub's boarding house for as long as you like. Or until you find something that suits you better. Just let Shirley know when you'll be there to eat. Her place is on Gold Street, just around the corner. The town will pay the bill. Same at Callahan's eatery. Three meals a day between those two places, to your liking."

"Any houses for sale?"

"Matter of fact, there's a small one on the street behind the church that might suit you. Another set back to the north aways. It's a family home, though, probably not to your liking. Family that owned it moved to Colorado. The man built that big brick building as an investment and ended up never putting it to use."

Nate stood and replaced his hat. "When do I start?"

"You can start tomorrow. Randall Parson has until the end of the week, and he can show you around."

The narrow man in the outer room blinked at Nate's guns as he passed through. Nate nodded and took his leave.

Shirley Staub was an attractive fair-haired woman

several years older than Nate's thirty-five, but she wore a wary expression after opening the door to him.

Nate immediately adjusted his saddlebags to remove his hat. "Nathaniel Harding, ma'am. I've come to board for a spell."

Her expression relaxed. "Yes, Sheriff Harding, the councilmen told me you'd be arriving. I have a room ready for you." She ushered him inside. "I put you close to the back stairs. That way should you have to go out of a night, you can leave through the rear without disturbing the other tenants. I have two elderly gentlemen, a lady schoolteacher and two sisters who are residents. The other rooms are only occasionally occupied. This is the parlor. You're welcome to share it with us of an evening."

He glanced at the long narrow room furnished with a spindly settee and several chairs gathered around a cold fireplace.

"The dining room is here. Breakfast at six, dinner at noon and supper at six. The regulars are set in their ways, mind you, so you'd best use this place here." She touched the back of a chair.

"The necessary is out back, of course, through the kitchen right here. And these are the back stairs."

Nate followed her up and stood aside while she opened a door. "This is your room. You can take water up with you at night for washing, but I'd like for you to bring the dirty water down in the morning. I change and wash bedding once a week. There's a laundry across the street for your clothing. We do have a bathing chamber behind the kitchen. I have a boy who helps with water on Saturday afternoons."

"Thank you, ma'am. The room is adequate."

"Well." She brushed her hands together as if she was finished with her task. "Welcome to Thunder Canyon, Mr., er, Sheriff Harding."

With his hat against his chest, he nodded. "One more thing, ma'am. Where can I get a bath and a shave today?"

"There's a bath house on the street behind us and back toward Main. You can't miss the shingle." She left him alone.

Nate closed himself inside the room and glanced around. Nothing fancy. He dropped his saddlebags to the floor. Plain iron bed frame and a piecework quilt— mighty tempting after a stretch of sleeping on the ground. On one wall stood a chest of drawers, and on the other a table holding a pitcher and bowl. Under the window was another table with a chair pulled up to it that served as a desk.

He couldn't remember the last time he'd set himself up in a room without knowing when he'd be leaving. The longest he'd stayed anywhere in years had been six months ago, when he'd been shot and taken a hard fall from his horse. He'd done a lengthy stint recuperating in a doctor's home.

That had been when he'd decided fifteen years of man hunting was enough. Fifteen years of being on a horse, sleeping on the ground, tracking wanted men and bringing them to justice had been more than enough. He was good at it. But he'd seen the worst side of life, dealt with the dregs of humanity, and he was weary.

Compared to what he'd been doing, sleeping in a bed, cleaning up the dance halls and keeping the peace in this town was going to be as easy as a ten-cent whore.

"HE'S HERE," HELENA SAID, in her dramatic Polish accent.

Lily glanced at the door, which hadn't opened. "Who?"

"The bounty hunter. He's in town. Bernard Kendrick saw him going to the bath house yesterday. George Lynch said he has a black beard and he wears a Colt."

Bernard Kendrick had a vested interest in the new sheriff—he owned the Big Nugget. George Lynch was the barber, and he and his son ran the bath house.

"Then he went into Wesley Clark's hardware store and bought bullets. Mr. Clark said he possesses a menacing look."

Lily wasn't going to get in a dither over a new sheriff. She ran a clean establishment, had no bone to pick with the law. "I'm sure we'll see him sooner or later."

"We have nothing to fear, do we, Lily?" Helena asked. Her lovely dark eyes had crow's-feet at the corners, though she was probably only five or six years older than Lily. She had once worked for Antoinette and had very little use or respect for men. The Shady Lady was her safe haven and Lily her dear friend. Lily couldn't tolerate the uncertainty in her eyes.

"We have nothing to fear," she assured her with a brief hug. "The sheriff is here to protect us from the bad guys, remember?"

"I find men difficult to trust."

"So do I, Helena. I never want to have to rely on a

man. And I won't have to. Neither do you. You and I, we have decent skills to earn our way."

Helena and Mollie had taken over Lily's laundry position and were paid by the other women to wash and press their clothing. Helena often sang of an evening, and the patrons paid her well for the gift of her voice.

"We have money in the bank," Lily reminded her. "But nothing is going to happen to the Shady Lady. It's mine free and clear, and as long as I'm around, you have a home."

"You are a generous, kind-hearted person, Lily. Those uppity women don't see that, because if they did, they would know you are an angel sent from above."

"I don't know if I'd go that far," Lily said with a laugh. "But I'm for sure not the devil they think I am."

Boots sounded on the floorboards. "Package came on the train for you, Miss Lily."

The two women turned toward the front door as young Mitch Early carried in a flat crate about four feet long. "Mr. Brennan said I should bring this on over to you, so it didn't sit in the store room."

"Well, that's good of you, Mitch," Lily replied. "Would you like a cold sarsaparilla while you're here?"

"Yes'm, Miss Lily. That would hit the spot right nice." His glance took in the corners of the room and the hallway leading toward the entrance to the house next door.

Lily smiled to herself. It was no secret that Mitch was sweet on Celeste Kinney, a young woman who'd been with Lily for about a year.

"Let me go ask Celeste to shave some ice for you."

Lily stopped. "Maybe you'd like to come to the kitchen with me and wait for her while she does it."

He grinned and followed her down the hall and through the open doorway. They only locked the adjoining door of an evening when there were customers in the saloon.

Celeste was humming as she peeled potatoes at the big oak table that ran down the center of the kitchen. Mollie stood at the stove browning meat for their dinner.

"Celeste? Would you mind shaving some ice so Mitch can have a cold drink? He's come all the way over with a package for me. A heavy one at that."

Celeste blushed prettily and wiped her hands on her apron as she stood. "Be glad to, Miss Lily. We could all use a cold drink."

Lily left them and returned to the saloon, where Helena was examining the flat crate. "Did you order something?"

Lily shook her head and found a hammer behind the bar. She used the claw to work the boards loose. After several minutes she had broken the crate open to reveal a carefully wrapped object.

Peeling back layers of batting, she discovered a framed painting.

Her eyes played tricks on her at first glance, because there seemed to be too much exposed flesh in the likeness of the woman she first viewed upside down.

Helena drew in a breath. "It's exquisite work. I've seen paintings of this quality in museums."

Lily walked around the painting on the floor until she

saw the portrait from the proper angle. Picking it up, she propped the frame against the brass foot rail on the cherrywood bar.

It was indeed a painting of a naked woman, as she'd first thought. No mistaking it. Curly auburn hair with ringlets about her ears and neck, blue eyes, a gentle, almost self-satisfied smile. Shocking. Scandalous. Beautiful.

Her.

The woman's ivory skin appeared soft and delicate, her breasts were full and rose-tipped, her waist narrow. Across her hip a sheer black veil exposed skin, but concealed her pubic area in dark mysterious folds of gauze. The woman's legs were long. She wore pearls on each ankle as well as around her neck.

"Lily, it's you." Helena turned wide eyes on her friend. "You didn't pose for this portrait, did you?"

"No, I didn't. Well, I did, but—but I had my clothes on. My gray skirt, remember? You saw—everyone saw that day. I sat for hours while Edward Mulvaney sketched and mixed colors. But I *had my clothes on.*"

Helena's lovely smile deepened the lines at the corners of her eyes. "You are beautiful, Lily."

Lily's cheeks were warm. "That's not really me."

"Of course it is."

"It's the way he imagined me."

Helena laughed then, a full-throated sound. "I would like to see the faces of the Intolerant Women's Prayer League if they saw this."

Lily laughed at her friend's twist of their title, and then at the thought of Meriel Reed's eyes bugging out when she got a gander at this painting. "Beatrice Gibbs would fall over in a swoon!"

She and Helena laughed until tears ran down their cheeks.

Old Jess came shuffling from the back room with a broom in his hand. "What's all the cacklin' about?"

He walked around the bar and stopped in his tracks before the painting.

"Jumpin' Jehosephat! That's a fine piece of art!"

Mildly embarrassed, Lily laughed harder, wiping tears from her eyes.

Mollie, Celeste, and Mitch Early joined the gathering a few minutes later, followed by the other women from various parts of the house who'd been drawn by the commotion.

Mitch blushed clear to the tips of his ears.

Rosemary, a woman who'd come to Lily for a job five years ago after her abusive husband had been killed in a brawl, studied the artwork with a look of incredulity. "How astonishing," she said at last. "He's captured your spirit, Lily. Your kindness, your determination and compassion. Right here on this canvas."

Lily studied the likeness of her expression again. "You see all that?"

The others murmured their agreement.

"All I can see is…are…"

"And how amazing that he drew you like that by using his imagination," Celeste said, pointing to the nude body.

Lily met her eyes. "Thank you."

Mitch cleared his throat. "You didn't pose for this?" he asked, color still high on his cheeks.

"She posed fully dressed," Mollie replied for her, and the others confirmed that.

Lily felt better knowing her friends and employees knew her well enough to realize she hadn't been naked in front of Edward Mulvaney. And if she had, she'd be grateful if she looked that good, she thought with another sideways glance.

"Lily and I were imagining the reactions of the uppity wives if they saw this painting," Helena told the gathering, and they laughed.

Mitch picked up the painting and carried it behind the bar, where he propped it on the counter. "It belongs back here. For everybody to see."

"Oh, I don't know," Lily objected.

"Yes," Mollie agreed. "It's the perfect place."

Lily looked at the nude woman and felt a brazen sense of defiance. "It's not illegal." Displaying the painting would be impudent. Challenging. Daring. She couldn't help a smile. "People might not even know it's me."

Mollie and Helena exchanged a skeptical glance and a grin.

"And after all, this is the Shady Lady Dance Hall," Lily said. "She looks like her namesake."

The others clapped.

"Let's celebrate with sarsaparilla," Celeste suggested. "We'll toast to the Shady Lady."

She and Mollie carried trays to the bar and all of them raised their glasses to the woman in the portrait.

The painting became a symbol of liberty for Lily that day. She would not be intimidated. Nor would she cower to those who accused her of imagined sins. She would be the confident, independent woman others saw. And she would not let any of her friends down. She was, after all, Lily Divine.

CHAPTER TWO

THE DOORS HAD BEEN OPEN for nearly an hour, and half a dozen men were sitting at a table playing cards when Big Saul hurried to Lily, where she sat at the end of the bar. Saul was over six feet tall and built out of solid muscle, but he had the mind of a ten-year-old. He'd been with Lily since his mother's death four years previous.

"Miss Lily, you gotta come. Little girl's hurt and askin' for ya."

Lily slid from her seat. "Where is she?"

"Came to the back, she did. I was stackin' wood by the stove." He ran and she followed.

Saul didn't have a key to the adjoining door, as he and Old Jess lived over the dance hall, so Lily followed him out back to the alley and in through the rear of her house.

"There she is. There's the little girl."

Lily took one look at the girl, who wasn't all that little. She appeared to be about fourteen. She wore a baggy dress and thin shawl, and her brown hair was limp and tangled. Her left eye was nearly swollen shut and the bruising extended to her jaw.

"Thank you, Saul. You did the right thing to come

and get me. I'll take care of her now, and you go help Old Jess."

"Yes'm, Miss Lily." He exited back the way he'd come.

Lily approached the girl, who stood trembling beside the cold stove. "It's okay, sweetie," Lily said to her. "What's your name?"

The girl's skittish gaze flicked around the room and back to Lily's face. "Violet."

"What happened to you, Violet?"

She didn't reply.

Lily went to the ice chest and used the mallet to knock a small chunk from the brick. She wrapped it in a thin rag. "Will you let me put ice on that?"

Violet nodded.

"Sit here, sweetie."

Violet sat on a bench and allowed Lily to touch the ice to her injury. She winced and sucked in a breath at the touch. "I…I heard you give girls jobs. Can I stay here?"

"I hire grown women, not young girls."

"I'm not a child. I can work. I work for my pa all the time. Please." She reached out and gripped Lily's forearm. "You have to let me stay."

The desperation in her voice and her eyes took Lily back to a time when she'd feared for her own safety. Lily felt the girl's desperation as though it were her own and knew in that instant that she had to help her.

She placed her hand over Violet's. "You're going to be all right now."

After a moment Violet lowered her gaze and loosened her grip on Lily's arm.

"Take this." Lily left her holding the ice and prepared

a basin of soapy water. "Let's wash some of the blood away and see if you need stitches."

"I ain't goin' to no doctor."

"Let's just look, okay?"

Violet let her wash the side of her face. There were older bruises along her neck and cheekbone, bruises that were already fading and sickly green. "Who did this to you?"

Tears formed in Violet's fearful blue eyes. "I didn't have supper ready when my pa got home. He gets real mad if I don't have everything ready. I wasn't feelin' so good…my…my woman time, you know—and I laid down for a minute. I didn't mean to sleep. When I woke up he was yellin' and shakin' me. I tried to get away, but he pushed me and I fell against the table. I can't go back there."

Lily felt ill at the thought of a grown man—a father—hurting this girl. Lily blinked back her own tears and busied herself rinsing out the rag, so Violet wouldn't see. She'd been only two years older than this girl when her father had traded her to a man for a share in a miner's claim. She understood the feeling of helplessness gripping Violet.

"Please don't make me go back. I'd work real hard for ya, I swear I would."

Lily knelt before the girl and looked into her eyes. Antoinette had been Lily's savior years ago. She wouldn't be alive today if the woman hadn't come to her aid. "Of course you shouldn't go back. We'll figure out what to do."

"If he finds me, he'll beat me for runnin' away." Her

eyes pleaded with Lily, and Lily's heart broke with compassion.

"Don't you worry, sweetie. He's not going to find you. As long as you're in my place, you're safe. I'll see what I can do to help you. Let's get you upstairs and into a nice soft bed. I'll find you something to eat, and you can rest all you like."

Lily ushered the thin girl into one of the unoccupied bedrooms. The tawdry decorations had been disposed of, the wallpaper replaced and the rooms made to suit the respectable house it was today. Lily was blessed with an abundance of rooms, along with money for food and clothing, and she shared them with anyone who needed help. "You can stay in here for as long as you like."

Violet glanced around at the lace curtains, the quilted counterpane and the rugs on the floor. "This is the nicest room I ever saw."

Lily pulled down the covers and helped Violet out of her shoes and stockings. "There are nightshifts and extra clothes in the bureau there, you help yourself. Big Saul is going to be down in the kitchen tonight, sort of standing watch. I'll be back with food and some milk."

Violet nodded, and Lily left the room, closing the door behind her. Violet wasn't the first female who'd come to her for help, but she was definitely the youngest. Most women who sought her out were escaping abusive husbands, or they were soiled doves looking for a fresh start.

Violet was just a young girl who should have been under her father's protection rather than a stranger's.

But life wasn't fair, and women weren't treated as equals. Oftentimes they were no more than possessions.

The thought infuriated Lily.

After preparing a tray and seeing that Violet was comfortable, she assigned Big Saul to a position in the kitchen, instructing him to keep an eye out for strangers and not to let anyone in.

When Lily returned to the saloon, Helena hurried forward and caught her hand. "He was here!"

"Who?"

"The new sheriff. He asked for the owner. Said he'd be back another time. The whole place got quiet when he came in. Lily, he's a menacing-looking man if I ever saw one."

"I had something else to handle." She explained to Helena about Violet.

"What will you do?" Helena asked.

"I don't know. I'm afraid if I went to the new sheriff, he'd give the girl back to her father, and I won't let that happen. I think I'll send a telegram to the governor and ask for his help to protect Violet."

The next morning she prepared Violet a bath in the downstairs chamber and waited outside the room while the girl washed her hair and bathed.

Mollie found a blue dress small enough for Violet's waist and hemmed the skirt. The area around Violet's eye was swollen and bruised, despite the ice, but the cut hadn't required stitches. Mollie and Helena told Lily they had a difficult time looking at the poor girl's face without crying. Molly made a poultice and applied it while Violet again rested.

That afternoon Lily sent a telegram to the governor in the state capitol. It could be days before she got a reply.

Molly's poultice had taken down much of the swelling by the time Violet came out of her room for supper and stayed to help the women in the kitchen. She was a sweet-natured thing with a soft voice and a willingness to pitch in. Every time Lily looked at her she saw herself, and she was determined that Violet's abuse would stop now. She stayed with her most of the evening and once again missed the sheriff.

The next day was Friday, and that evening the saloon was filled with patrons. Lily watched her girls as they accepted coins for dances and helped Old Jess pour drinks. The sheriff would undoubtedly be back, and she didn't plan to miss him again.

A man she didn't recognize pushed his way up to the bar and asked for a bottle of whiskey. Lily took his money and handed him the liquor.

"Name's Jack Brand," he said, and she could tell he'd already been drinking. She'd have to tell Big Saul to keep an eye on this one. "Been doin' some checkin' and I think you and me got a problem."

"And what would that be?"

"I got a little girl who's missin'. I think you know somethin' about it."

Warning bells went off in Lily's head. Anger rose up inside her. This was the man who had hurt Violet. "Why would I know anything?"

"I heard tell you take in strays. Women who think they're too good for their menfolk."

"I don't talk about my private business."

He grabbed hold of her wrist. "It's my business if you got my kid stashed away, lady."

When he touched her, another man's angry face swam into Lily's vision and made her skin crawl. "Let go of my arm right now."

"Hand over my kid."

She tried to pull away. "I don't know what you're talking about."

"You're lyin'."

Old Jess caught wind of the struggle, and slid a sawed-off shotgun from beneath the bar. "Let go of her, mister."

"I ain't movin' till I get my kid."

The music stopped and the attention of everyone in the room focused on the scene transpiring at the bar.

"Let's take this outside," Lily said calmly. "Jess, put the gun down."

Jess lowered the barrel.

Jack Brand released Lily's wrist. Infuriated, she rubbed it and walked around the end of the bar. Men who bullied women didn't deserve to draw air.

Brand grabbed his bottle by the neck and carried it outside.

Lily nodded to Jess, and he understood the signal to get Saul.

"Play something, Isaac!" Lily called and followed Brand outside. Behind her a lively tune resumed on the piano.

Out on the boardwalk, the man pulled the cork and took a swig of liquor.

Lily kept her distance. Saul would join them in a moment, and the troublemaker would be on his way.

"Where's she at?" Brand asked, taking several steps forward.

"I don't know who you mean."

"You know damned good and well who I mean. My daughter, Vi'let. You're hidin' her." He gestured up at the windows above the dance hall. "Up there. Vi'let! Vi'let, you come down here right now!"

From the other end of the street, Lily could hear the Bible thumpers warming up in front of the Big Nugget. The unmistakable sound of their tambourine echoed along the storefronts. She had to get rid of this man before the choir made their way down here.

Saul came out and stood at Lily's side. "You need me, Miss Lily?"

"Only if Mr. Brand here doesn't move along," she replied.

"You can't keep my daughter," he said and shook his fist at Lily. "I'm goin' to the law. You can't steal children and get away with it."

"I didn't steal anyone."

"She's a runaway and you're hidin' her. That's against the law."

The singing grew closer.

At that moment she wished she was a man. Jack Brand's face became the face of another. A man she'd stab again if she had the chance. She clenched her fists at her sides. "No law against beating children though, is there?"

"I knew you had her!" He drew back his fist, but Saul

stepped toward him to prevent him from lunging at Lily.
Lily scrambled aside.

Brand used the split second before Saul reached him
to howl and heave the bottle of whiskey toward Lily.
She didn't have time to react. It struck her head with a
dart of pain and shattered against the wooden post at her
side. Whiskey showered her ear, neck and shoulder,
and glass lodged in her hair.

Someone screamed.

Lily saw stars for a full minute. She reached out
blindly and caught the post to hold herself upright.

Saul had Brand on the ground and restrained him by
sitting on his chest.

The singing had stopped and the women now gathered in a tight cluster, staring in abject horror at the
scene before them.

The doors burst open behind Lily and several men,
as well as Helena and Celeste, spilled onto the boardwalk.

"Lily! Are you all right?" Celeste hurried to her side.

Lily blinked and tried to focus on Celeste's face.
"I…I think so."

Confusion reigned, with the women chattering and
more people coming out of the dance hall to join the
commotion.

Celeste picked shards of glass out of Lily's curly hair.

Brand bellowed at the top of his lungs for the big oaf
to get off his chest.

The women quieted, and a hush settled over the gathering as attention focused on a man who'd ridden up and
was climbing down from his horse.

He was a big man, tall and broad-shouldered. He wore a hat and a holstered revolver, and he carried a rifle. When he stepped into the light from the gas lamps, a tin star glistened on his shirt.

Lily's head throbbed and the glare from the badge hurt her eyes. She frowned.

"Trouble here?" he asked.

"It was a street brawl right before our very eyes," Meriel Reed said, aghast. "The shame of it!"

Once again the women burst into mortified chatter.

The sheriff silenced them with one hand in the air. "Who was fighting?"

"That man," Blythe Shaw said, pointing to Brand. "And…and *her!* Lily Divine. She was screaming like a fishwife."

"Did anyone else see what happened?" the sheriff asked.

"I seen it," Big Saul said.

"He's just a big dummy, don't listen to his account," Beatrice Gibbs ordered. "We definitely saw what happened, and she provoked the man."

The other women agreed with accusing nods and murmurs.

Lily's temperature rose a notch at Beatrice's cruel dismissal of Saul. None of the Intolerants even knew Jack Brand or what he'd done to his daughter, but they were willing to take his side over hers. She stepped forward unsteadily and lurched toward the gathering of women. "Don't you witches have something better to do than haunt the streets at night? Go home and warm your husbands' beds. You're a bunch of…"

The vision of the women before her swam, and the throbbing in her head increased. She swayed on her feet.

"…of puritanical hypocrites."

Someone gasped.

"Just look at her! She's inebriated!" Meriel said with a disdainful sniff and covered her nose with a hankie as though Lily was a bad smell she could filter.

The last thing Lily remembered was looking at the sheriff, who scowled at her as though she was a fly in his coffee. Her vision blurred and she slumped to the ground.

NATE PUSHED ASIDE the gathering of dance hall girls who had rushed to the woman's aid. He hauled her up by pulling on one arm until he got her upright, and then he threw her over his shoulder.

"Stop that! Wait!"

"What are you doing?"

"I'm locking her up," he said. "Drunk and disorderly on a public street."

"She's not drunk!" a small black-haired woman cried, following close behind.

Nate ignored her. "Keep him there until I get back," he told the giant on top of the man on the ground.

He grabbed his horse's reins and walked toward the jailhouse, Lily Divine slung over his shoulder, a gaggle of colorful saloon girls following in rustling shiny dresses.

Nate tied his horse to the hitching post in front of the jail and carried the saloonkeeper who reeked of whiskey inside. Two of the women followed him, objecting all the while. He opened a cell door and unceremoniously dropped the limp woman onto the cot.

"You can't lock Miss Lily up!" the Indian woman cried, following him. "She did not break any laws."

"Unless you want to be in one of those other cells," he said, jerking a thumb over his shoulder, "you can leave me to my job."

A pretty woman with crow's-feet at the corners of her eyes joined them in the cell. She spoke in an accent he didn't recognize. "Mr. Sheriff, Miss Divine is a respectable business owner. She runs a clean business and breaks no laws."

"I guess that's up to a judge now, isn't it? Since I say she's drunk and disorderly and disturbing the peace. Come out of there."

"I'm stayin' until Miss Lily is taken care of." The Indian woman situated herself on the side of the cot with an obstinate flounce. He had visions of trying to pull these two females out of the cell against their will. His temple throbbed with a dull ache.

"Miss Lily needs a doctor," the other woman insisted. "She is injured, otherwise she wouldn't be unconscious. I'm going for Doc." She followed Nate out of the cell.

"Suit yourself." He swung the iron enclosure shut, locking two women in and one out, and headed back outside. Nate untied his horse and rode it back down the street to where the big man still sat atop his prisoner.

"I'll take him now," he said.

"Is Miss Lily okay?" the big man asked.

"She's sleepin' it off in a cell."

"She's gonna be mad," he replied.

Nate hoisted the other man up by one arm, took the stranger's revolver and tucked it into his waistband. "What's your name?"

"Jack Brand. That saloon woman's keepin' my kid. She's holdin' her somewhere in there." He jerked his head toward the dance hall.

"That so?" Nate asked the other man. "Is there a child in there?"

The big man shook his head vehemently. "Only little girl is Violet. Miss Lily gave her food and washed her up."

"That's her!" Brand shouted. "That's my kid! I knew she was in there! Let me go after her."

"Not tonight. We'll get this settled tomorrow when everybody's sobered up." Nate handcuffed Brand's hands behind his back. "Where's your rig?"

Brand nodded toward a horse at the hitching rail. "Black nag there."

Nate glanced from the horse to the big man. He'd picked up on the fact that he was almost childlike in his speech and actions. "What's your name?"

"Big Saul."

"Saul, will you take Brand's horse to the livery and ask Wade Reed to put it up for the night?"

"Sure thing, Sheriff."

Nate hoisted Brand onto the back of his horse and led it toward the jail. He placed the drunk in a cell, well away from the one the dance hall woman and her friend occupied, and locked the door.

"You ain't gonna let her get away with this, are you? She can't just take my kid."

Nate met the Indian woman's eyes, but answered Brand. "We're not even talkin' about this till morning, so shut up and get some sleep."

"I know my rights."

Nate wished Parson was here, but the former sheriff had already gone home for the night.

The door opened and the pretty foreign woman entered, followed by a man carrying a black bag. "This is Doc Umber. He must see Lily."

"Is there somethin' you can do for imbibing too much whiskey now, Dr. Umber? Advances in medicine and the like?" Nate asked.

"Never known Miss Lily to tie one on," the doctor said without a smile. He walked toward the row of cells. "Let me in, please."

Nate grabbed the keys and unlocked the iron-barred door. The doctor, with the woman on his heels, entered the cell.

"Miss Lily?" the doctor said, kneeling beside the cot.

"She's out cold," Nate told him.

Both women sent him scathing looks.

"She does reek of whiskey, Mollie," Doc said softly.

"There was broken glass in her hair," Mollie replied.

Doc examined Lily's face and head. "There's a knot here," he said. "In her hairline near her temple."

Mollie's tears dripped on Lily's skirt. "Will she be all right?"

"I'm sure she will," Doc replied. He took a small squarish bottle from his bag and passed it beneath Lily's nose.

Lily's eyelids fluttered, and she opened them to look at the doctor. She raised a hand to her head. "Holy hell!"

"Lily!" Mollie cried. She picked up Lily's hand and pressed it to her cheek.

Lily blinked in confusion. "Where am I?"

"You are in jail," Mollie said. "The new sheriff locked you up. Helena brought the doctor."

Lily sat up then, aided by her friends. Her hair was a mass of wild auburn ringlets that had fallen loose and hung down her back. She blinked at the doctor and at Mollie, then turned her gaze to Nate, who stood outside the cell. Her electric-blue gaze narrowed on him, and he experienced a lightninglike jolt of wary surprise.

"Why am I here?" she asked.

"Drunk and disorderly conduct."

"I'm not drunk, and I was *not* disorderly. There was a man causing a ruckus in my saloon, and I took him outside to handle it. He attacked me." She raised a hand to the knot at her temple and winced.

"It's your word against mine, lady," Brand called from the other end of the hall. "I came for my daughter and you refused to give her to me."

"I don't know what you're talking about," she replied.

"Saul told me there was a girl you'd fed and cleaned up," Nate said.

She turned that blue gaze on him again, and this time Nate couldn't catch his breath. An ocean of defiance and anger shone in those eyes, and right now the hostility was directed at him. "I've sent a telegram to the governor, asking for his help," she said. "That man belongs in a cell. He beat a child half to death."

"Why didn't you come to me?" Nate asked. "Why wait for the governor?"

"What would you have done?"

"Listened. Assessed the situation."

"Would you have protected her?"

"I can't say. I don't know the circumstances."

"I wasn't willing to risk that you wouldn't have," she replied.

The doctor stood. "She should have some ice on her head and get some rest."

At that moment the door opened and Big Saul entered the office. "I did like you said and got his horse put up."

"Thanks." Nate gestured for him to come closer.

Saul lumbered toward the cell and spotted Lily awake. "Miss Lily. You're okay!"

"You said you saw what happened in the street tonight," Nate interrupted. "Is that right?"

"Yes, sir."

"What happened between Mr. Brand and Miss Lily?"

"Mr. Brand was real mad and yellin', and Old Jess sent me to make sure nothin' happened." He lowered his head and then looked up at Lily sheepishly. "I'm sorry, Miss Lily. I wasn't fast enough."

"It's not your fault," she assured him.

"What weren't you fast enough to stop?" Nate asked.

"That man, he threw his whiskey bottle at Miss Lily. It happened real fast, after Miss Lily asked him to move along. I grabbed him and sat on him soon as I could. But it was too late, 'cause Miss Lily got hurt."

The enormous man looked like he was going to cry.

"It's okay, Saul," Lily repeated gently. "I'm fine, really."

"Who're you gonna listen to?" Brand called. "Some big idiot?"

Saul looked at the toes of his shoes.

Lily shot daggers at Nate. Even the doctor and the two women looked at him as though he was the one who'd spoken those cruel words.

"I'll see you back to your place," Nate said at last.

Brand howled in outrage from his cell. "You cain't let her go and leave me in here! I got rights!"

Mollie helped Lily to her feet and walked behind her out of the cell. The doctor and Helena followed, Brand cursing at their backs.

"I was wondering when we'd meet." A note of sarcasm laced Lily's tone.

"I've come by the Shady Lady, but haven't seen you."

"I've been busy."

"Apparently. I heard about you from the mayor and Sheriff Parson. You have a lot of friends in this town."

"Enemies, as well," she replied. "Talk had it you had a beard."

"I got a shave the first day in town."

The group exited the jail house and walked along the dark street toward the dance hall.

"I'll leave the women to look after you now," Doc Umber said. "Come by my office tomorrow, Lily. I'll have another look at your head."

"Thanks, Doc. Helena will get you a drink before you head home."

Helena scowled at Nate and led the doctor toward the saloon.

Lily fumbled in her pocket, discovering her keys were missing.

Nate dangled the brass ring in front of her.

She took them from him and opened the front door of the house next to the dance hall. They entered a large foyer with striped wallpaper, a gold-framed mirror and a chandelier.

Nate glanced around. He'd been expecting red velvet and gaudy furnishings.

"I want to see the girl."

Lily Divine met his gaze with a straightforward stare. "You can't take her out of here."

"I won't. We'll wait for the governor's reply."

"Why do you want to see her?"

"It's my job to know what's happenin' in Thunder Canyon."

Lily glanced at Mollie. "You go on back to work. You can come up and check on me later."

Mollie gave Nate a sideways glare and left them alone. If looks could kill, he'd have been dead that night.

Lily led him up the front stairs. The steps were carpeted, the runners held in place with brass rods, and the stained oak banisters had been polished to a sheen. She led him along a hall with muted floral wallpaper and glowing gas lamps to eventually stop before a room. She knocked.

"Come in."

Lily opened the door. "Violet, I've brought someone to see you."

"Who is it?"

Nate couldn't see around Lily, but the voice of the girl sounded uncertain.

"It's the sheriff, but he's not here to take you."

"What's he doin' here? How did he find me?"

Nate pushed open the door. A girl, older than he'd anticipated, backed away. She wore a pretty blue dress, and her hair was clean and neatly braided. But her face.

His gut clenched at the sight of her face.

She was probably quite pretty, but one entire cheek was black and blue, and her eye was swollen.

"Yesterday that eye was puffed almost shut," Lily told him.

Nate controlled his reaction for the girl's benefit. The closer he stepped, the more marks he saw. A row of fingertip-size marks on her neck indicated someone had had his hands on her throat. The sight and the thought sickened and angered him. She bore a scrape on her chin and her lip was scabbed. Now he understood Lily's indignation.

"Did my father come?" she asked, her voice thin with terror.

"Yes," Lily replied.

Violet's face crumpled in despair, and she slumped to the edge of the bed. Sobs racked her slender frame.

"He's in jail." Lily moved to her side and comforted her with an arm around her shoulders. "He's locked up for the night."

Violet peered up through tears and beseeched Nate for confirmation. He nodded.

"What about tomorrow?" she asked. "He'll come for me then."

Nate had seen men beaten, and unfortunately he'd seen his share of women with scars of abuse, but this was the first time in his experience he'd seen them on a girl so young, and with the signs of abuse so recent.

"He did this to you?" he asked.

She nodded.

"It wasn't an accident?"

"Weren't no accident that he grabbed my neck and punched me. Wasn't the first time, neither."

A knot formed in his gut, but he wasn't a judge or a jury. "Where's your ma?"

"She died. Three years ago."

"Brothers? Sisters?"

She shook her head. "I had one sister. She was tiny and cried a lot. My ma sent her away and told Pa she died. She said it was for the best."

Nate looked at Lily and found her expression a combination of compassion and outrage. He steeled himself to do only his job.

"I can't go back," Violet told him. "He'll beat me for runnin' away, and it'll be worse than this."

Nate found himself wanting to make promises, wanting to reassure her. "We'll wait and see what the governor says. Until then you stay right here with Miss Divine."

Violet nodded, relief obvious on her battered face.

Outside in the hallway, Nate faced the dance hall owner squarely. "Let's set something straight."

"Let's do."

"She's here for protection."

"Yes, thank you."

"She's not material for your stable."

"Pardon me?"

"Don't put her to work."

Lily Divine's eyes blazed with a fire plainly visible in the light of the hissing gas lamp on the wall. "I run a clean establishment, Sheriff. This is a home." She gestured with one hand toward the hallway. "Look for yourself. Right now. Leave no doubt in your corrupt mind. My girls dance and serve drinks. We don't pleasure men."

"Don't waste your speech on me."

"I would never, *never* impose that life on a young woman, and you don't have to believe me or approve of me. The Shady Lady stands for freedom from the tyranny of small-minded men. I can compete with the other dance halls and I don't have to sell women to do it. The other owners don't much like me, either, matter of fact, but that hasn't stopped me yet."

He turned and headed for the stairs.

"How typical for you to see what a man has done to her, and then warn *me* against harming her," she called after him.

He stopped on the top step and turned to face her. "We're not on opposite sides regardin' Violet," he told her. "You're just gonna to have to trust me."

She laughed, but there wasn't any humor in the sound. "Let me know when hell freezes over."

Nate continued down the stairs.

She was incredibly convincing, but he hadn't been born yesterday. He had a feeling his dealings with Lily Divine would only get rockier. He wasn't here to make friends, after all.

God help him.

CHAPTER THREE

"WE HAVE A SHIPMENT at the freight station," Lily said to Old Jess and Saul the following afternoon.

"I'll get a wagon from the livery," Jess offered. "Me'n Saul kin handle it."

"I'm perfectly capable of helping," she told him.

Jess squinted at her. "You got a pretty good knot on your noggin there."

"That's so, but I'm fine." She turned and glanced at her reflection in the mirror behind the bar. The skin around her left eye had drawn a little tight due to the swelling, and her temple bore a bruise, but her appearance was nothing compared to that of the girl scraping carrots in the kitchen right that moment.

The entire household had taken a liking to young Violet and had welcomed her into their protective midst.

Lily tucked in a loose strand of hair and smoothed her floral-print shirtwaist into the waistband of her dark-blue skirt. She ran upstairs for a bonnet and joined the men on their trip to the freight station.

As luck would have it, she entered the building to find the new sheriff conversing with Mitch Early, who stood behind the counter.

Mitch spotted her. "Afternoon, Miss Lily!"

"Hello, Mitch." And after a pause, "Sheriff."

The man in the dark trousers and cream-colored shirt turned to face her. The star on the front of his shirt winked in the sunlight streaming through the window. He was every bit as large and as intimidating as he'd been the night before. He'd had a recent shave and from the spot where Lily stopped, she could smell the bay rum. The scent curled around her senses in a manner she didn't like.

He touched the brim of his hat in deference to her presence. "Miss." Taking a couple of steps back, he gestured for her to approach the counter.

She glanced from his hand to his face. "Have you finished your business?"

"Yes. I'm waitin' for Mitch to have time to haul my belongings to the boardin' house."

She stepped past him.

Mitch pushed a piece of paper forward, and she picked up the invoice. "I'll bring this back after I look over the delivery."

She joined Jess and Big Saul in the rear of the station and stood in the back of the wagon, counting and arranging as they loaded crates of liquor. More than once she felt eyes on her, but resisted the urge to turn and see if the sheriff watched them.

Crates counted, she returned the list to Mitch and signed for the delivery.

"How's the head today?" the sheriff asked.

She focused her gaze on him, gauging his interest. "Hurts to the touch. I couldn't brush my hair on that side."

He studied her, his hazel-green gaze flickering over

her hair. She resisted the urge to reach up and set to rights the ringlets that had fallen out of the knot.

"Brand still locked up?" she asked.

He nodded. "I spoke to a few of your regulars last night. Said they saw him grab you. Said he looked hoppin' mad and you took him out of doors to talk to him."

She nodded. "I told you that's what happened."

"Is Violet okay?"

"You saw her. What d'you think?"

"Doesn't matter what I think. Since you contacted the governor, matters what he thinks."

"Can you keep Brand locked up until we hear back?"

"Unless the judge comes first."

"The judge would let him go. And he'd make Violet go back with him. I've seen Judge Adams's justice."

"Nothin' I could do about that, you know."

Lily knew. And she knew she needed a plan to help Violet if she didn't hear from the governor or if he wouldn't help them.

"Good day, gentlemen."

"Bye, Miss Lily," Mitch called. "Give my regards to Celeste."

She joined the men who waited for her in front of the station and climbed up to ride with the crates in the wagon bed on the short trip back.

"Stop here," she called to Jess. He reined the horses to a stop and she hopped down in front of the mercantile. "I'll be along in a bit."

The wagon pulled away and she entered the store.

Lily made her way past barrels and counters and brooms and kegs until she came to the dry goods section. There she perused the bolts of fabric, looking for something suitable for Violet. She selected a white cotton sprigged with dainty purple flowers, a yellow check and a pale green sateen. After finding lace and buttons she liked, she carried her selections to the counter.

Blythe Shaw had seen her approach and had deliberately moved away to stand in the doorway to the back room. Blythe behaved as though she hadn't seen Lily.

"Mr. Shaw!" Lily called, unperturbed.

Howard had to step around his wife to heed Lily's call. The woman whispered something, and he cast his wife a frown but continued past.

"Afternoon, Miss Lily," he greeted her. "How many yards of each would you like?"

She told him and as he measured and cut, she said, "I've need of threads in these colors if you have some that match."

Howard turned to the enormous spool cabinet behind him and pulled out half a dozen colors.

He'd been helping Lily for years before Blythe had come to Thunder Canyon, and he'd always been friendly and polite. Lily did ample business in his store, buying supplies for her kitchen and ordering readymade clothing and shoes from the catalogs.

Lily selected three spools. "Do you have a lady's hair brush and comb set? Also, I'd like three bottles of White Rose Face Wash, some shampoo paste and tooth powder." She followed Howard's motions as he searched the shelves and found the items she'd asked for. A bottle labeled Old Reliable Hair and Whisker Dye caught her attention. "One of those, too, please."

"Black or brown?"

"Black, please."

Without blinking an eye, Howard set the bottle with her other purchases and tallied them up. "On your account?" he asked.

"Do I have anything on it now?"

"No, you just paid last Thursday."

"Yes, that's fine, thank you."

"Thank you, Miss Lily. Would you like these things delivered?"

"I can carry them."

Howard wrapped her purchases in brown paper, then tied them with string, and she picked up the bundle. "Have a nice afternoon. You too, Mrs. Shaw!" she added.

Howard glanced toward the doorway. His wife had disappeared. The man met Lily's eyes in a wordless apology. Lily offered him a warm smile and turned to leave.

She had a mind to bring her girls and sing in front of the mercantile that very day, just to give Blythe a taste of her own medicine. They could load the piano on a wagon and have Isaac play. But Howard was a good man, and Lily would never do anything impolite to him. It was a nice image though, and the vision carried her across the street with a smile.

"Somethin' funny about that package you're carryin'?"

Lily turned to find the sheriff standing in the recessed doorway of Callahan's restaurant. "No. No, I was just thinking about something."

"I could use a laugh."

"I was trying to decide which songs we would sing if I loaded the piano and my girls on a wagon and we did an impromptu tour of Main Street. 'Golden Slippers' comes to mind, but 'Little Brown Jug' has a certain appeal. Anything you're partial to?"

He didn't look at all amused. "You wouldn't."

"I wouldn't say never."

"If anyone complained, I'd have to arrest you."

"So if I complain about the Intolerants, you'll arrest them?"

A muscle in his jawed ticked. "Don't put me in a bad position."

"Wouldn't be the first time I'd seen the inside of your jail, now, would it?"

His eyes narrowed as he studied her, and Lily discovered she quite enjoyed irritating the man.

"Have a pleasant afternoon, Sheriff."

"Don't cause problems," he said to her back.

She waved over her shoulder. "I wouldn't dream of it."

Lily hummed "Camptown Races" as she strolled away, her thoughts already elsewhere. There was much to be done that afternoon and in the days that followed.

A man she'd never seen before stood outside the Shady Lady as she approached. Near his feet lay a satchel and a canvas bag. He was average height, with tawny curls under a cap, and when he smiled at her approach, she saw that one front tooth overlapped the next. His smile was charming, however, and Lily returned it.

"How do, miss." He whipped his cap off and stepped

forward. "Name's Thomas Finch. I'm travelin' through and lookin' for work."

"I have plenty of help, Mr. Finch. Maybe Howard Shaw over at the mercantile could use a hand."

"Oh, no, miss, I came here especially, 'cause I heard o' your place and I hoped to spend a few evenin's in your dance hall." He leaned over his bags and pulled out a banjo. "Listen to this."

He adjusted a string, then picked out a tune with his fingers flying. The melody was "Old Zip Coon," and Lily found herself tapping her foot. She'd never seen anyone who could play a banjo with such dexterity. He would definitely add to the lively atmosphere of the Shady Lady.

"I can sing a mite, too," Thomas told her. He changed the tune and sang "I Will Take you Home Again, Kathleen." His mellow tones were such a clear tenor that Lily's throat got tight.

"How long did you say you'd be staying?" Lily asked. She ushered him inside the front doors.

From his position on the boardwalk down the street, Nathaniel Harding watched Lily enter her saloon with the stranger. The doors closed behind them.

THOMAS FINCH was an amazing banjo player. His enthusiasm and energy inspired Isaac to try out new tunes, and by the second evening, they were playing together as if they'd always done so. The girls made more money dancing than they ever had. Thomas sang occasionally, and when he did, the crowd hushed to listen to his voice. The dancing stopped, and even the crustiest old miners got tears in their eyes.

"Save those," Lily told him when he came to the bar for a glass of beer. "Sparingly on the slow songs, Thomas. We want happy customers."

He grinned and drank the beer Old Jess slid toward him.

Sheriff Harding pushed through the bat wing doors and made his way to the bar. A few heads turned at his arrival, but Randall had always come in of an evening, so a lawman was no surprise.

Harding stopped beside Lily.

"Sheriff, this is Thomas Finch, our new banjo player."

The sheriff and Thomas shook hands. "Heard you play last night," Sheriff Harding told him. "You're good."

"Thank you. My daddy taught me."

"Miss Lily, can I have a word with you?" the sheriff asked.

Lily led him toward the hallway and used her key to let them inside her kitchen.

"What's on your mind?"

"Judge Adams arrived on a late train."

Lily's heart sank at the news.

"He'll be here for two days," he said. "I have to present Brand to him."

Lily had hoped to hear from the governor first, but she was prepared for the worst. "Thanks for letting me know."

"I understand the judge holds court early. Can you be at town hall first thing in the mornin'?"

"I'm sure Brand will give the judge an earful. But I'm not offering anything. I'm not even going to accuse Brand of assaulting me."

"Shouldn't you be there to defend yourself?"

"Against what? I haven't done anything wrong."

"You do have the man's daughter, Lily."

"He'll have to prove that, won't he?"

He stared at her as though trying to figure out what she was pulling. "Won't that be easy enough?"

The sheriff had been upstairs. He'd seen Violet. "I had hoped that you would help me," she said. "But I guess you can't compromise your job. Even for justice."

Their eyes met, and his were dark with an unknown reaction to her accusation. The silence of the kitchen was a contrast to the noisy dance hall next door. A muscle ticked in his jaw, but he said nothing.

"You do what you have to do, Sheriff, and I'll do what I have to do."

"When Brand accuses you of hidin' his daughter, Adams will come lookin'."

Lily shrugged. "My place is always open. I told the Intolerants the same thing. Come in, look around. Have a drink."

The sheriff studied her. The hazel green of his eyes was a color that seemed too bright for his dark countenance. His hair was black as midnight, and he was one of those men who grew a shadow of a beard by evening.

"They say you were a bounty hunter before you came to Thunder Canyon."

"That's so."

"What are you doing being a sheriff, then?"

"Startin' over."

His reply surprised her. "I have a healthy respect for that. A body should be able to start fresh."

The tinny sound of the piano changed. Isaac was playing "Pickles and Peppers."

"Got me a dandy banjo player, didn't I?"

"He's got a real way," Harding agreed. "I'll see you in the mornin'."

"You probably will."

The sheriff slid back the bolt. "I'll take my leave out this way. 'Night."

"'Night, Sheriff."

She bolted the door behind him.

Lily didn't like locking horns with the sheriff. She'd never broken any laws in running her business, and Randall Parson had never had reason to question her practices. The recent scrutiny of her dance hall had been brought on by the women in town, she knew that well enough. They were the ones pushing for their so-called morality, and she'd been trying to lie low.

But she wasn't going to let Violet go back to her father just to keep from ruffling a few feathers. Tomorrow would reveal where she stood.

Lily wasn't afraid for herself. Violet was the one who had the most to lose.

THE FOLLOWING MORNING Nate turned from pouring a cup of coffee at the stove on the side wall in his office as the door opened.

A large man in a dark-brown suit entered the room, accompanied by a younger man who carried a satchel. Judge Adams had pure white hair, though his skin didn't appear wrinkled or aged. His mustache was a shade grayer, and his eyebrows startlingly black. After he'd introduced himself and his assistant, Mr. Ulrich, he settled on a chair, leaving the other man standing near the door. "What cases do you have for me today?"

Nate took a packet of papers from his desk drawer. "There's a family waitin' to adopt a niece. We can drive out to their ranch later." He ticked off a few other cases waiting for the law, and then gestured to the holding cells. "And him. Name's Brand. I brought him in for disturbin' the peace and threatenin' a saloon owner. Threw a whiskey bottle at the owner, too."

"Who was it? Bernie Kendrick? Someone's always got a bone to pick with him."

"No, Your Honor, it was Lily Divine."

His black eyebrows shot up. "Lily? What happened?"

"Jack Brand accused her of hidin' his runaway daughter. Miss Divine denied it. People who were there at the time said Lily took him outdoors. After that, the reports of witnesses don't agree. Big Saul claims Brand threw the bottle without cause. The women who were singin' in the street at the time say she provoked him."

"Singing in the street, you say? Saloon girls? A theatrical troupe of some kind?"

"No, Your Honor. The Women's Temperance Prayer League is a bunch of wives who want to clean up the saloons. Get rid of gambling, whoring, the like."

Judge Adams rolled his eyes. "Lord protect us from righteous women."

"I locked up Miss Divine, too, but after the doc checked her out, I let her go. She wasn't drunk like I first thought."

"I'll have a talk with your prisoner. Bring him out here."

Nate picked up the keys and a pair of handcuffs and went back to open the cell door. "Judge wants to talk to you. Mind your manners." He secured the handcuffs on Brand's wrists behind his back and led him into the office.

The judge listened to Jack Brand's story.

"So, you say Lily Divine has your daughter?"

"Kidnapped her, she did."

"From where? Where did you last see her?"

"At my place."

"So, Miss Lily came to your place and took your daughter away?"

"No, it weren't like that. Vi'let ran off and that harlot's hidin' her."

"Why would she do that?"

"Ain't it a fact she hides women from their menfolk? I heard at the Big Nugget that one of the whores left her job there to work for Lily, and Bernard can't do anything about it. Women can work where they like, Sheriff Parson told 'im."

"What does that have to do with your daughter? How old is she?"

"Fourteen. Plenty old enough to cook and take care o' the place. She's mine to marry off when I see fit, but nobody can steal her from me."

"So your daughter ran away?"

"Damned if she didn't."

The judge leaned back and the chair creaked beneath his weight. "Just what did she run away from?"

"She don't like to cook and clean. She's lazy as they come. Lazy as her ma was."

"You claim Lily Divine is hiding her from you?"

"She's there. I know Vi'let's there. Won't have that harlot turnin' my daughter into no whore."

"What's your daughter look like?"

Brand stopped talking and blinked. "What'dya mean?"

"What does she look like? That's a simple question."

"Brown hair. Kinda mousy lookin'. Hangs down her back. She's skinny. Got freckles on her nose."

Judge Adams looked to Nate. "Sheriff, go to the Shady Lady and ask everyone to stand outside in the street. All the women and the barkeep, everyone."

Nate followed the judge's directions, pounding on the door until Old Jess opened it. "Judge Adams wants everyone outside in the street. He'll be here in a few minutes."

Jess left the door ajar and hurried back in as though he wasn't surprised at the request so early in the day. "Everyone out front!" he shouted. "Saul, go up and get the ladies. Bring 'em down."

Ten minutes later Nate led a cursing Jack Brand down Main Street behind Judge Adams, his assistant, and Mayor Gibbs. Nate noted movement behind a couple of windows, and one by one shop owners and tradesmen came out to watch the proceedings.

In front of the Shady Lady, four men and ten women stood in a crooked line. Nate noticed right off that the women were dressed for evening, rather than day, in bright satin dresses that showed arms, ankles and acres of cleavage. Their hair was dressed and adorned with pearls and feathers, and all of them were powdered, wearing lip rouge on their cheeks and kohl around their eyes.

Judge Adams walked directly to a particularly colorful Lily. She had on a bright-red dress and a black feather in her hair. Strands of beads draped her neck.

"Mornin', Miss Lily."

She offered him a smile. "Judge Adams."

"You had a bit of a dispute at your place, I hear."

"That's right."

"Mr. Brand here claims you've hidden his daughter. A young girl, skinny with brown hair. Name's…what's her name again?"

"Vi'let," Brand replied.

"Violet," the judge repeated. "We've come to take a look."

"Go right ahead, Judge. Will you have time for dinner today? Saul trapped 'possums and I stuffed them with sage dressing. It smells heavenly in the Shady Lady right about now."

Nate listened to the judge and Lily discuss a noon meal and scanned the faces of the townspeople who'd stepped off the boardwalks and crowded in to hear what the commotion was about.

Meriel Reed and Blythe Shaw were straining their necks and giving the saloon girls harsh looks that would shrivel lesser women.

Mayor Gibbs finally made an attempt to get back to the subject at hand. He turned to the prisoner. "You see your daughter here?"

The judge moved away from Lily and came back to stand near Nate.

Brand attempted to step forward. Nate held him in place. "That's close enough."

Brand eyed the row of saloon girls sullenly. A couple of the women returned his stare, while others offered friendly smiles to the bystanders.

Nate met Lily's eyes and found her expression confident.

"Do you see your girl?" Nate asked Brand.

The man sneered at Nate. "No. She has her hid, I tole ya."

Nate let his gaze move from one woman to the next, just like the judge was doing at that moment. He recognized Mollie and Helena, the two women who'd come to the jail and insisted on a doctor for Lily. He made out a few of the others he'd seen dancing with customers and spotted a couple of females he'd never noticed before. One of those two had blond hair and generous breasts that spilled above her dress.

The other had black hair, cut in a straight style below her ears with thick bangs across her forehead. Her eyes were lined with kohl and her lips were cherry red. Her waist was thick and her hips curved like an hourglass under the bright-green dress.

Nate looked at her again, his suspicions fully realized. The "woman" with the black hair was Violet. The minute her identity registered, he shot his gaze to Lily.

She wore that calm, almost self-satisfied expression he was learning meant trouble.

Judge Adams turned to Brand. "I don't see anyone fitting your description. Sheriff," the judge ordered, "you and Mr. Ulrich go indoors and search every room."

"You stay put," Nate told Brand before walking toward the dance hall.

"You'll need my key," Lily told Nate, and dangled her brass ring out before him.

Nate reached for the ring while their gazes clung. Her eyes were a more vivid blue because of the kohl outlining them. He couldn't help looking at her lips, tinted a shiny red. And then his gaze quite naturally dropped to the front of her gown, where the curvaceous tops of her breasts were exposed to the sun. Skin, pale and soft looking, made his mouth go dry, and the valley between her breasts tugged a reluctant reaction in his groin. He took the keys and forced his gaze away from the woman.

He and the judge's assistant went through the saloon and store rooms. He used the key to open the house, and they methodically searched the kitchen, parlor, bath chamber, bedrooms, and every last nook and cranny.

The room where Lily had taken him to see Violet looked just like every other bedroom. A bed, a bureau and lamp, a few dresses in the wardrobe. It could belong to anyone.

Nate hadn't been in that many family homes in his life, but his impression of the Shady Lady and Lily Divine took another gut punch. Cleanliness and order prevailed. Room by room, he discovered the place was outfitted and decorated for practicality and hominess. There was no red wallpaper anywhere. No clothing strewn about, no half-empty liquor bottles in any of the bedrooms, nothing that indicated its use in the sale of flesh.

Lily had obviously staged the whole lineup of women, right down to their gaudy attire. The odd thing was how incongruous their appearance was with the interior of the place where they lived.

She'd either taken the time to wipe the interior of the house clear of any indications that it housed prostitutes or it was decorated like no whorehouse he'd ever seen.

Nate paused inside the largest of the bedrooms, knowing by the size, the amount and quality of furnishings, the adjoining sitting room…and the scent…that the space belonged to Lily.

The furniture was ornately carved hickory, stained and polished to a sheen. The enormous headboard and footboard on the bed, worthy of a madam, would have seemed tawdry had they been combined with fringed brocades or bright silks, but the counterpane that covered her bed was a simple quilt, made from calicos and checks in shades of blue and white.

A huge armoire topped with hatboxes stood against one wall, and Nate walked forward to open it. Someone could hide inside, he told himself. He knew he wasn't going to find anyone, but curiosity drew him.

The wooden rod held a strange assortment of prim shirtwaists and skirts on one end and bright dance hall costumes on the other. A shelf held feathered hats, ankle-high boots, satin shoes and a wooden jewelry chest. He recognized the fragrance that enveloped him as the one that defined Lily, though he'd never consciously acknowledged it before.

"Anything?" Mr. Ulrich asked from the doorway.

He closed the armoire. "Nothing."

Nate knew they weren't going to find a girl, but the assistant had to return to the judge satisfied that no one was hiding in the house.

They returned to the street, where the judge had moved from the glaring sun to a bench on the board-walk. The mayor stood a few feet away.

"No one in there," Nate assured them.

Mr. Ulrich concurred.

"Are you satisfied, Mr. Brand?" Judge Adams asked.

Brand sneered from where he stood in the sun in the dusty street. "I ain't satisfied the whore didn't hide her."

Lily's chin raised a notch, but she kept her silence.

"It's apparent your daughter ran away," Judge Adams said, getting to his feet. "If you truly want to find her, I suggest you seek elsewhere. You may not go near the Shady Lady Saloon again. In fact, Mr. Brand, I find you have no further business in Thunder Canyon. Do you have a horse?"

"It's at the livery," Nate told him. "I'll get his belong-ings and meet him there."

"Get your horse and leave town. If the sheriff sees you again, he will detain you until my return. You don't want to see me again." To Nate he added, "You may re-lease him."

Nate unlocked the handcuffs, and Brand headed in the direction of the livery, grumbling and rubbing his wrists.

"Keep an eye on him till he's gone," the judge said.

"Would you like a drink with your dinner, Judge?" Lily asked, slipping her arm through the crook of his and leading him toward the dance hall. "Our new banjo player could play something special for you. We'll open early today in your honor. What do you say?"

"I say, what are we waiting for? Sheriff, join us later. C'mon, Mayor."

Nate watched the gathering of colorfully dressed women and the few men make their way inside. The doors swung shut behind them. If Judge Adams had any idea of what had just happened, he obviously didn't care. Nate was left with the question of whether or not the judge suspected Brand's daughter had been among those women. He hurried to the jail to get Brand's few possessions, including the coins he'd had in his pockets, then followed to give them to him and make sure he got his horse.

There was some discrepancy over the amount Brand owed Wade Reed for stabling the black, but Brand grudgingly paid it and rode out of town.

Back at the Shady Lady, the piano and banjo players were performing a lively tune, and the judge was watching as Mollie danced with Mr. Ulrich. The man's cheeks were pink, and he held himself stiffly.

Mayor Gibbs had settled down to a game of cards with Doc Umber, who'd shown up while Nate was gone. Two of the girls sat with them, and one lit the mayor's cigar with a match.

Beside the dance floor, Judge Adams clapped his hands and bounced one foot on the floor in time to the music.

"You sure you don't want to dance?" the woman with the accent asked him.

"Oh, Helena, my knees wouldn't last the day if I

danced. And I still have to do some traveling. Show me a Polish dance."

"Not to this music."

"To something else, then."

"No, it makes me too sad."

Judge Adams looked to Nate. "Did you know Helena was an actress back in her country of Poland?"

Nate shook his head.

"Back east, too, isn't that right?" the judge asked.

She nodded. "A long time ago."

"How did you come to be here?" Nate asked.

The pretty woman looked at him. "I trusted a man," she said. "He was involved with bringing opium into the country, and he made it look as though I was the one. It took all my savings and more to defend myself. I lost everything and ended up working for Antoinette Powell, the woman who once owned the bordello next door."

"I remember those days fondly." In a few words, the judge revealed his connection to this woman in another capacity.

Helena looked away, but then seemed to gather her courage and faced both men. "That was another life. I have a different life now. It's good."

So far Nate hadn't seen a thing that indicated there was anything other than dancing, poker and drinking going on in this establishment. But he now knew first-hand that Lily Divine was a master at deception. He had no doubt that she was hiding everything she didn't want him to see.

He moved to stand in front of the bar, and his gaze was drawn to the painting on the back wall. He'd glanced at it before but hadn't wanted to stare while the room was filled with patrons. Now he took a good look and recognized Lily.

A slow heat started inside and worked its way to his extremities. Lily...naked. He couldn't say he'd never imagined Lily without her clothes on. She was a beautiful woman, and he was a man. But until today he'd fought back every last thought of her as a woman and worked hard to see her as a business owner, someone he had to deal with as part of his job.

There was nothing hiding her femininity in the portrait. Breasts he'd glimpsed today were proudly displayed for any and all to view. Her skin seemed to glow, and her hair looked as though she'd just been made love to.

And that smile. Nate experienced it all the way to places he couldn't afford to have involved.

Lily came from the rear hallway just then, carrying a tray of sandwiches and a bowl of apples. Lily's gaudy appearance today still startled him. Even during the evenings in which she worked in the saloon, he'd never seen her wear a costume like the other girls or known her to wear color on her face. Today's appearance was all part of an elaborate ruse.

And it had worked.

The black-haired girl was conspicuously missing from the dance hall, but so were several of the others. He'd bet anything that if he went upstairs in the adjoining house at that moment, he'd find Violet in the same room she'd occupied before. Probably scrubbing her face and removing padding from her clothing.

Lily set one of the tables and placed a platter of

savory-smelling meat and stuffing in the center. The judge moved to take a place and eat.

The saloon owner then approached Nate. She glanced from the painting to his face, her composure undisturbed. "Please join the judge. Dinner is on the house." She studied him a moment. "You didn't tell the judge."

"About what?"

"About…anything."

"He didn't ask about anything."

She placed her hand over the back of his then, her fingers warm and soft. She'd probably caressed a hundred men far more intimately, but regardless, his chest ached with the sweetness of her touch and the disturbing thoughts that followed.

"Thank you," she said.

The shape of her lips, the feminine scent that enveloped her, the feelings she caused inside him all warred with the knowledge of who she was and how she made her living.

But the fact that she wasn't ashamed of anything about her life was what tipped his confidence. He looked at her and saw the woman in the painting.

He was asking for a lot of trouble.

CHAPTER FOUR

EACH DAY breakfast was served at ten in the kitchen of the house. After the dance hall closed, Lily's help worked late into the night cleaning up, so their mornings didn't start early. Occasionally there were a few hangovers, but as a general rule, none of her help drank overmuch.

This morning the girls were cheerful, mostly because of the scheme they'd pulled over on Violet's father.

"I din't say nothin', Miss Lily," Saul told her proudly.

Lily had suffered pangs of remorse about instructing Big Saul to say nothing about Violet. She felt as though she were encouraging a child to lie, but she hadn't been willing to risk that the big fellow would unwittingly give away Violet's whereabouts. "It's never good to lie, Saul, but we had to protect Violet, you understand?"

He nodded. "Yes'm."

"I think we should get in the habit of addressing our newest friend by a different name, though," Lily suggested. "That is, if you're planning to stay with us." She looked to their latest boarder. "Are you?"

Violet nodded. "Oh, yes. I'd very much like t' stay. Thank you."

"What shall we call you?" Mollie asked.

Violet blinked as she thought. "Well…" Her fresh dark hair and bangs made her eyes look very blue. The area around one was still pitifully discolored. "I've always thought Francesca was a pretty name."

"Very French," Helena agreed with a nod.

"And it goes with the dark hair," Celeste added.

"Francesca it is, then," Lily said. "Ladies and gentlemen, meet Miss Francesca Dumont."

Thomas stood and bowed in a sweeping gesture. "I shall have to write a song in your honor, Miss Francesca."

Violet stood, in keeping with the good nature of the naming ceremony, and made a curtsy. "Thank you, all of you." She wiped appreciative tears from her eyes. Her chin trembled for an instant before she said, "I'll work to repay my debt."

"You have no debt," Lily hastened to tell her. "You've already been pitching in, so I figure you started your new job a few days ago. You'll earn your keep, plus get paid at the end of the week just like everyone else. But we do have rules to abide by." She thought a moment. "Normally the help is allowed two free drinks a night if they want them."

"You cain't save 'em up, though," Old Jess said with a wink.

Everyone in the gathering chuckled.

"But you're too young, so no drinking for you." Lily made a point of looking to Old Jess to make sure he understood her edict. He nodded his compliance.

"No men upstairs," Helena said, continuing the rule list.

Violet's cheeks reddened, and the women laughed.

"It's funny, is it not?" Mollie asked. "Half the townspeople think this is a bordello, but there are no men allowed."

"It's a good rule," Helena said. "This is a place for second chances. There are many of us who appreciate feeling safe and being free of men."

"We honor privacy," Lily told her. "No one enters another's room without permission. If you want to borrow something, you ask. If you need anything, you come to me. Anyone caught stealing will be asked to leave."

"It's like family," Rosemary told Violet. "Closest thing most of us ever had, in fact."

The others agreed with nods.

"Chores are divided up monthly, and Helena is in charge of that schedule," Lily continued. She glanced from one woman to the next before she spoke again. "I think Francesca is too young to dance with the customers. How will the rest of you feel if she doesn't share that part of the work?"

"She can wash glasses and help Old Jess clean up," Mollie suggested.

The others agreed.

"I want to do my share," Violet said with a worried frown.

"If you are still here in a year or two, you may dance and play cards with the customers," Helena said. "For now you are too young."

Lily was pleased that the others shared her belief. "Never leave the dance hall with anyone," she cautioned. "If a man approaches you, alert me or Jess or Saul, and we'll handle the situation."

Violet nodded her understanding, and Celeste gave her a hug.

"Thank you so much." Emotion laced Violet's voice.

"We have a garden in a plot of land Miss Lily owns at the end of the street," Helena told Violet. "We're weeding this afternoon, and you can help. Is your bonnet finished?"

"Mollie has it cut out, but I'll lend her one of mine," Lily said.

"Prepare for the church ladies to walk past and ignore us or scorn us with dirty looks," Rosemary told her.

Violet's blue gaze was questioning. "The church ladies?"

The women launched into an explanation of the Women's Temperance Prayer League's recent mission, so Lily removed herself to find a bonnet for Violet. When she returned, she found the girl alone, and used the opportunity to speak with her.

"What about school?" she asked. "Do you normally attend?"

"I went when I was small," Violet replied. "But then my father kept me home to work." A look of anxiety came over her features. "Please don't ask me to go," she said. "I'm older than all those children."

"Can you read and write?"

"Pretty much."

"Can you figure numbers?"

"I'm not very good at numbers. But they'd all laugh at me, Miss Lily. Please. Please don't ask me to go."

"It's okay, I understand. You don't have to go to

school. But I think you should work on writing and numbers every day. I'll order the proper books for you. I don't believe it has to be a woman's plight to birth a baby every year or be cook and laundress to a man and his hired help. You don't have to depend on a man to take care of you. Women end up in bad situations because they don't know any other way."

"I've heard some of the girls talk about how they got by before," Violet said. "It's a harsh living, they said."

"If that's not what you want, then you have to learn to take care of yourself."

Violet looked at her with admiration. "Like you do?"

"Plenty of western women are working on ranches and running shops of their own. If you're not lazy and you're smart, you can take care of yourself. We all need other people, don't get me wrong. But we need the right kind of people and the right help."

"You're a smart lady, Miss Lily. I'll listen to whatever you say."

"I hope I'm worthy of your praise," she replied and gave the girl a hug. "Now get along with the others."

Violet hurried to join the women, and Lily locked herself in her small study, where she kept the ledgers and a safe. After an hour of work, she carried a deposit to the bank.

Amos Douglas spotted her from where he sat with his office door open and came out to greet her. "Good day, Miss Divine. I understand you had a bit of excitement at your place when Judge Adams was in town."

She tried to avoid him, but it seemed the man looked for opportunities to talk to her. She tried to gloss over the incident. "It was a misunderstanding, but it's all smoothed over now."

"That's good. May I have a word with you in my office?"

Lily glanced around. She had a particular aversion to this man. She'd seen the way he treated his wife and held no respect for him. He might have power in the town, but if there was another bank, she'd move her money quick as the shake of a lamb's tail. "I guess so."

He ushered her in and closed the door.

"What's on your mind?" she asked.

"Please, have a seat. I'm just wondering if you're considering improvements to the Shady Lady."

She sat on the edge of a chair. "Improvements?"

"Yes. You know, new tables and chairs, perhaps a renovation to bring the place up to date."

"None of the furnishings are that old, Mr. Douglas. I outfitted the dance hall when I took it over—that was just seven years ago."

"Yes, well, one does want to keep up, the competition being what it is and all."

Lily knew all about her competition, and it wasn't fancy fixtures or decorations that drew customers to the other two saloons. "I think we're faring well enough."

"Should you need to expand or even build another place, I'd be pleased to help you with finances. Just keep that in mind. Your credit is always good at my bank."

"Thanks, but I don't need credit. You're certainly aware that the Shady Lady makes a tidy profit every week."

"Indeed. And a shrewd businessman expands into more property and more businesses."

"What kind of business would you suggest I invest in? I'm not one of the most popular people in Thunder Canyon right now, you know. I don't know how much support I'd have."

"You would have my support."

"Well, thanks." Eager to get away from him, Lily stood.

"Miss Divine, be aware that my wife is not one of those militant do-gooders working to shut down your business."

"I am aware." She knew more about his wife than Amos Douglas thought she did. "Thank you."

Catherine Douglas was one of the few women in Thunder Canyon who'd been here for years and wasn't part of the newly formed resistance. Because of their husbands' businesses, it was unwise for any of the wives to try to hurt Lily's, but it would probably be most unwise for the wife of the banker. Half of Lily's savings were held in this bank. And she was sure that even if Catherine had a mind to join the Intolerants—which Lily knew for a fact she didn't—this man would discourage her any way he saw fit.

"Well, have a lovely day. Should you need anything, don't hesitate to come see me."

His eagerness to lend her money was strange, but not uncommon. He'd said similar things on more than one occasion. Lily shrugged it off. He knew how much money she held in his bank, and she suspected he wanted a chance to dip into some of it. The day she asked him for anything would be a frigid day in hell.

At the end of the street, her ladies were weeding the garden in the afternoon sun. Lily stopped to visit with them and look over the summer vegetables. "What is that you have there, Francesca?"

Violet held up a basket of ripe red tomatoes.

"I'll look forward to those at dinner."

Out of the corner of her eye, she caught movement at the mercantile as the shade was drawn down over the window. Probably not as much to hold out the afternoon sun as to shield Blythe Shaw from their contaminating presence, she thought, and chalked up the rudeness to those Bible thumpers.

Beatrice Gibbs exited the mercantile just then, turned her face aside and walked past. Lily watched the woman approach the sheriff's office.

"I'll have cold lemonade ready when you get back," Lily told the women and made her way home.

A TELEGRAM HAD BEEN DELIVERED to Nate that morning, and he read it over again. It was from the governor, asking for a report on the Brand girl. Nate hated paperwork, but it appeared as though the law was taking the situation seriously, and it was his duty to respond with the facts so the governor could make an informed decision.

He looked up from the stack of papers on his desk as the door opened and a buxom woman in a blue dress and matching hat entered the jail office.

He stood.

"How do you do, Sheriff," she said affably. "I'm Mrs. Peyton Gibbs, the mayor's wife."

"How do, ma'am."

"I trust you've found your lodging adequate."

"The boarding house is fine, yes."

"That's nice. I understand you're thinking about purchasing a house?"

"That's so."

"Well, that's just lovely. There's nothing like one's own home to make one feel at home, is there?"

She'd just spoken in circles, but he nodded as though she'd made sense.

"I'd like to make you feel more welcome and invite you to our home for dinner tomorrow evening. The mayor and I desire to get acquainted with you."

"Thank you, ma'am. That would be nice."

"Lovely. Seven o'clock, then. It's the big house with the red shutters on First Street."

"I'll be there."

She turned and swept out of the office with a swish of skirts, like a queen making a royal exit.

Nate moved to peer out the window, observing that she passed the garden lot across the street without so much as acknowledging the women who toiled in the sun.

His gaze took in the rows of beans and mounds of blossoming melon plants. He'd noticed the well-tended garden right off, and after inquiring about the owner found it no surprise that the property belonged to Lily Divine. Quite an ingenious watering system had been set up, with troughs fed by a mountain stream in the nearby hillside.

The women from the Shady Lady didn't seem to notice that Mrs. Gibbs had passed by without a greeting or sideways glance—or if they had, they had ignored her as well.

Mitch Early paused on his way past the garden, and

Celeste offered a smile. The two spoke for a moment, and then Mitch backed away with a jerky wave. Celeste shaded her eyes with a hand and watched as he passed to the other side of the street on his errand.

One of the other women must have teased her, because Celeste picked up a dirt clod and tossed it at her.

Nate had been in hundreds of frontier towns, had frequented his share of saloons and dance halls, and he'd never given much thought to the women who worked in them.

He'd never stayed in one place long enough to notice the distance regulated by the other women or the lowly place the saloon girls had been given in society. Working women were a class all their own, but a fact of life. They followed mining camps and railroad construction and westward expansion and were simply a part of western civilization.

Maybe he should feel bad that he hadn't held any convictions one way or the other about them. It sure seemed to matter now, and a big part of his job hinged on them.

Nate didn't think about women much, period. At least, he hadn't until he'd met Lily Divine and her houseful of soiled doves. If ever he had need of a woman, he didn't think, he just took care of the itch. There'd only been one woman he'd ever let into his head—and his heart. And that had been a lifetime ago.

Being in Thunder Canyon was the new life he'd wanted, though. Now he had to deal with it.

THE FOLLOWING EVENING Nate paid for a bath and a shave, then dressed in the best clothes he owned, dark trousers and a white shirt and string tie. He walked to the Gibbses' home.

A slender girl with a white apron over her dress and a matching cap covering her red hair answered the door. She took his hat and ushered him into the parlor.

"Hello, Sheriff." Peyton Gibbs greeted him with a hearty handshake.

"Evenin', Mayor."

"Dinner will be ready shortly. Have a seat."

Nate glanced around and settled on an uncomfortable brocade settee.

"I haven't had a chance to commend you on the way you conducted the incident with the Brand fellow. The society women were up in arms, weren't they?"

"The whole thing was a big mistake."

"It ended well. Thank goodness the judge came when he did."

The last Nate had seen of the mayor that day, he'd been playing cards at the Shady Lady. Nate would bet a penny to a dollar that the man's wife didn't know.

"I mailed a letter to the governor this afternoon. He asked for my account of the incident. I suspect he intends to provide some sort of protection for…the missing girl."

"Sheriff Harding!" Beatrice Gibbs entered the room, dressed in a blue satin gown that rustled as she walked. Nate thought the gown was too formal for a simple dinner, but what did he know?

Nate stood. "Mrs. Gibbs. You look lovely this evening."

"Why, thank you," she said with a blush that stained her cheeks blotchy red. "Dinner is served. Shall we move into the dining room?"

She hooked her arm through Nate's and led him into a room set with a long table draped with pristine linen and laden with white china. A candelabra held half a dozen burning tapers. The mayor had followed and moved to stand behind his wife's chair.

Another woman appeared from an opposite doorway. This one was young and pretty and dressed in a yellow gown. She wore her dark-blond hair in sausage curls that lay against her long slender neck, and her round eyes were a grayish blue. She smiled hesitantly.

"Sheriff, please meet our daughter, Evangeline. Evangeline, this is Sheriff Harding."

She made a little curtsy. "How do you do, Sheriff?"

"Pleased to meet you, Miss Gibbs."

Beatrice ushered them to their places, seating Nate beside Evangeline. Nate pulled out her chair and then seated himself. He glanced uneasily at the gold-plated flatware and the crystal glasses, then at the young woman beside him.

She spread her napkin in her lap and he did the same.

"Where are you from originally, Sheriff?" the young woman asked as the serving girl held a platter of roast beef between the two of them.

"Born in the Oklahoma Territory," he answered and took several slices of meat. "Lived a little bit of everywhere since then."

"What's your favorite part of the country?" she asked.

"Every state has its share of exceptional scenery," he

told her. "Colorado's pretty. Kentucky's green and fertile. I'm partial to Montana and Wyomin', though."

"So you've decided to settle here in Thunder Canyon?" Beatrice asked.

"Yes, ma'am. I believe so."

Once their plates were filled, Mrs. Gibbs picked up her fork to eat, and Nate followed her cue.

"I've eaten on the trail and in saloons for so long that I'd forgotten what good food tasted like," he said. "This is a treat."

Her smile broadened with pride, then she cocked her head and asked, "Does Shirley Staub offer a decent menu?"

"She cooks fine meals."

"I always say the presentation is half the joy. I like to set out my good things."

"Everythin' looks real nice, ma'am."

Beatrice smiled, and they continued eating.

"Evangeline returned from tutoring in the East only a few months ago," Beatrice told him. "She spent a year at a young women's finishing school."

"Whereabouts, miss?" Nate asked.

"Connecticut," Evangeline replied.

"So you've seen some of the country, too."

"That's it, I'm afraid. The stops along the rails weren't much to look at. I did spend a few weeks in Chicago with my mother's aunt on my way home, however. She and Mother's cousins showed me the sights. I attended the theater."

"We women are bringing civility and society mores to Thunder Canyon," Beatrice said. "We plan to have an elegant restaurant soon, and even our own theater. Maybe the brick building on Main Street could be put to good use."

"You women could never afford that," her husband chided. "Douglas bought that from the builder and has had to pay the taxes on it ever since. He'll want a gold mine in exchange."

"Well, whatever we do, Montana isn't going to remain uncivilized and heathen. We're modern-thinking people, Sheriff. The days of the lawless frontier with its oases of sinful pleasure and dens of iniquity will soon be driven into our past."

"That's quite a job you're speaking of there," Nate said. "Thunder Canyon is a mining town."

"The miners have their tents and camps in the hills and along the streams. They can just keep to themselves."

"It's their gold and their money that started this town." How could she dismiss the origin of the place where she was living? He looked to the mayor, but the man was studying the pile of glazed carrots on his plate. "It's still their money supportin' the economy," Nate pointed out.

"Not for long," she replied with conviction. "We don't need their money. We're generating a thriving community here."

Again Nate looked to Mayor Gibbs. The woman was being unrealistic if she thought the place would thrive without the miners. Who would support her fancy restaurant and a theater? "You'd better be lookin' for a whole lot more residents, then," he told her.

The mayor continued to eat and stayed out of the discussion.

The serving girl poured coffee for the men and tea for the ladies.

Mrs. Gibbs got up and returned with dessert, a fluffy white cake served with juicy ripe strawberries and sugary red sauce.

"Evangeline made the cake, didn't you, dear?" Beatrice served thick slices.

Her daughter nodded.

Nate took a bite. "It's the best dessert I've had since I don't know when."

The young woman blushed and lowered her gaze to her plate.

Nate enjoyed every bit of his dessert, but refused a second piece. He finished his coffee.

"Let's retire for a smoke, shall we?" Peyton suggested.

"That's a disgusting habit, Mr. Gibbs," his wife said, but he ignored her and led Nate to his study, where he closed the door and opened both windows.

He handed Nate a cigar and then lit it with a match he struck against a flint on his desk.

"Men built the saloons and the liveries and the stores," Peyton told Nate through a haze of smoke. "Womenfolk brought schools and churches. Takes both to make a flourishing town."

"I see your point. But I don't see the town bein' much without the miners and the saloons. I've seen other towns where the gold ran out. The people up and moved on and there was nothing left. You have to have money comin' in."

"The women would think it was all their doing if suddenly the miners or the dance halls were gone."

Nate chuckled.

"In time there will be more ranchers. There's money in horses and cattle, too. Amos Douglas is working on building up a substantial ranch."

Nate slanted his head in concession to the mayor's point. "I guess it's good to have a plan in case the gold ever does run out."

The mayor nodded.

"I'm walkin' a fine line here," Nate told him. "Between the wives and the dance halls. You know it, because you put me here."

Mayor Gibbs leaned back in his chair. "Better you than me, son. Better you than me."

Not very encouraging words, he thought. The more Nate was around these people, the more he wondered what he'd gotten himself into.

CHAPTER FIVE

AN HOUR LATER Nate strolled the boardwalk, coming to the front of the Big Nugget and pushing through the doors.

Heads turned in his direction. The place reeked like smoke and whiskey and unwashed bodies, definitely a step down from the Shady Lady. He nodded a greeting and walked to the bar, his heels encountering grit on the filthy wood floor.

"Evenin', Sheriff." Bernie Kendrick ran his own bar. He poured a shot and slid the glass toward Nate. "On the house."

"Thanks." Nate picked up the whiskey and the rot-gut smell burned his nose before he ever got it to his lips. In contrast, Mayor Gibbs had served him smooth Kentucky bourbon.

Nate downed the shot so he didn't offend the saloon owner, but it burned his throat and landed on top of his dinner with a vengeance.

The women who accompanied men at the card tables were thin, with harsh expressions and weary eyes. No one danced to the music, and the piano player looked as if he would fall off the stool in a drunken heap at any moment. The clash of notes the man was pounding on the keyboard sounded more like a cat running over the keys than a song.

Bernie said something to one of the girls, who then ran up the open stairway and disappeared to the second floor. No doubt warning the men and women upstairs not to come down while the sheriff was present, he surmised. Nate was already convinced that there was money being exchanged for favors in the rooms above. He just didn't know what he was supposed to do about it.

His job was to be visible and vigilant. To *look* like he was cracking down. Well, he was visible, making an appearance in each dance hall at least once a night. He was vigilant. He knew what was going on. Cracking down? Unless he had instructions otherwise, or complaints, he was keeping things on an even keel.

Nate spoke to a few miners, listened to one of the girls tell an off-color joke, then nodded his goodbye to Bernie and left.

Things were much the same at Zeke Taylor's saloon, the Three Moon Palace. Nate avoided the bar so he wouldn't be obliged to accept a drink. The inside of the "palace" was a crude structure with rough-hewn walls, and floors that hadn't been scrubbed since Moses was a baby. Nate's skin crawled when he thought about the women and the rooms upstairs.

At a table in the corner two men argued over a hand of cards, and Nate waited around until the dispute was settled without incident.

He gratefully walked out into the fresh air and took his time making his way to the Shady Lady. As he reached the entrance, he glanced inside. The place was twice as full as the other saloons, and it was easy to see why. The drinks cost just as much, but the whiskey was better, the place clean and the atmosphere lively.

He entered the room and heads nodded in acknowledgment. He spotted Lily at the bar and settled on a stool close by. Avoiding looking up at the painting, he looked at her instead.

The low neckline of her green satin dress revealed tantalizing crests of cleavage that made his head feel light and his other parts feel heavy. She'd wound a rope of pearls around her throat a few times, and her hair was caught up by tortoiseshell combs studded with rhinestones.

With one hand on her hip, she smiled. "You look like you could use some cheering up. I have just the thing for you."

He raised a brow and watched as she poured a shot of rye into a glass of cider and then twisted a slice of lemon into the mixture. He'd bet neither of the other saloon owners ever spent a penny on a lemon.

"This is Buffalo Bill's favorite drink," she said, pushing the glass toward him.

"You've served drinks to William Cody?"

She grinned. "Passed through on one of his buffalo hunts."

Nate didn't know whether or not to believe her, but he tasted the drink and enjoyed it even more than he had the mayor's bourbon. "How'd you know I'd like it?"

"I have a knack for knowing what men like," she replied with a wink.

He studied her but didn't see a suggestive gleam in

her eye or any hint of double meaning. His body reacted all the same. How a whore could tie him in a double knot, he didn't know. But he didn't like his weakness.

The dark-haired girl came through the doorway behind Lily and loaded dirty glasses into a small crate. The girl glanced over at Nate, then quickly away.

Without thick powder and rouge, the purpling under her eye was visible. She didn't appear the same, because of her hair color and the way it had been cut, but there was no doubt in Nate's mind that this girl was Violet Brand.

"New girl?" he asked.

Lily nodded. "Francesca, this is Sheriff Harding."

The girl gave him a sideways glance and a nod, then carried the crate into the back room.

"Not very friendly, is she?" he asked.

"She's shy." Lily made herself a drink like Nate's and came around the end of the bar to sit beside him. "I don't do this often, but it's a good drink on a warm summer night."

He had the opportunity to note that the hem of her dress decently covered all but her ankles, and he breathed a sigh of relief. Her delicate floral scent drifted to where he sat and melted his resolve.

His gaze unerringly rose to the portrait of the nude Lily, where he observed the pearls and her breasts for a moment, then forced his attention back to the drink in front of him.

He shouldn't be thinking about Lily Divine naked. Shouldn't notice the way her dress pushed up her breasts or molded her slender waist. Shouldn't have *any* personal thoughts about her at all. He thought about her comfortable-looking room upstairs, the carved hickory bed and patchwork quilt, and wondered if that was where she took customers.

The whiskey he'd slugged back at the Big Nugget still burned in his belly, but now the heat had spread. He took off his hat and wiped his brow with a handkerchief.

"Warm night," Lily observed.

He nodded.

Nate let his gaze wander the room, resting on a customer here and there, recognizing Doc Umber, the Callahan fellow who owned the restaurant where he ate many nights, and Wade Reed, who sat at a table playing cards with Helena and two miners.

The livery owner's presence didn't really surprise him. There wasn't much other entertainment in town. But it did amuse him that the husband of the woman who led the Women's Temperance Prayer League was playing poker and sipping a beer.

As though his thoughts had conjured it up, the sound of the women's nightly caterwauling drifted through the doorway.

He turned to meet Lily's eyes and saw a bright fire light in their blue depths.

"Excuse me, Sheriff." Lily slipped down from the stool and strolled to the doorway, where she pushed open the bat wings and stood in the dark opening. "Choir's a mite slim this evening," she called to the group. "Some of the ladies find amusement elsewhere?"

She'd be better off to ignore them rather than taunt

them, he thought, listening to their haughty replies and glancing at Wade Reed, who'd just heard his wife's voice and suddenly seemed interested in the rear hallway.

Lily turned back to the room and called to the man at the piano. "Play something lively, Isaac!"

Nate got up and strode toward Lily. "Just shut the doors and ignore them."

"Like they're ignoring me?" She called out again, "It's warm in here, isn't it? Come dance by the doorway, so you can feel the night breeze. Mr. Ridley, will you dance with me?"

A grinning rancher joined Lily in the doorway, and a few at a time, others joined them, until a dozen dancers frolicked just inside the entrance.

Nate skirted the perimeter of the group and edged his way out into the night. He couldn't even hear his boots on the boardwalk above the clomping of the feet inside, the piano music, and the women who shrieked a hymn at the tops of their voices on the street. "*'Bringing in the sheaves, bringing in the sheaves…'*"

Meriel Reed had edged up near the boardwalk and was peeking under the bat wing doors to get a better look. "*'We shall come rejoicing, bringing i-i-in the sheaves'!*"

Nate observed the gathering of women with a sinking feeling. He didn't see how any of this would bode well.

Finally their song wound down.

"Let us pray for the sinners!" Blythe Shaw called.

The women gathered in a circle, held hands and bowed their heads.

Nate didn't know how God could hear their silent prayers over the clamor coming from the dance hall, nor why they'd want the competition. "Shouldn't you move your prayer meetin' to the church?" he asked.

"This is where we're needed to do God's work," one of the wives replied. "This is a battleground, and we're here to wage war against sin and drunkenness."

"I was just in there," he told them. "I didn't see much sinnin' going on."

"The whole place is a den of iniquity and evil," Blythe told him. Her eyes narrowed. "You'll do well to remember who you're working for, Sheriff Harding."

"I'm workin' for the people of Thunder Canyon, you can be assured. And when I see someone breakin' the law, you can bet I'll take care of it."

"See that you do," she retorted. "Let's move on to the next battlefield, ladies."

As the gathering moved away, Nate noted that Beatrice Gibbs hadn't been in their midst that night. He couldn't recall ever seeing Evangeline with them, but he'd never had his attention called to her until that evening, so he might not have noticed.

Behind him, Lily stepped out onto the boardwalk and joined him near the stairs. "Guess they didn't like our music."

"Why do you taunt them?"

"Why do they harass me?"

"They think you're doing something sinful in there."

"And that's my business, isn't it? I was here before those women packed their fancy dresses and uppity ways and came hunting husbands. I washed smelly laundry, served drinks and earned my place in this town. I've shoveled more snow and horse dung off that street out there than they've seen clouds in their useless lives. I built my dance hall from the ground up and paid for every board and beer glass with hard work." Conviction was evident in her determined tone.

"It's your kind of work they're objectin' to, Miss Lily," he said respectfully. "Don't you see that?"

"I'm not ashamed of what I do, Sheriff. It's more shameful to rely on a man for your next meal and a roof over your head than it is to control your own life."

"But you *do* rely on men, lots of them," he replied. "The Shady Lady wouldn't be in business if it wasn't for men."

"Wrong." She faced him with angry passion in her eyes and conviction in her expression. "I rely on customers, the same as Wade Reed and Howard Shaw and Amos Douglas. I choose who sets foot in my doors and I set the rules for their behavior while they're inside. *I* am not the one *sleeping* with a man to keep my so-called respectable place in their home. Which of us are truly whoring ourselves, Sheriff?"

He stared at her, the accuracy of her statement sinking in. Again, he'd never thought that much about the plight of women. And he damned well wasn't sure he liked it now that she'd made him think—made him see things he didn't like. Things he knew weren't fair.

"I know how to deal with men," she told him, intensity in her voice. "You call them out. You see yourself as an equal, and you make them see you that way, too. But those women?" She gestured in the direction the singers had gone and shook her head. "I don't know how to deal with them. They don't look at themselves honestly. They're living in some sort of fairy-tale world where they're good and every one else is evil."

She glanced up at the dark heavens, and he studied her profile against the luminous gas lamps. Her delicate beauty belied a strength and conviction she didn't bother to hide.

She looked back at him then. "Real evil is a person controlling another person's will and life and livelihood, man or woman."

He saw what she was talking about, and her insight scared the hell out of him. Right here, right now, she made more sense than anyone he'd met in this town so far.

"My job is to keep the peace, Miss Lily, not to pass judgment."

"I'm pleased to hear that. Because passing judgment based on ignorance or narrow-mindedness is wrong." She observed him a moment in the light from the doorway, and the tension seemed to seep out of her. "Come in and finish your drink."

He followed her inside, where the activity had reverted to normal after the display for the Women's Temperance Prayer League. They finished their rye and cider drinks, and Nate thanked her before moving on. "I'd better wander back to the Big Nugget and make sure the women didn't cause a ruckus."

Lily nodded a goodbye.

Before the evening wound down, Nate ended up

with two drunks in cells. He'd hauled them in after one had broken a chair over the other's head in a disagreement over a card game at the Three Moon Palace.

Sometime after midnight both prisoners were snoring soundly, so he locked up and made his way toward the boarding house.

A sound caught his attention, and he noticed a woman walking toward the livery. Recognizing Lily's curly hair, he followed.

She entered the livery, and minutes later the door opened again. She led out a horse, mounted deftly and rode away from town.

Was there trouble? Nate decided to follow to see where she was headed, so he quickly saddled his roan. She was only a few minutes out, and the moon was bright enough to catch up and keep her in sight without getting so close that she would hear him.

What was she up to? What reason did she have to ride out so late at night? Either something was wrong or she was up to no good, and damned if he wasn't unnaturally curious as to which.

He followed a trail along a valley that led to a stream bubbling in the otherwise-silent night. Ahead Lily dismounted and tied her horse to a bush, then disappeared along the bank.

Belatedly, Nate wondered if she was meeting a man. Why would she find the need to hide the encounter unless the man was married and didn't want to be seen with her?

He slid from his mount and held his hand over the roan's nostrils, so it wouldn't smell the other horse right off and whinny. Silently he hobbled the animal and crept forward.

The horse she'd ridden shook its head at his approach, and he quieted it with a whisper and by rubbing its neck.

Nate moved forward, making his way around trees and bushes. He came upon a flat rock where the green dress she'd been wearing lay in a heap. Without thinking, he reached out and touched the slick, cool fabric.

At the contact, a buzz started in his head. Immediately he glanced around for a man's clothing. She had come to meet someone. Someone special, if the rooms in her place weren't good enough. Curiosity about the identity of the man overcame his better judgment. He assured himself he needed to know what was going on in his town.

He peered in the direction of the gurgling water and took several silent steps.

An unmistakable click warned him he'd made a grave mistake. The sound of a drawn hammer. The hairs on his neck stood up. Because of his curiosity, he'd been sloppy. Someone had a revolver aimed at his back.

"Stop right there." Lily's voice.

Damn! How had he gotten so careless?

"Hands up, mister."

Slowly Nate raised both hands in the air. She wouldn't shoot him. Would she? Had he interrupted something he wasn't supposed to see? Had he frightened her?

"Toss your gun down real slow."

He was faster, but he couldn't risk startling her. Still, he couldn't let her take his gun. Slowly he lowered his right hand toward the holster on his hip. At the last second he spun, lunged toward her and locked his fist around the .45 she held.

She emitted a startled cry, but clung to her Colt in a death grip. The struggle soon had his arms wrapped around her as he fought to keep her from shooting. He was larger and stronger, and in moments he overpowered her, taking the gun away and subduing her struggles.

The next thing his brain registered was that her dress was over there on that rock, and he was holding her near-naked body against him. She was soft and warm and disturbingly feminine. The crush of her breasts against his chest ignited a disturbing reaction, one that angered him at his weakness. "What the hell are you doing?"

"Sheriff?" The question came out as a breathless discovery. "What the hell are *you* doing?"

"Keepin' you from shootin' me in the back, I reckon." He released her and took a step back.

She stood in the illumination of the moon, wearing a corset, stockings held up by black garters, and the ever-present pearls around her neck.

The sight of her scantily clad form, even in the darkness, sent messages of sensual alert to the rest of his body.

"Did you follow me?" she asked.

"Had to see what you were up to. Who you were meetin'."

She placed her hands on her hips, seemingly undisturbed by the fact that she wasn't wearing her dress. "And what business is that of yours?"

"It's my business if you're in trouble—or if you're not safe."

"And if I was meeting someone, I'd be in trouble? Or unsafe? Who did you imagine my partner to be?"

"I had no idea."

"Of course you didn't." She edged farther away from him. "Because there isn't anyone. It's a hot night, and on nights like this I come for a swim." She reached for her garters. "Turn away."

When he realized she meant to remove her stockings, he jerked into motion and faced the opposite direction. "Alone?" he asked.

"Yes, alone. Not that it's any concern of yours. I can take care of myself."

The image of her stripping away the rest of her clothing added twenty degrees to the already-simmering night. "Like you did just then? I had you overpowered."

"I could have shot you in the back first."

That fact still rankled him, and so did the fact that she was rubbing it in. "But you didn't."

"Aren't you grateful?"

He ignored that question. "So you came to swim?"

"Yes. And if you've seen enough, I intend to do just that."

The bushes rustled.

Nate turned to catch only the glimmer of her hair and a pale shoulder as she disappeared around an outcropping of bushes on her way to the stream. A few minutes later he heard the sound of water splashing. His imagination went wild.

Lily Divine naked in the moonlight.

That painting in the Shady Lady was burned into his aching mind and he could see her vividly right now. For the first time, he envied the man who'd painted it. And the men who accompanied her up to her room to take their ease in her lush body.

Nate realized he still held her Colt. He walked toward the rock where her clothing lay and placed the .45 on top of her garters and stockings. The backs of his knuckles brushed the fabric, finding it still warm.

Against his better judgment, he followed the path she'd taken. He couldn't see much of her, only her head and shoulders above the surface of the water. The moon reflected circles of shimmering light in ever-widening rings around the spot where she splashed. She was humming "Beautiful Dreamer" as though she hadn't a concern in the world.

"I left your gun!" he called.

The humming continued.

Nate turned his back with resolve and trudged back to where the horses stood. Something wouldn't let him leave her here alone. Maybe she had come by herself plenty of times. Maybe she wasn't afraid. But he wouldn't feel comfortable riding back to town without her. Occasionally he heard water splash. He tried not to think about Lily in her corset and stockings, or about her naked body covered only with droplets and goose bumps, but it was futile.

The seeds had been planted in his mind, and he

couldn't uproot them. Best he could do was keep snippin' off the shoots as they tried to grow.

Finally the sound of her footsteps in the grass alerted him that she was returning. He turned to discover Lily once again garbed in the green dress. She carried something, and it dawned on him after a moment that what she held was her underclothing. Her dark hair lay in a mass of wet ringlets across her shoulders.

She didn't seem surprised to find him waiting beside the horses. "You can see I survived. And I didn't break any laws or conspire with any outlaws."

He watched as she mounted with a swish of satin and settled herself in the saddle. He stood close enough that he could have reached up and touched her bare calf, and his palm tingled with anticipation at the indulgent thought. He could smell her hair and skin, and the scent ignited his senses.

With purpose, he swung onto his roan, and they headed for town. When they reached the outskirts, Nate reined to a halt. She kept riding forward but glanced back over her shoulder.

He held up one hand in a farewell.

Lily turned away and kept riding.

Nate kicked his horse into a run back toward the stream. It was a hot night. He could use a swim, as well. And now he knew the perfect spot.

THE FOLLOWING MORNING at home, Lily answered a knock at the front door. After suffering a restless night, she'd given up trying to sleep, so she'd been up and dressed for hours.

A man stood outside, dressed in a well-cut suit that appeared to have seen better days. There was a mended tear in one shoulder, and the opposite sleeve was unraveling at the cuff.

"How do, ma'am," he said, removing his hat. "Marcus Pinkerton."

"It's miss," she replied. "Miss Divine."

"Miss Divine. I was directed to your establishment—"

Lily's defenses went on alert. Many men had been mistakenly guided to her door. "I run a dance hall, Mr. Pinkerton, and we're open for drinks and card games of an evening only."

"I don't wish to impose, miss, it's just that I've been trying to raise a bit of cash, you see." He seemed embarrassed at his next words. "I'm taking my family across country and we've run into a bit of hard luck."

Lily stepped out onto the walk beside him and noticed his wagon for the first time. It was a fine rig, one of the best made, in fact, and a woman sat on the seat, two children peering around her shoulder.

"What is it you think I can do for you?"

"I have a few pieces of furniture for sale. Unique items, and I'm not asking much. Just enough for supplies and a doctor."

"Is someone sick?"

"No, no. My wife has blisters that have become infected. She probably just needs some ointment and a bandage."

Marcus Pinkerton's face was bright red now, and

Lily understood his need to spare his pride by selling something to provide for his family.

"I'll have a look at that furniture," she said.

The man led her to the rear of his wagon and climbed up to haul out a few pieces carefully wrapped in blankets. He exposed them for Lily's inspection. Quite garish furniture actually, and she tried not to grimace when she looked at the selection.

"This table is from Japan," he told her, indicating the table with ugly cast-iron elephant legs. It had ivory tusks as crossbars and a marble top. "It weighs too much to keep hauling," he said sadly.

"I can see that it would." Lily glanced at the weary face of the woman and the worn clothing of the children. They appeared to be a once-affluent family who'd indeed seen some difficult times. She'd never started out with money, but she certainly knew what it was like to be dragged from one site to the next without a place to call home.

"Are you a miner?" she asked out of curiosity.

"No, miss. I was an importer back east. My partner swindled me out of a tidy sum, and I'm moving my family to start over. My wife's brother has land for us."

She looked from his face to his wife's. "I doubt anyone in Thunder Canyon has seen anything like this," she said of the table. "I know I never have."

She made the man an offer, and his eyes shimmered with unshed tears. She went inside to take money from her safe and returned to find a lamp had joined the table on the boardwalk.

"My wife wants you to have this, as well."

Lily glanced at the black fringed shade and smiled.

She handed Mr. Pinkerton the cash and he carried her table and lamp indoors. She wished the family well and watched their horses draw the wagon down the street.

She gave the hideous table and lamp a regretful glance and left them where they stood in the foyer.

She'd no sooner reached the kitchen when a tap sounded on the rear door. "You'd think we were running the freight depot," she muttered.

Only Mollie and Violet were in the room, and they continued their morning tasks as Lily answered the knock.

Lily discovered a woman with a lace-trimmed shawl draped over her head.

"Can I help you?"

She nodded, though she didn't look up, and Lily was unable to see her face. She wore a yellow and white dress with ruffled lace at her wrists and a wedding band on her left hand.

"I need someplace to stay," she said.

Lily turned to the women inside and said, "Excuse us a moment, ladies, will you please?"

Mollie and Violet moved their pans from the stove and left the room.

Lily invited the woman into the kitchen and closed the door, knowing instinctively that getting her inside would lend her a measure of safety. "Do you need a doctor?"

The woman peeled the shawl from her head. Lily recognized Catherine Douglas, the banker's wife.

CHAPTER SIX

SHE'D BEEN CRYING. Her eyelids were red and puffy, but she also bore a fresh bruise along her jaw and her lip was cut and swollen.

"Catherine," Lily said.

"No, no doctor," she replied. "I just need a place to stay for a night or so."

Lily masked her anger and quickly filled a basin of warm water. "Follow me. Ladies, I'm done in the kitchen," she called. "Thank you!"

She led Catherine upstairs. "No one will disturb you here in my room. You'll be safe."

This wasn't the first time the woman had come to her. Lily wished she could wring her own justice from men who abused women. If that suddenly became possible, Amos Douglas was high on her list.

"What happened?" she asked.

"Amos was angry when he came home last night," Catherine said. "Something to do with the bank, but I'm not sure. He didn't like the meal and the children were quarreling. He gets frustrated, and then he sends the children to their rooms and shouts at me because I'm not disciplining them well enough. I am having difficulty handling them, I admit. I just don't know what to do."

"They see their own father being disrespectful, so how are they supposed to respect you?" Lily asked angrily.

"He's not a bad person," Catherine said on a sob. "He's never laid a finger on the children."

"He hits you," Lily replied. "That doesn't make him a saint." She bathed Catherine's face. The woman was older than Lily, with lovely features and porcelain skin. "This happened last night?" she asked.

Catherine nodded. "He left this morning. I was afraid he would come back after the children had gone to school."

"Perhaps it's time you take the children and get away from him," Lily suggested.

"I have no money of my own to support us, and Amos would find me. It would only be worse then."

"I could help you," Lily told her. "We could get you far away from here."

Catherine shook her head, tears streaming from the corners of her eyes. "I can't. John will be going to university soon, and I couldn't pay for that. I couldn't support the girls by myself."

Lily took Catherine in her arms and hugged her. "You can always come here. I'll do anything I can to help."

"I know. I know. Thank you, Lily."

Lily released her and got out a dressing gown. "Why don't you lie down and I'll bring ice for your lip."

Catherine seemed relieved to have Lily look after her. She lay with the sheets pulled to her chest and Lily rested a scrap of cloth filled with ice against her lip and jaw.

"You know how helpless I feel, don't you, Lily?"

Lily looked into her eyes without responding.

"I've never asked you this before. Have you been in a situation like mine? Has someone hurt you?"

Lily's hands fell still. She didn't share her story with many people. Only a few of the other women knew Lily's background.

"When I was a girl," she began softly, "my father dragged me and my mother from one camp to another. I worked long days panning for gold beside him. Sometimes the streams would be so cold I wouldn't be able to feel my feet until they started to throb during the night."

"That sounds awful," Catherine said. "I had a very pampered childhood in comparison."

"My mother died when I was sixteen," Lily continued. "My father traded me as a wife to a miner for a share in his claim."

Catherine's eyes revealed her shock and sympathy.

"After that I worked in the mine, and I cooked for both of them and did their laundry. My husband beat me whenever it struck his fancy, and my father didn't do anything about it. He was happy with his half of a worthless mine."

"How did you get away, Lily?"

"My husband died," she said simply. "Ownership of the mine went to my father and I ran away. I came here."

"That's when you met Madam Powell?"

"Antoinette gave me work in her kitchen and taught me how to make my own way. I learned that the miners paid well for having their laundry done, so I started my own business and saved nearly every penny."

That's when Lily had become friends with Mollie and Helena. But while she appreciated that the other women were also making a living, she recognized that they held as little respect for themselves as did the men to whom they sold their favors.

"What happened?" Catherine asked.

"Do you remember when the cholera epidemic struck the town? Several of the girls died, and Antoinette got sick, too. She was never well after that. I took care of her and the business. When she finally died, she left me everything."

"And you added on the dance hall and gave the women respectable jobs."

Lily nodded. "Not that anyone believes that."

"I do. I've been here with you." Catherine took a deep breath and adjusted the ice pack on her face. "I admire your courage, Lily. You've come so far on your own."

Lily stood and tidied up the stand near the bed. With a heavy heart she added, "I didn't have children to concern myself with. That's an added worry for you."

Catherine had been lying with her eyes closed for several minutes. Now she opened them and asked, "Where is your father, Lily?"

"He used to come into the saloon from time to time. Usually looking for a drink or money. He died a year or so back."

"So you own the mine?"

Lily gave Catherine a sidelong glance and admitted, "A lawman from Bear County sent my father's things. The deed was among them."

She still remembered how she'd felt when she'd seen that piece of paper. The ache still gnawed at a hollow place in her chest. The Queen of Hearts represented her value in her father's eyes. He'd traded her dignity for his share. "Yes, I'm the owner of a worthless played-out mine."

"I'm sorry, Lily."

She hung a towel on the rack beside the water basin. "It was a long time ago. I really don't think about it much anymore."

But it had shaped her. Driven her. Bolstered her and given her the impetus to create her own sense of self-worth.

"Rest," she told Catherine. "I'll bring your supper up later."

That evening she waited for someone to question her about Catherine's whereabouts. If Amos had gone to the sheriff, surely the sheriff would come looking here. He'd learned from the incident with Violet that Lily was likely to harbor a runaway female. But Lily had her doubts that Amos Douglas would go to the lawman about his wife. He wouldn't want to sully anyone's opinion of the town banker's character or family.

When Nathaniel Harding made his rounds, Lily was helping Old Jess open a crate of whiskey that Big Saul had just carried in and left behind the bar. She finished using an iron crowbar to loosen the lid and placed the tool under the counter, well away from reach.

"I'll take one of those Buffalo Bill specials," the sheriff said, leaning against the end of the bar where he could stand and see the entire saloon, as well as Lily's full length.

Lily filled a mug with cider, then grabbed the neck of the rye bottle. After twisting a slice of lemon into his drink, she handed it to him.

"Warm night," he said, raising the mug in a toast and taking a sip.

She couldn't help wondering if he was thinking about the night before, when he'd followed her. Did he wonder if she'd be going for another swim soon? It still rankled that he'd followed to see what she was up to. Apparently, he would always consider her under suspicion.

She wished she could tell him about Catherine and seek his help in protecting the woman, but things just didn't work that way. If the sheriff knew she was hiding Catherine from her husband, he might feel obliged to turn her back over.

It wasn't right. It was just life.

"Howdy, Sheriff." Spooner Brennan, who worked at the freight office, sidled up to the bar to stand beside the sheriff. "Mizz Lily."

"Evenin', Spooner. What'll you have?"

"Beer." Spooner glanced at Sheriff Harding. "Hear you bought the Pierson place."

In surprise, Lily looked to the sheriff for his reply.

The sheriff nodded. He met Lily's gaze, then glanced away. "News travels fast."

"Your boots're gonna echo in that big place," Spooner declared.

Lily filled a mug from the keg of beer behind her and set it before Spooner. The Piersons had been a family of seven who'd moved to Colorado some time ago. The house was a nice one and undoubtedly hadn't been cheap, especially with Amos Douglas selling the property.

The sheriff didn't have a reply; he merely shrugged.

Spooner sipped his beer and wiped foam from his upper lip. "You thinkin' about a family, Sheriff?"

Nathaniel Harding pierced him with a quelling look. "I'm thinkin' about a little privacy," he replied. "Don't get much at the boarding house. Or anywhere else, for that matter."

Lily hid a smile and moved away.

The Intolerants were late that evening, so the sheriff missed them while he was there, and Lily simply closed the front doors when she heard the women approaching. As soon as they'd moved on without incident, she once again opened the room to the night air.

It was well after ten when Amos Douglas pushed through the bat wing doors and made his way to the bar. At the sight of him, immediate anger rose inside her, but she forced herself to remain calm.

He ordered a beer and nodded in her direction. "Evening, Miss Lily."

She set down the rag she'd been using to wipe a table and moved to stand behind the bar in front of him. Amos didn't frequent her establishment often, but hers was the only one he did occasionally stop by. She figured he had his own supply of liquor at home and only dropped in from time to time to keep a finger on the pulse of the community.

The fact that he hadn't been here for months until tonight, when his wife wasn't home, didn't escape her.

"How's the family?" Lily asked.

"Fine, all fine," he replied, lying through his teeth.

"Those children of yours must be close to grown," she said.

"John's nearly finished with his schooling," Amos replied. "Next year I'm sending him east to attend university."

"And your daughters?"

"Margaret and Trudy are beauties like their mother. They'll make fine wives one day."

Of course the girls were being groomed to be wives and mothers. Women from wealthy families didn't work. "I'm sure you'll be selective in who you allow to marry them," Lily said. "Wouldn't want any harm to come to either of them."

He gave her a hard stare. "They will marry well."

Lily studied the man's unruffled composure, wishing she could expose his hidden disposition and bring him to justice. But there was little justice for the women of this land, and the fact set her teeth on edge. Five minutes in the dark with him in handcuffs and her wielding a big stick would take the edge off her temper. The thought brought a grim smile to her lips.

"And your lovely wife?" she dared. "How is she?"

"She's well, thank you."

"Give her my regards."

"I'll do that. And, Lily?"

She cocked a brow.

"Don't forget my offer. Improvements, furnishings, even a new location. If you should need anything, you come to me."

"As you can see, I'm doing quite well," she replied.

"Your establishment is of a caliber above any other," he agreed. "But remember, it takes effort to keep it that way."

Currently all her effort was focused on not knocking out a couple of his teeth, she thought, and walked away before she said anything she would regret.

The clamor of metal against wood echoed above the sound of the piano, and Lily turned to find the bizarre spectacle of a horse and rider entering the Shady Lady. The man in the saddle ducked his head to come through the doorway. Once inside, the horse shied, its rear hooves clomping against the floorboards. The man swung his hat and whooped.

"I hit a vein!" he hollered. "Gold!"

The frightened horse skittered sideways, knocking into a chair, from which a miner picked himself up and darted away. The table tipped, sending cards and coins flying.

Lily ran forward and grabbed the horse's bridle to keep its head down and to prevent further destruction. The animal used its rear feet to step sideways, and led Lily in a circle.

"Get this horse out of here!" Lily shouted at the rider. She recognized him as a miner who came through on occasion, but she didn't recall his name.

Thomas Finch came to assist Lily by grabbing the other side of the horse's bridle and taking the reins from the rider. Together they led the animal out through the doorway and down off the boardwalk into the street. Lily released the horse and stepped away. "Won't have you breaking up my place," Lily called to him. "I hope you had the sense to go to the assayer's office and the bank before you announced to the town that you'd hit a vein."

The man got a stupefied look on his face and stopped waving his hat.

Behind them, patrons poured out of the saloon onto the walkway and into the street. The man was swamped by other miners, all asking questions.

"Fool will be lucky if someone doesn't knock him over the head for any gold he has on 'im," Old Jess said from beside her.

Lily shook her head. "A little caution would have served him well." She turned to Thomas and Helena. "I'll be back in a little while."

She hurried toward the sheriff's office, not expecting him to be there, so she was surprised when she entered the building and he turned from pouring a cup of coffee from an enamelware pot on the stove. "Miss Lily. Would you like some coffee?"

"No, thanks. There's a fool miner who came riding into the Shady Lady announcing to one and all that he's hit a vein. I have a suspicion his gold and maybe even his person are in danger now. Suppose you could lock him up until morning, when he can get to the assayer's?"

The sheriff set his cup on the top of his desk and grabbed his hat from a hook beside the door. "Sounds like a wise idea."

He accompanied Lily back to her dance hall, where people still milled in the street.

Lily discovered a few customers had gone back inside and Old Jess and Saul had set the table to rights. The card players were squabbling over who had had which cards and how many coins each had had in their stacks.

From the corner of her eye, she caught Amos Douglas returning from the hallway that led to the back. The adjoining door to the house next door and the back door of the house were always locked, so she knew he'd been unable to get into the house to find his wife. But he'd undoubtedly tried.

He had the perfectly believable excuse of using the outhouse, and she would only look suspicious if she questioned his whereabouts.

Half an hour later, as the evening returned to normal, Lily found an opportunity to slip next door and check on Catherine. The woman was sitting on an overstuffed chair in Lily's sitting room, an unopened book lying on her lap.

"Amos was downstairs until a few minutes ago," Lily told her.

Catherine pursed her lips before sighing and speaking. "I must go back to my family."

Lily didn't argue with her. She took a seat on the ottoman.

"I can't stay here," Catherine explained. "I'm thankful for your help, Lily, but I can't stay any longer."

"Where does he think you go?"

Catherine shook her head. "We never speak of it, and he doesn't insist I tell him. He usually behaves as though nothing has happened."

"Not even an apology?"

She shook her head.

"I insist you wait until morning, when he's gone to the bank. Tonight he's had several beers, and I wouldn't feel safe letting you go."

"All right," the other woman agreed. "What was the commotion I heard earlier?"

Lily explained about the miner who'd ridden his horse into her saloon. "Tomorrow there will be prospectors coming out of the hills, claims being filed and grub-staking going on. There's always a big rush when someone hits a vein, no matter how small. Everybody thinks they're gonna be the next to get rich."

"Meanwhile few actually find gold, but you get rich selling whiskey and dances," Catherine commented.

Lily laughed at Catherine's accurate account.

Tomorrow she would place an order for more whiskey and fresh kegs of beer. Maybe she'd buy all her girls new dresses and shoes while she was at it. Nothing like a fresh influx of miners to keep things lively.

NATE NEVER HAD A MORNING he didn't have to go to the jail house or a night he didn't have to make rounds of the businesses. But most of Sunday was his to do as he liked. He hadn't cared much while he'd been staying at the boarding house, because he didn't fit in with the other boarders, but now that he'd bought a house, he valued the free time.

The house had been in excellent condition, with three fireplaces, four bedrooms and a large kitchen and pantry.

He'd been browsing in Wesley Clark's hardware store one afternoon when the man had offered him a bed and chest of drawers for next to nothing. Nate had purchased a few additional pieces of furniture from a fellow who lived on the fringe of town and made tables and chairs.

He had more than he'd owned for years, but the house was still large and hollow. He'd had lumber delivered and spent his morning building shelves in the pantry and more for storage in his bedroom. When the tasks were finished, he looked at the work he'd completed and his mind took him back to another time, another house—a small one with comfortable furniture and handmade rugs and checkered curtains.

He hadn't always played a lone hand. Hadn't always lived on the trail, hunting men. There'd been a time when he'd had a home and a family. He didn't let himself think on those times. He'd had his revenge. He'd left the past behind. But there were times—like now—when the present was such a hollow reflection of the past that he couldn't help but make comparisons.

This house wouldn't always be empty. He'd looked through the catalogs at the mercantile and ordered lamps and kitchen items, but they wouldn't arrive for another week or two. How much difference a few more material things would make he didn't know. A home was more than furniture and dishes, and that fact kept eating at him.

He'd been invited to a birthday party for Constance Thorndike at the Temperance Hall that afternoon, so he cleaned up his mess early and heated water to wash and shave. His house had a bathing chamber near the kitchen. Heating water to fill the tub took too long and it was a hot day, so he used only one kettle of boiling water and enjoyed a refreshingly cool bath.

He couldn't help thinking of Lily swimming in the stream on hot nights, and he remembered his own visit to the secluded spot.

The disturbing woman came to mind often, and it was an effort to push those sensual thoughts away. The more time he spent in his big empty house, the more he had thoughts of bringing someone here to live with him. It was time he put the past behind him for good and started to enjoy the years ahead. He was young enough to have a wife. Perhaps a couple of children. There had to be more to his existence than just enduring.

It was time to think about change. Time to look around.

Nate had purchased a stack of new shirts at the mercantile and then taken them to the laundry to be pressed. He put on a blue one now and tucked the tails into his black trousers.

He'd polished his boots and brushed his hat the night before, so he looked as shiny as a new penny when he stepped off his front porch and made his way to the Temperance Hall.

The building wasn't much more than a big empty room, set with tables at one end and chairs along the walls. Wade Reed had told him that the Women's Temperance Prayer League had purchased the land to build their own hall as an alternative to the saloons.

One corner held a raised wooden platform and an organ. Reverend Bacon's wife was warming up by playing something Nate didn't recognize. As more people arrived, a fiddle player and a man with a harmonica joined her.

The Gibbs family arrived, and the mayor greeted Nate with a handshake. Even the mayor's male assistant was there, accompanied by a tall, toothy young woman.

Nate tasted the bland punch, knowing beforehand it wouldn't contain alcohol. This was the Temperance Hall, after all.

"Hello, Sheriff Harding."

"Afternoon, miss," he greeted Evangeline Gibbs.

She was as pretty as a ripe peach in a pale silk dress with acres of ruffles around the hem and more at her shoulders. Her dark-blond hair was gathered on her head and adorned with pearls and what looked like a brooch. Delicate pearl earbobs dangled from her lobes.

Nate immediately thought of Lily in her ropes of pearls and not much else. It took effort to banish the seductive image.

"Have you tried the punch?" he asked.

"Not yet."

Nate filled a cup for her and she thanked him.

"It's refreshing on a warm afternoon," she said.

"At least the nights are cool here," he observed. "Some places I've been, the nights are as blistering as the days."

"That would be most uncomfortable. Have you been to Texas?"

"I have."

"Oklahoma? Nevada?" At his repeated nods, her eyes widened. "What were you doing in all those places?"

"Hunting men," he told her honestly.

"Did you catch many outlaws?"

"A good number."

"What about Indians? Have you fought them?"

"Made friends with those I could, rode clear of the unfriendlies," he replied.

"Are they fierce and frightening, the unfriendly ones?"

"You might say that."

"I confess I've read a number of dime novels. Such adventures are told. Do the Indians really cut off people's scalps?"

"And carry them on their spears or their belts," he answered. "Most of the tribes have been forced to the reservations now, though."

"Thank goodness for that."

He wasn't going to get into a conversation with this sheltered female about the indignities the tribes had suffered or who the land originally belonged to, so he held his tongue.

With a rustle of stiff fabric, Beatrice swooped upon them in another of her blue satin dresses. "I shall hold your cups while the two of you dance," she announced. "Go on with you. Enjoy the party."

Nate handed over his cup of punch and led Evangeline to the area where several other couples were dancing in time to the organ music. Her cheeks were flushed when she curtsied and extended her hand.

"I'm not much of a dancer," he told her.

"I haven't danced with many gentlemen," she admitted. "In school the girls danced together and pretended."

"Well, then pretend most men are as bad as I am."

Her silver laugh was a surprise he enjoyed hearing.

Evangeline was as inexperienced as he was awkward, which made him feel less so. After a few minutes they managed a fairly fluid two-step, and Nate took care not to tromp on her toes.

Two more musicians with banjos and fiddles joined the group as ranch families arrived, and the music turned more lively. Nate partnered Evangeline for two square dances before Meriel Reed introduced him to her cousin, Lucinda, and Nate danced an obligatory reel with the dark-haired young woman.

The musicians took a break, and Reverend Bacon sang "Carry Me Back to Old Virginny" while his wife accompanied him on the organ. The crowd applauded, then the reverend took a good-natured bow and he and his wife made their way to the punch table.

Evangeline stood talking with her friends. Occasionally, one of them glanced his way, making him suspect he was the subject of their clandestine chatter.

The gaggle of women seemed so young and innocent. He was sure he was an oddity in their midst—a hardened bounty hunter who'd lived on wits and endurance most of his life, while they'd been learning to serve tea and tarts and do needlework. He observed them with interest, returning the curious stares. Their naiveté appealed to his desire to leave his old life behind.

Thoughts that had been simmering in the back of his mind for weeks and months were now rising to the surface for consideration. He wanted a fresh start. He wanted more. He wanted to feel like a real person.

Evangeline's gaze met his across the space that separated them, and Nate liked the way she made him feel. Hopeful.

CHAPTER SEVEN

NATE TESTED A SMILE on the gathering of females, and most of them reacted with blushes. He couldn't remember a time he'd been the center of attention without a loaded .45 in his grip. It felt strangely revitalizing.

"You're quite the popular fellow," Reverend Bacon commented from beside him. "A man like you is a rarity in Thunder Canyon."

Nate glanced around. "I see a few unmarried ranchers."

"Ah, but it's not only your unmarried status that intrigues the young ladies. Those others don't possess your air of mystery and romance, because they're not the exception."

Nate shrugged off that notion. "Nothin' mysterious or romantic about me."

"Obviously, the females think differently." The reverend sipped from his cup of punch. "I'd like to extend a welcome for you to come to Sunday services, Sheriff. I haven't seen your face in the congregation as yet."

"I've never been much of a churchgoer, Reverend. No offense."

"None taken. But God is concerned about your spiritual well-being, and He welcomes all into His house."

"If God reined in some of His more enthusiastic supporters, we'd all get along a little better," Nate replied.

"I assume you're referring to the Women's Temperance Prayer League? They are exuberant, aren't they? We're admonished not to be lukewarm, and those ladies are not lukewarm."

"Seems there's something about not being judgmental, too, but I'm not as familiar with the principles of faith as you, so I might have it wrong."

"You don't have it wrong, Sheriff. Temperance means restraint and self-control. However, some of the more passionate campaigners don't always apply that to themselves."

"Miss Lily calls them the Intolerants," Nate mentioned offhandedly. Seemed he was thinking about the woman half the time, and now he was bringing her up in party conversation. To the town preacher!

"I regret to hear that. I'm sure she feels threatened."

Nate thought any threats she felt were justified, but he kept a lock on his tongue this time.

"Because of her strong independent nature, Lily is greatly misunderstood," Reverend Bacon said. "If people knew her better, they would know what a kind and generous heart she possesses and wouldn't think the worst of her."

Surprised, Nate eyed the reverend. "And you know her well enough to say this as a fact?"

"It's my job to love and care for all of God's children. Some are easier to love than others, of course. When it comes right down to it, Lily and I are very similar. It's natural for us to share a bond."

What could the town preacher and the owner of a dance hall have in common? They dispensed spirits of completely different sorts.

"You're looking at me as though I've spoken heresy," the reverend said with a chuckle.

"I reckon I'm just surprised."

Shirley Staub joined them then, curtailing the conversation, and Nate was disappointed. He wanted the reverend to elaborate on his earlier statement.

"We miss you at the boarding house," Mrs. Staub said, "but I'm pleased you've decided to become a permanent citizen of Thunder Canyon by purchasing your own home. There's a strong sense of community here, isn't there?"

They were joined by the Reeds and Meriel's cousin, and once the musicians were back on the platform, Meriel encouraged Nate to dance with Lucinda.

He managed to extricate himself after one turn around the floor and invited Evangeline to join him for the next few dances.

Darkness had fallen, and though the saloons were closed, Nate still had to check the stores and businesses. "I'm obligated to make rounds along Main Street," he told Evangeline. "It's a quiet night, though. Completely safe. Would you care to join me for the walk?"

"I'd be delighted," she replied.

He grabbed his hat. They strolled along the storefronts, and Nate checked each door. At the corners he left Evangeline standing on the boardwalk while he hurried around to the rear and checked the alley side, then returned.

"All's well," he told her as they stood in front of the darkened hardware store.

"Everyone feels safe with you watching out for our town," she told him.

"I'm doin' my job," he replied. He led her along the boardwalk with no direction in mind. They came to the empty three-story building and Nate checked the doors and windows.

Evangeline studied the facade. "You bought a house, so I assume you're planning to stay."

"It's time I settled down, called someplace home." They moved on. "This is as good a place as any. Better than most."

"It's amazing you'd choose to come here when you've been so many interesting places."

"What you call interestin', I call wearin'. Some places just suck the life out of you. Some people do, too. I came here to get away from that."

They arrived at the end of the street, with the Shady Lady on their left. Lights illuminated the windows of the enormous house attached to the dance hall.

"Like to see my house?" he asked on impulse, then had second thoughts realizing her parents wouldn't approve of her going to a single man's house. "Maybe it wouldn't be appropriate."

"No, I don't think it would be," she replied with disappointment in her voice.

Nate thought a moment, trying to remember what was acceptable. It had been too long since he'd been around people who observed proprieties. "We need a chaperone, don't we?"

She nodded.

"I'll figure out something. For now, I'll take you back to the hall."

They strolled until they reached the Temperance Hall, where music still played.

He removed his hat and held it over his chest. "I'll wish you a good evening now."

"Good night, Nathaniel."

Turning away, he settled his hat on his head.

SUNDAY EVENING Lily answered a knock on the kitchen door.

"I need a job."

Lily looked at the middle-aged woman dressed in a worn skirt and frayed shirtwaist. She'd never seen her before. The woman stood in the alley behind the house.

"Come in." Lily opened the door wider and gestured for the woman to move into the kitchen. "What kind of work do you do?"

"Farm work. We have a place to the south. I can cook and clean and sew and do just about anything. Make soap, too."

All the household tasks in Lily's house were filled by the women who lived there. The woman looked down on her luck, but not the sort who'd work in a dance hall.

"I promised my daughters new coats and shoes before winter if they worked hard making butter. We've been selling the butter to Mr. Shaw."

Lily gestured for the woman to take a seat at the table.

"Yesterday I found that my husband took the cash we'd been saving."

Lily dreaded these stories. If the man had gambled this woman's savings in her saloon, Lily'd pay it back forthwith.

"What did he need it for?"

"Bought himself a racehorse."

Lily walked to the end of the table and back. "I'd like to give you a job, but my girls take care of the house. I have people hired for the dance hall."

"I just thought I'd try." She stood.

"Wait. You can bring me butter. I'll buy as much as you can make. And soap. I'll buy yours. Do you have eggs?"

The woman's weary face crinkled into a smile. "I do."

"Well, you'll have those coats and shoes come winter." She paused. "You should start yourself an account at the bank. Or I could save up for you in my safe."

"He's not takin' away from my children again," she agreed.

They made arrangements for delivery and payments, and Lily saw her to the door.

She'd have to own ten businesses to give work to all the women who sought her out. Or at least two or three, she thought.

A swim sounded good that evening, so she locked up the house and took her time walking along the boardwalk.

No one answered her knock on the door of the house next to the livery. It was late, and it was Sunday night, but Wade Reed had always obliged her by saddling a horse and waiting for her return. In exchange she gave him a bottle of his favorite vermouth every time she ordered fresh supplies.

Lily had just turned away when the door behind her opened.

"I thought you must be sound asleep," she said, turning back with a smile.

Wade stepped out and pulled the door shut behind him, but he didn't head toward the livery. His movements seemed nervous.

"Something wrong?" she asked.

"I'm sorry, Miss Lily," he began.

"What is it?"

"I'm just afraid I can't accommodate your rides of an evenin' anymore."

Lily looked at him in confusion. "You can't?"

He shook his head. "It's my wife, you see. She's the leader of the Women's Temperance Prayer League, and she doesn't think it's fittin' for me to be doin' business with you. I'm sorry, Miss Lily, but please understand— I have to live with the woman. She can make my life hell if I don't do this. I feel bad, truly I do."

Lily took a step away, absorbing his words and his hurtful decision. She wasn't good enough for the livery owner to do business with? "I suppose you won't rent me a buggy or a wagon whenever I need one, either."

"I'm sorry, Miss Lily."

"You know I need a wagon to pick up my supplies, Wade." Angry, she turned and headed away from the building.

"I'm real sorry," he called. "Don't take it personal."

Lily stopped in the middle of the street and slowly

faced the man. "Personal? Don't take it personal? How am I supposed to take it? You're refusing me as a paying customer. I have nearly fifteen people working for me, and we rent from you aplenty. But you're turning that away because your wife doesn't think I'm *fit* to do business with? *That's* personal."

He took a pleading step forward. "Don't get mad, Lily. I wouldn't never do this if she wasn't hell-bent on closin' the saloons. I like you just fine."

"Don't take *this* personal, Wade. Go. To. Hell." Furious now, Lily whirled and marched toward her home, leaving Wade standing in the street.

Inside her kitchen, she made herself a cup of tea and sat at the table, fuming. She needed the use of a wagon and horses for hauling supplies. Meriel Reed wasn't going to put a dent in her business or her determination. On the other hand, Lily could sure damage Wade's. An idea came to her, taking the sting from her temper. After thinking her dilemma through, she finished her tea and went to bed with a plan.

First thing in the morning, she woke Big Saul and asked him to deliver notes to Zeke Taylor and Bernard Kendrick. Lily set about her tasks. The lesson books had arrived, so she saw to it that Violet was working on her numbers and asked Mollie to help prepare food.

Midmorning both saloon owners showed up at the door of the Shady Lady. She invited them in and offered them sandwiches and coffee.

Zeke chewed on the sliced beef with obvious appreciation. "What's the occasion, Lily?"

"I've run into a problem with Wade Reed," she told

them, glancing from one man to the other. "Have either of you been denied horses or wagons yet?"

Zeke shook his head, but Bernard said, "I sent a boy over this mornin' and he came back sayin' something about Wade not having a wagon to rent. I thought that was bull, but I figured I'd just go myself later."

She explained what Wade had told her the night before. "Those women intend to cut us off and shut us down," she said.

"They cain't do that," Zeke said. "Not all the business owners are as stupid as Reed. Or as henpecked. He's bitin' off his nose to spite his own face."

"We don't know that the others won't be swayed by their wives, so we need to stick together," Lily told them. "We need a plan of our own, and we have to show the town council we won't be bullied."

"What the hell can we do?" Bernard asked.

Lily flattened her hands on the table and leaned forward. "I've got a philosophy that's done me well, and it's gonna carry us through this. Don't be dependent on anyone. Don't owe anybody. If you can do somethin' yourself, do it."

Zeke frowned. "What're you talkin' about?"

"We own businesses and property in this town," Lily stated. "Combined, we probably own more than anybody except Amos Douglas."

Bernard shrugged. "So?"

"So we buy our own horses and wagons and we take care of them ourselves."

Zeke scratched his nose. "That'd be a hell of an expense, Lily."

"Not if we share the cost and the upkeep. We hire a liveryman to keep up the place and the animals. Who knows, we might even decide to rent out a few wagons of our own!"

Zeke looked persuaded at that suggestion, but Bernard shook his head. "I don't know. That's a lot of work."

"Bernard." Lily stared into his face. "Work is how you get things. It's how you succeed. If we let the Women's Temperance Prayer League get away with this—let Reed knock us down—then what's to stop Howard Shaw or Clive Callahan or Wesley Clark from letting their wives talk them into refusing us supplies or dinners? What's next?"

Bernard's surprised and angry expression showed she'd made her point.

"But if we *stop* them," she continued, "if we show them that not only can we do without their services, but we can hurt their business because of it, they'll have to rethink their plans."

"I'm in," Zeke said. "What do we need to do first?"

"We need a permit," she replied.

"What if somebody objects?" Bernard asked.

"Who's gonna object?" she replied. "We're just starting a business. Besides, if anyone does have a complaint, Amos Douglas has been hounding me to expand. He'd support our project. I'm not sure why, but he would."

Bernard nodded. "What else?"

"We'll have to order wagons and purchase lumber for a building. We'll decide where we're building these

stables and draw up a legal contract that says we will
share the expenses and the profits." She thought a moment. "I own some land past the edge of town that I inherited, but in bad weather, that'd be quite a walk to go
get a horse. I own the plot where my garden is—not
enough land though."

She and Zeke both looked to Bernard.

He leaned back and scratched his neck. A minute
ticked by. "I got a couple acres right behind the Big
Nugget," he said finally. "Nothin' on 'em but a few
trees. Room for corrals even."

Lily whooped with excitement, and the three of them
shook hands.

They made plans as they ate, and Lily made them
what she'd come to think of as her Buffalo Bill specials
after the sheriff's tag.

"Damn, Lily, what'dya charge for these? I might
have to try makin' 'em," Zeke said.

"I hear you might want to try scrubbing your floors,"
Lily told him honestly.

The man looked at the clean floor of the Shady Lady,
then nodded. "Maybe so."

EARLY ONE MORNING the following week, Nate stood in
front of the mercantile beside Howard and Blythe Shaw,
watching a wagon laden with lumber roll past.

"What in tarnation is goin' on?" Howard asked, leaning on his broom.

Shipments had been coming in on the train, and several unfamiliar men were making deliveries and working on a structure behind the Big Nugget. So many

wagons had rolled past that a new street was being pressed into the earth beside the saloon.

"Seems a building permit was taken out," Nate replied. "Clive Callahan heard it holds a company name. Wynn or some such."

The sounds of distant hammering could be heard along Main Street as the building in question was being constructed.

Everyone in town was curious, but no one seemed to know what in blazes was going on. Late the night before, Nate had studied the framed structure, surprised at its size. It wasn't built like a house, and an enormous fireplace and chimney had been constructed out of river rock.

A stove or a small fireplace would do for anything other than a forge, and he'd come to suspect that was exactly what was being built.

"My guess would be a livery," he said.

Blythe stared at him, and Howard's eyebrows shot up. "Cain't be," the man said. "Town this size don't need more'n one livery."

Nate shrugged. "I'm just tellin' you what it appears to be."

"I hear you're taking Evangeline Gibbs to supper tonight, Sheriff," Blythe said, changing the subject.

She wasn't the first person to mention his plans. News spread faster than an epidemic in this town. He nodded. "Yes'm."

George Lynch had told Nate that his son, Joel, who worked as a barber with his father at the bath house, had an interest in one of Evangeline's friends. It had been the perfect opportunity for Nate to speak with Joel and arrange for them to take the young women to dinner. With the other couple along, they'd be chaperoned, and Nate could show her his house without her parents around.

"In fact, I'd better go lock up my office and get on over to George's for a shave."

"Have a lovely evening," Blythe called as he stepped off the boardwalk.

On his way across the street, he touched the brim of his hat to greet a pair of ladies.

When he reached the barber shop, Joel Lynch spotted him and nearly tripped over his own feet on his way forward. "Sheriff!"

Nate studied the eager young man. "Your pa around?"

"He's cleanin' the stove. You want him?"

Nate hung his hat on the tree with a nod. "No offense, but I have a care for the skin on my face, and you're lookin' a mite jittery there."

"Pa? Sheriff wants you to shave 'im!"

A chuckle reached them from the back room. "I'll wash up and be there momentarily."

George shaved Nate with his usual agility. "Joel's been moonin' over Tess Prescott for weeks, Sheriff. You done us all a favor by gettin' the two of 'em together."

"Seemed a mutually advantageous arrangement," Nate replied as George wiped lather from his chin.

"Should we rent a carriage for the ladies?" Joel asked. "I was wondering about that all morning. What will they expect?"

"Everywhere we need to go is within a few blocks," Nate replied. "I'm sure they won't mind the walk. Seems more trouble going for a carriage and returnin' it than just usin' our feet."

"Hot bath is on the house tonight," the barber said.

"I'll take you up on that. It'll be a pleasure not to heat my own water at home."

After bathing, Nate hurried to his house to dress in his good trousers and a clean shirt. He met Joel at a pre-arranged corner on Main Street, and the two of them walked to the mayor's expansive two-story home.

The maid answered the door and led them to Peyton Gibbs's den, where he sat in an overstuffed easy chair.

"Good evening, gentlemen. Come in and have a seat."

Joel glanced around the room, taking in the dark wood-paneled walls and the expanse of bookcases. A painting depicting a hunting scene hung over the dormant fireplace.

"What do you make of the new structure?" the mayor asked.

Nate shared his theory, and Peyton puffed on the stem of his pipe. Smoke curled around his head. "You're perceptive. And dead-on. Anything built within a quarter mile of Main Street requires a legal document. Lily Divine secured the building permit, and it indicates a stable is going up."

Nate heard the man's clarification with surprise. "*Lily* is building a stable?"

"The project isn't hers alone. The land belongs to Bernard Kendrick. Along with Zeke Taylor, the three of them are building the stables."

"Why?"

"Seems Wade Reed turned away their business. Part of the Women's Temperance Prayer League's plan to close down the saloons, I hear."

The information sank into Nate's mind slowly. The livery owner had refused to rent horses and buggies to the saloon owners. Reed's wife had to have been behind the plan. Wade didn't seem the sort to turn away business from hardworking paying customers—especially those who'd hired his horses for years.

"It's all perfectly legal," Peyton added. "I have a bad feeling that at least one group in town will take exception, but there's not a damned thing they can do to stop them."

"The Intolerants, you mean."

"Who?"

"The Women's Temperance Prayer League."

The mayor shrugged.

"Does Wade know that she—that they—are building their own stables?"

"I haven't talked to him. Only one other person besides you two knows what the permit says and who paid for it. That's my assistant and he doesn't mingle much."

Nate couldn't help admiring Lily's ingenuity, but he had a feeling the members of the Women's Temperance Prayer League would be up in arms over this setback to their battle plan.

The mayor glanced toward the doorway then, and the whisper of women's skirts rustling preceded Evangeline and Tess into the room. The fragrance of lily of the valley wafted on the air.

Nate and Joel stood to greet the young ladies.

Evangeline wore a yellow silk dress with a lace insert at the neck and a white sash at her waist. Her blond hair was gathered at the back of her head in long curls. She was fair and slender and pretty as could be.

"We'll be goin'," Nate said to Evangeline's father.

"Have a nice time," Peyton told the group.

Nate suspected a comment was expected of him, so as he and Evangeline strolled behind the others, he said so that they couldn't hear, "You look fetching this evening."

In the glow of the late-day sun, she blushed and lowered her lashes. "Thank you."

They reached Callahan's restaurant and selected a table near the front window. Nate held Evangeline's chair, and taking a cue from Nate, Joel scrambled to do the same for Tess. The men seated themselves across from the young ladies. Mrs. Callahan placed utensils and napkins before them and took their orders.

The conversation remained polite and impersonal. Tess shared amusing stories about their group of friends, and Joel hung on every word she spoke.

"What does your father do?" Nate asked her. He wasn't familiar with her family.

"He works for Mr. Douglas at the bank," she replied. "He's very good with figures. I'm afraid I don't share his talent. He tutored me in numbers when I was in school, and I was miserable. Evangeline has a head for accounts, though."

Nate looked to the young woman for confirmation.

Evangeline blushed again. "Mother says it's not attractive for a woman to be too smart."

"I disagree," he told her. "Why should a woman pretend to be less than she is, just so a man can feel smarter?"

His comment quite obviously pleased her. She smiled, and dimples appeared on either side of her mouth.

Their food arrived, and they enjoyed the special of the day—roasted chicken with new potatoes and green beans. Nate ate at Callahan's nearly every day, so this was no treat for him. On Mondays and Thursdays the Shady Lady offered a supper, but other than that, this was the only place to get a meal.

Clive carried out cups of coffee. "Evenin', ladies. Gents."

"Evenin', Clive."

The owner set a bowl of sugar in front of Nate. "Suzanna made apple pies today," he said, referring to his wife. "Slices are on the house."

They thanked him, and his wife returned with their dessert.

Nate noticed that neither Evangeline or Tess touched their coffee. "You gonna drink that?"

"I don't care for coffee," Evangeline said. "Please, drink it while it's hot, if you want."

He added sugar and enjoyed a second cup. After watching Nate, Joel did the same with Tess's cup of coffee.

The restaurant wasn't busy. Only a few other patrons arrived and left while Nate's party was there. He didn't feel as though they were creating a spectacle, so he didn't mind lingering.

Nate's meals were included in his salary, but once they were finished, he paid for Evangeline's dinner. Joel paid the other couple's share, and they took their leave.

"I thought we'd walk to my place now," he told the ladies, "so Miss Gibbs can see my house."

"Oh, lovely!" Tess said. "I'd like to see it, too."

They strolled along Main Street, passing the darkened storefronts and crossing the street to walk on the opposite side as they came abreast of the Shady Lady. The dance hall was relatively quiet, but it was still early. The sound of Isaac's piano playing was a tinny echo along the street. Half a dozen horses were tethered to the hitching posts.

Evangeline peered at the saloon.

Nate spoke aloud what he'd thought before. "I've noticed you don't accompany your mother on her evening missions."

"Singing outside the saloons?" She shook her head. "My father asked my mother and me not to become involved, though she ignores his wishes. I don't feel any personal threat from the dance halls, actually. Goodness knows I've sat through enough of the women's meetings to know I should. Perhaps it's because I was gone for a few years, but I just don't feel connected to their cause."

Joel and Tess walked several feet behind them, involved in their own conversation.

"Do you think it's something I should be involved in?" Evangeline asked.

"I admire you for deciding your interests for yourself," he replied.

"Thank you for that. It's not easy. Mother badgers me to join them at least once a day."

The home Nate had purchased sat on the north side of town, away from the businesses and with no other houses nearby. They reached it a few minutes later.

He unlocked the front door, which held an oval beveled-glass window, and ushered his company inside. After reaching into his pocket for matches, he lit the gas lamps on the walls. The night wasn't completely dark yet, but it would be within the hour.

They stood in the small foyer, which was empty of rugs or furniture, and their feet echoed on the floorboards.

"This is the parlor," he said, going ahead to light lamps. He'd picked up two chairs and a side table for the room, but it was still woefully bare.

Evangeline studied the room, as though planning how it could look, and—perhaps—wondering why he'd wanted her to see it.

He was wondering that himself.

Was he actually considering taking her as a wife and bringing her here? He'd thought about it—no denying that. He'd been in Mrs. Staub's boarding house, and he'd seen the Gibbses' home as well as those of a few other people who had invited him by. A real home appealed immensely, as did someone with whom to share it.

Nate pictured Evangeline in this house with him. In his life. In his bed. Nothing about any of those images put him off.

She met his gaze then, a pink stain on her cheeks, as though she could read his thoughts.

"Come on, I'll show you the rest." He led them into the dining room, the kitchen, the pantry he'd recently built, and lastly the study with its brick fireplace.

"Bricks!" Evangeline said in surprise. "Most fireplaces out here are stone and river rock."

"I suspect the owner who built the place was well-off," he replied.

Joel spoke up for the first time. "He was a surveyor. Had a place down by the watchmaker's. He had worked for the railroad for several years, came here for a time. He built the brick building on Main Street, but changed his plans and moved on to start another company."

"What was that building intended to be?" Nate asked.

"He had a hotel in mind. Someone might take up where he left off as the town grows."

Nate showed them the four upstairs bedrooms and then asked if the ladies would like tea. "I got ice today, but I'm not sure how much is left."

"Tea would be nice," Tess replied.

"I set a few chairs on the porch," Nate told them. "Eventually I'll get a swing and maybe a rocker. Why don't the two of you sit out there and enjoy the night air, and Miss Gibbs can help me."

Evangeline accompanied him to the kitchen, where earlier he had steeped tea and left the pan on the cold stovetop. "I'm not much of a cook. I can get by, but nothin' fancy."

"Where are your glasses?"

"Jars in that cupboard," he told her.

She located the jars while he chipped ice in a basin.

She gathered the chunks and filled the containers, then sweetened the tea with a generous scoop of sugar before Nate poured it.

"Better taste it," he told her.

She sipped from a jar. "Strong and cold."

"Passable?"

She smiled. "Yes."

"Miss Gibbs," he began.

She looked up uncertainly.

A nagging hesitancy kept him from committing himself by asking if she'd consider allowing him to court her. The words would make a planned relationship seem final, and that finality didn't sit well with him. He couldn't explain his discomfort, but it held him in check.

He felt as though he had to be careful around her, in what he said and the way he presented himself, and he was mildly uncomfortable with the restriction. Something inside just wouldn't let him promise more than he was ready to give.

"Perhaps we could take a Sunday drive," he ventured.

Her gray-blue eyes seemed to assess his intent. "We could have a picnic after church," she offered.

He nodded, at ease with that arrangement.

"Will you join my family in church this week?" she asked.

Was this some sort of test? "Want to make sure you're not…spending time with a heathen?" he asked.

She blinked in surprise. "No. I mean, I don't think so. I just thought…well, that it would be a way to… show your good intentions."

That brought him up short. *Good intentions?*

CHAPTER EIGHT

WHAT *WERE* HIS INTENTIONS? He wasn't sure, and he didn't like the feeling of not being certain of his next move. Planning well and taking precautions had kept him employed and *alive* for a good many years. He was out of his element in this town and with this young woman, but he wanted the change. Now he had to acclimate to it.

He set the filled jars on a wooden tray. "What do you think I intend, Miss Gibbs?"

"I'm not sure, Sheriff." Her cheeks were ablaze with embarrassment.

"I assure you I don't have designs to sully your reputation or your…innocence," he stated bluntly, because he didn't know any other way. "I just hoped to get to know you."

She wouldn't meet his eyes. She nodded. "I believe you."

"I'll come to church," he said, making up his mind. If he was going to be part of the community, he needed to take part in their activities.

Still without looking at him, she nodded.

Nate picked up the wooden tray, and she followed him through the house to the porch.

LATER THAT NIGHT, once he'd seen Evangeline and Tess back to the Gibbses' home and Joel had gone his own way, Nate toured the boardwalks. The saloons were just closing up, and at the Shady Lady, Big Saul swept dust out onto the walk and then off into the street.

"Evenin', Sheriff," Big Saul said with a boyish grin.

"Busy evening?" Nate asked.

"Yes, sir. Got a peck o' miners in town lately."

There had been an influx of miners since Pete Jenkins had announced a strike nearby.

"Not too late for a drink," a female voice said from the doorway, and Nate glanced over to see Lily silhouetted in the opening. She wore a wine-colored dress with a low neckline and her arms were bare.

Nate took her up on her offer, entering the saloon and moving a stool to the end of the bar.

Lily made them each a rye and cider and sat beside him.

"I hear you're gonna be in the livery business," he commented.

She turned to face him. "Seems so. The town knows already?"

"Not yet. I just found out from the mayor today. Joel Lynch was with me, so by tomorrow plenty more will have heard."

Lily's lips curved into a self-satisfied smile. "I'd love to see a few particular faces when they hear."

"Howard…or Blythe Shaw?"

She tilted her head with a smile.

"Wade Reed…or *Meriel?*"

"Most definitely, Wade *and* Meriel."

Nate couldn't help a chuckle at the thought. "Might be worth tellin' 'em myself."

She shrugged. "Suit yourself."

"Is it true, then, that Reed turned you away?"

"It's a fact. Said it wasn't anything personal, that he had to live with his wife and she'd make his life hell."

"Seems he might be sorry."

"I intend to make certain." She sipped her drink. "Until our rigs are here, I'm paying for deliveries from the train depot to my place. Spooner charges an arm and a leg to use his wagons."

"How long do you think it'll be?"

She lifted the hair from her neck with a tired sigh. The warm evening had created charming corkscrews of curls around her face and ears. "Another week or two." From the bar, she picked up a black fan edged with lace and fanned her face. "I can't even go for a ride until I have my own horses and a place for them."

"Can't go for a swim, you mean?"

"I'll get by. It's just a nice quiet way to end a hot crowded night in this place." She dropped her hair back down and shrugged. "My private time in summer. Though I've dipped a time or two when the stream was frigid in the spring and fall."

Without thinking, Nate said, "I can take you. To the stream."

She stared at him. "You?"

He nodded. "I'll give you a ride."

He thought she was going to say no, because she tilted her head and lowered her chin as though she would shake her head, but she surprised him. "Okay."

"Now?" he asked.

"Give me a few minutes to lock up."

Nate finished his drink. "I'll saddle up. Meet me out front."

She picked up their glasses, and with a nod to Saul, Nate headed out.

Wade Reed had given him a key to the stables, so he let himself in, saddled his horse and rode out without disturbing the man.

With toweling over her shoulder, Lily waited on the boardwalk. He rode right up beside her and slid his left foot out of the stirrup, so she could use it to climb up. She settled behind him, her hands at his waist, and moved her foot so he could get his back in the stirrup. He turned the horse's head and urged their mount away from town.

The bright moonlight revealed Lily's bare knee, where she'd drawn her dress up so she could sit behind him. If he reached down, he'd be able to touch her skin. He thought of the vast difference between this woman and the one he'd been with earlier that evening. Lily's reputation was never in question. She wouldn't in a million years think of asking for a chaperone while in his company.

She'd once stood before him in her underclothing, and though it had been dark, he would bet a month's wages she hadn't blushed. There was a painting of her bare naked over the bar in her saloon, after all. Nate suspected any number of men had been alone with Lily, seen her naked, and had paid to enjoy her intimately. Once the erotic image of Lily with a man had formed in his head, he couldn't dislodge it.

Unwise thoughts to allow while in the saddle, he admonished himself as he slid into extreme discomfort. But he couldn't resist looking at her knee again.

His physical reaction was undoubtedly due to the fact that the only women he'd known over the past years were of Lily's sort. He had to redirect his thinking if he was going to make a different life and think about a new wife and family.

They reached the tree-lined stream, and Nate led the horse down the gently sloping bank. He raised his leg over the horse's neck, so he could dismount first and help Lily down.

"I'll wait right here," he told her.

"Sure you don't want to swim?" she asked over her shoulder as she made her way toward the stream. "There's plenty of water, and it's nice and cool."

"I had a bath today," he said, but she was already gone. This wasn't about bathing, this was about cooling off and relaxing. Why not? He hung his hat on the butt of his rifle in its sheath.

Nate walked in the direction she'd gone and found Lily's garments on the flat rock. He tugged off his boots and unbuckled his holster, then removed his shirt. Closer to the bank, he stripped out of his trousers and waded into the cool water a safe distance away from where Lily splashed. In the middle of the stream where the water was over his head, he spent several minutes diving down and then coming up to leisurely float on his back.

Their activity had disturbed the small creatures that normally would have been croaking and chirping, and the night seemed eerily still except for the sound of the water splashing on stones farther up the stream and the hoot of an owl.

He explored the smooth rocks along the stream bed with his feet, while deliberately not turning to see what Lily was doing. Eventually, though, he couldn't resist and looked for her.

She had stepped out of the water and was drying herself behind a clump of shrubbery that permitted glimpses of her skin through the skimpy branches. As she moved he saw a thigh, her back, her foot and ankle…and his mind filled in the rest.

"I usually sit on the bank and dry a little before I put my clothes back on," she called to him.

"Don't let me bother you."

With one length of toweling wrapped around her, she took a seat on the grass and dried her hair with another.

"You gonna let me borrow that?" he asked, standing nearby in waist-high water.

She tossed the towel toward him, and it landed on the bank. She turned to look the other way, and the fact amused him. He chuckled as he waded out and grabbed the towel.

"What's so funny?"

He dried himself as well as he could with the already-damp towel, then wrapped it around his waist. "You. Acting shy."

"What makes you think it's an act?"

"Your body is in plain sight over the bar for all to see."

"Yours isn't."

He laughed again.

He sat down a few feet away from her and let the tantalizing warm night air flutter over his skin and hair.

After a few minutes, the creatures resumed their normal night noises, frogs jumping into the water and croaking from the banks, crickets chirping and animals making tiny rustling sounds in the tall grass.

Lily sat with her face turned up to the sky. "Peaceful, isn't it?"

He agreed. The sounds were familiar and comforting. "I've spent most nights of my life camped under the stars, good weather and bad."

"You've always been free to do as you wish," she said.

There was a measure of envy in her voice. "I reckon so. What about you?"

"I'm free now."

"There's somethin' to be said about now. New starts and all."

"Is that what you're truly doing? Starting over?"

Nate nodded. It was strange how he always ended up talking to this woman. Saying things he never intended to say, things that he'd never said to anyone before. He guessed the quality made her good at her job. She made a man comfortable, set him at ease.

Her shapely shoulders and slender arms were pale in the moonlight, and she sat with her knees drawn up. She wasn't wearing a stitch but that towel. He wished it was daylight so he could see her eyes, the shape of her delicate feet, the way her hair shone.

He needed a woman. Plain and simple. His powerful reaction to this one made the fact obvious.

"You ever think about starting over, Lily?"

She turned to face him, and he wasn't sure if his use of her name delayed her response or if it had been the question. "I did start over, Sheriff. The Shady Lady is my second chance. My independence."

"Is there anything more you want? Besides the Shady Lady?"

"Such as?"

He paused a moment before saying, "A family."

She straightened her shoulders and raised her chin. "I have a family. Mollie and Helena, Old Jess and Big Saul. Francesca now. We have each other. Are you gonna tell me my idea of a family is wrong?"

"No. As long as you're happy." He plucked a long stem of a weed and twirled it between his fingers. "Most females want a husband is all. Children."

She was quiet again.

He'd probably said the wrong thing. It wasn't likely that a whore would find much of a husband. Maybe having everyone else's husband was plenty more than enough.

"I had a husband once," she told him.

That revelation stunned him into silence.

"I wouldn't wish that fate on my worst enemy," she went on. "Well, my worst enemies do have husbands, I guess." She opened both hands to gesture as she said that. "Serves them right."

She'd been *married?* He stared at her.

Lily could have bitten off her tongue for telling him that. He was looking at her as though it was hard to believe someone like her could have had a husband, as if the title itself meant something honorable. Next thing she knew, he'd be poking and prying into her past, and it wouldn't be in her best interests for a lawman to know she'd stabbed and killed the man she'd been married to.

"What happened to him?"

Here it came. "He got what he deserved."

The sheriff blessedly didn't question her further. She glanced over and couldn't help admiring his muscled shoulders and back. His body was a palette of shadows and his face a solemn mask of mystery. She normally saw him with his hat pulled low, but now, even though it was dark, his wet slicked-back hair revealed his chiseled and handsome features.

Nathaniel Harding was a man to make a woman weak in the knees—even a woman who didn't want or need a man.

In seven years Lily hadn't looked twice at one man. Not until this sheriff had arrested her attention and disturbed her peace. She had wondered, though. There were a couple of the girls who claimed sex had been pleasurable for them—exciting even. Lily didn't buy it, but she had to wonder why some couples seemed happy. She would never trust a man, but she was curious.

Apparently, she held a slim thread of trust for the sheriff—maybe it was his badge, or the fact that he actually behaved like a gentleman around her—because she wasn't afraid to be here with him, not even in this intimate situation.

"Don't act so shocked, Sheriff. It's insulting."

"No insult meant. I just—didn't know, that's all."

"Now you do. And you're thinking I was a poor widow driven to prostitution."

He said nothing, confirming her perception. She had the inkling that he found her repulsive because of what he thought she did for a living.

"You still think me'n my girls are in the sportin' business, don't you?"

He tilted his head to the side in lieu of a reply.

"You think my customers buy more than liquor and dances."

"I really can't say, Lily."

"Come home with me."

"What?"

"Come see for yourself. If I ran a whorehouse, there would be men there. In the upstairs rooms—with the women."

"Unless you warned them ahead of time."

"Warned them about what? It's not illegal, so what would I be afraid of? You could pop in the Nugget right now and get an eyeful, but you couldn't make any arrests."

"Why's it so important to you to prove this to me?"

She didn't know. She wished she did. She'd never cared a whit what anyone thought before, and she sure didn't know why she should start with Nathaniel Harding.

"Ask anyone," she said. "Ask any man in town if he's ever bought favors at the Shady Lady."

"And any man would deny it."

Lily hit the ground in frustration. "Well, hell."

He laughed, and the sound irritated her.

"What's so funny?"

"You."

She stood and marched toward her pile of clothing

with as much dignity as she could muster wrapped only in a towel. Her skin was cool and dry now, and she worked her way into her pantalettes and dress, but carried her corset and stockings in a fist as she moved to stand beside the roan. She couldn't get into a corset alone and never wore one on her return trip.

A few minutes later, she turned at the sound of the sheriff walking toward her. He'd dressed and buckled on his holster. He reached around her to pluck his hat from where it hung on the butt of his Remington. His nearness created an unexpected flutter in her chest.

"I'll get up first and then help you up," he said. He was standing so close she could feel the heat of his body against her cooled flesh.

She should have stepped away, but her feet weren't cooperating with her head.

She could smell him, the clean fresh scent of man and night air that clung to his hair and skin. The image of his sleekly muscled arms and shoulders in the moonlight rattled her composure and made her heart skip a series of beats. Her head felt curiously light.

She studied the lines of his face, her gaze dropping to his mouth. She'd never been kissed. Not really kissed. Not with any feeling or tenderness, and she somehow instinctively knew that this man could satisfy her curiosity.

She imagined leaning into him…closing her eyes… absorbing his heat…tasting his mouth…

"Oh, hell," he said in a rasp.

Lily had closed her eyes in that moment of fantasy, and the dream became reality when the sheriff's mouth came down over hers. Not tender by any means, but not rough or abrupt, either. The feel of his lips against hers engulfed her senses.

He urged a response from her with the melding of their mouths and the velvet stroke of his tongue against her lips, until she opened her mouth and tentatively returned the stimulating caress.

Lily pressed her palms flat against his shirtfront, absorbed his warm strength and discovered the hard plane of his chest. Her fingers grazed the tin star, and she brushed her hands upward to encircle his neck and cling to him.

The sheriff's hands circled her waist and drew her flush against his body. In that revealing instant, all she'd been robbed of came into distinct focus. This thrilling delight was what the girls had described. This yearning, this compulsion for physical and spiritual unity, was what a woman should feel for a man—a husband.

The wholesome honesty of somehow feeling precious and desired was a pleasure she'd never known or felt.

Never. Ever.

Not even her own father had valued her or anything she had to give. Her husband had taken her with force, had never cared for her or treated her with respect.

The dignity she felt in this man's arms was the last thing she'd expected and probably the last thing he'd intended, but it was there all the same.

He ended the kiss, burying his face in her neck and splaying his hands across her back to keep her so close she could feel the beat of his heart as though it were her own.

Lily clung to him, opening her eyes to the stars in the

night sky, expecting them to have changed or fallen after such an earth-shattering experience. But the stars were still in place. The frogs still croaked along the stream bank, and she was still Lily Divine. But a changed Lily Divine. One who knew exactly what she'd been missing. And precisely what she could never have.

The sheriff's breath against her ear sent shivers across her shoulders, and her breasts were supremely sensitive against the fabric of her dress. She realized she'd dropped her corset and stockings without a thought, because she was pulling him close with both hands at his back.

He straightened then, to look into her face. His thumb stroked her cheek in a delicate caress, and she gazed into his eyes in the darkness, wishing for light so she could read his expression. Night was okay, though. If it was regret, she didn't want to know.

She feared suddenly that he would apologize or tell her that this had been a mistake, and she didn't want to acknowledge that just yet. She made the first move and pulled away, bending to grab up her corset and stockings. She made a halfhearted attempt to tame her hair, which was drying into a wild mane of curls.

"Go ahead, Sheriff." She gestured to his horse. "I'm ready."

He looked at her curiously, but he stepped away to pick up his hat and settle it on his head. With a creak of leather, he set his foot and pulled himself into the saddle, then reached for her.

Lily tucked her unmentionables under one arm and grasped his hand to swing up behind him.

With the taste of him on her lips, his smell in her head

and his solid, warm body before her, she wrapped her arms around his waist and enjoyed the last moments of closeness as they rode back.

The sheriff took it slow, as though he wanted to make the most of the ride, as well. When he reined the horse in before her house, he started to dismount, but she stopped him with a hand on his shoulder. "Stay."

She managed to swing her leg across the horse's rump and dismount, landing on her wooden doorstep. She adjusted her skirts and bodice and looked up at him with her chin raised.

"Just so you know, Sheriff... I'm not sorry."

"Neither am I, Lily."

His words made her want to cry. She took her key from her pocket and let herself inside, quickly closing the door behind her and leaning against it.

But she *was* sorry. Sorry that she knew now. Sorry she'd never have what she'd merely glimpsed and felt this night. There was nothing she could do to change her circumstances. Sorry was a waste of energy.

And Lily was an overcomer. She would get over this, too.

She wouldn't let a silly kiss change anything.

She was Lily Divine.

SUNDAY ARRIVED on the tail of Saturday night, just as he feared it would. Nate thought of all the things he'd planned to do with his free time, and then resigned himself. He'd promised.

He was going to church.

He dressed in his finest shirt and trousers, tying a new string tie at his throat and donning his polished boots and holster.

Seemed a mite odd to wear his gun to church, but he was the sheriff, after all. People expected to be protected, and he'd feel buck naked without it, anyway.

Reed's finest buggies were hired out this morning as townspeople arrived. A row of parked ranchers' wagons stretched along the road to the west, and people milled in the churchyard.

Nate approached the gathering and walked through the open gate in the white picket fence. It wasn't as though he'd never been to church before. He'd been married in a church. He'd been to funerals. He'd followed a wanted man into the midst of a revival meeting once and had nearly lost him to Jesus before he could get the handcuffs on.

Some of the looks cast his way were those of surprise, but most glances were friendly as he approached the stairs and the open doors.

"Good morning, Sheriff." Reverend Bacon greeted him with a firm handshake. "Welcome to God's house."

"Thanks."

Inside the small building, the church members were taking their seats on long wooden benches. Nate spotted the Gibbs family, and the mayor and Beatrice stepped out into the aisle so Nate could sidle in and sit beside Evangeline.

She wore a lavender-and-white-checked bonnet that matched her dress this morning, and she moved acres of skirts aside so he could sit. She met his gaze with a demure smile.

The reverend led all the verses and choruses of several hymns, and Nate knew where the Intolerants got in all their practicin'. The message was about David and King Saul, and Nate found the history part interesting. When he'd finished preaching and praying, Reverend Bacon announced a brief meeting for any townspeople interested as soon as the service was concluded.

Nate thought a town meeting held in the church was a mite unusual. It had been his understanding that most of the meetings took place at Lily's. He had a bad feeling about this gathering in particular.

Reverend Bacon stood at the front of the room to address the people. "You may have heard about the rancher who was injured by a horse last week. I'm sorry to tell you he died Friday."

Sympathetic murmurs passed through the crowd. Nate had heard about the accident, but hadn't known the man.

"Some of us have come up with a way to raise money for the family," he said. "And have fun at the same time. George, come up here and tell them about the idea."

The barber moved to stand beside Reverend Bacon. "I was thinkin' we could have us a base ball tournament. I got to thinking about it, 'cause I read about tournaments in the papers. What they do is charge a fee for each team to sign up. We could have teams, and the money we raise would go to the Stoddard family. Should help the missus hire help and keep the ranch going for the rest of the season."

"Isn't that a great idea?" the reverend asked. "A community fund-raiser."

The suggestion was met with approving voices, and it was suggested that George and the reverend find the sponsors and deposit the entry fees. The amount of the entry fee was decided quickly.

A few church members left after that discussion, and the children were still occupied in a game outdoors. The mayor came forward and brought up the subject of the new livery.

He adjusted his tie, appearing uncomfortable with his position in moderating the discussion. He opened the floor, and the members of the Women's Temperance Prayer League stood at the front of the room.

"We must show our opposition to this newest form of rebellion," Meriel Reed announced. "The saloon owners cannot get away with harming our respectable businesses."

"That's right," Blythe agreed. "If they get no support or customers, they can't continue this practice."

The butcher, an unmarried German immigrant, stood. "With due respect, ma'am—and ma'am—seems to me they wouldn't have been forced to start their own livery if the one already here hadn't turned 'em away. What's a person to do to get their supplies?"

"That's the idea, Mr. Hulbert." Meriel straightened. "By forcing them out of business, we will make them discontinue their sordid occupations."

"This is America," he replied. "They have just as much of a right to their occupations as any of us do."

"And where do you think the tax money for that new school building and the schoolteacher's salary came from?" a rancher asked, standing to speak his piece. "The saloons've been supportin' this town for years."

"We don't need their kind of money," Beatrice Gibbs said.

Nate exchanged a look with the mayor.

"We can raise money on our own," she went on. "We've already built the Temperance Hall from our box socials and quilt sales."

"Lady, that ain't a drop in a bucket compared to what the saloons bring in," another man said. "Do you know how much they pay in taxes a year? How much their fines add up to? Besides that, when miners come in to the saloon, they board their horses, they get a bath and a shave, they eat at Clive's place."

Clive and Suzanna Callahan nodded their agreement.

"And if they have some dust to sell, they do so and buy supplies from Howard." He looked at the mercantile owner. "How many miners outfitted themselves because of that Jenkins fella shoutin' about a strike?"

Blythe stood at that. "I don't have a problem selling to the miners. It's the women from the dens of iniquity we should turn away and discourage."

At that, Howard Shaw stepped up beside his wife and faced her. "Don't you understand? If the miners didn't have a saloon to come into Thunder Canyon for, they would go somewhere else!" he said emphatically. "We wouldn't have *any* of their business."

Shirley Staub spoke up then. "I haven't taken sides in this issue. I don't want to. But I run a place in town, too, and it seems to me that Wade is going to be hurt by his decision to turn away the saloon owners." She looked directly at Meriel. "Once their livery is running, people will have a choice, and that cuts into *your* living. If Clive turned them away, what's to say they wouldn't start their own restaurant? The Shady Lady already serves meals two evenings a week."

"Don't speak that name in the house of the Lord!" Meriel cried.

At that point Nate understood exactly what Lily had meant about these women being unreachable in their own narrow-minded little world.

Several people spoke at once, and chaos broke out.

After a few minutes of being unable to understand anyone over the commotion, Nate got up and walked to the front of the church.

CHAPTER NINE

"Enough!" Nate bellowed.

Silence ensued. One by one, every person looked at him.

The rafters creaked.

Reverend Bacon smiled.

"I know this is my first time to church and all, but *damn!* Don't you people know freedom and tolerance are what your fathers fought to the death for? Speaking your mind and having an opinion are fine. Fine! But trying to force people into your way of thinkin' and believin' is wrong."

"You were hired to do a job, Sheriff, not to tell us how to run our town," Meriel said.

He took an angry step forward and directed his words to her. "Any time the city council doesn't like the way I'm doin' my job, they can let me know. The men who hired me can have my resignation. My job is to keep the peace in this town. Hell, the most disturbance I see comes from right here." He pointed to the floor, indicating the whole of the gathering.

He glanced from face to face and zeroed in on Wade. "Mr. Reed, do you realize what you've done? This is revenue we're talkin' about! If your livery business suffers, what will the effect be on you and your household?"

"Well…things would be real tight."

"There wouldn't be much money to spend, would there?"

"I reckon not. Not if none was comin' in."

"And expenses like dresses and shoes and frippery for the house would have to be forgotten, do you suppose?"

Wade glanced from Nate to his wife, understanding dawning on his face. "Yep. A cut in what we sell means a cut in what we spend. That's a fact."

Meriel's face drew into a pinch.

Howard Shaw spoke up then. "If Miss Lily stopped ordering from the catalogs and buying her supplies from me, my profits would drop considerably. She's one of my biggest customers. Zeke and Bernie, too."

Blythe's angry expression scorched her husband and blistered every man in the room. "Is money more important than morals? Are we going to condone the practices of sin and evil by supporting them?"

The Thorndike man who worked at the bank spoke up for the first time. "Seems to me some of us have let our wives' perceptions of what is right and wrong dictate our better judgment. Is it our job to be telling others they are wrong or that their business is sinful?"

"The Good Book does teach us that we should lead by example and pray for our brethren," the reverend said.

"And get the plank out of our own eye," Clive Callahan added. His wife poked him in the ribs.

Thorndike addressed the subject again. "Mr. Shaw,

you sell bottles of liquor from your mercantile, as well as playing cards and dice. Mr. Clark sells guns and bullets, weapons that kill. No one is asking you men to stop selling your merchandise."

"I'm not going to deny anyone's business," Clive said. Suzanna nodded her agreement this time.

"Lily and the others are good customers," Howard said. "I'm not changing my practices, either."

Blythe scowled at her husband. The room got so quiet, Nate could almost hear her blood boiling. She gathered her skirts, marched stiffly to the bench where she'd left her reticule and then stormed down the aisle and out of the church.

Howard's grim expression showed that being between a rock and a hard place was mighty uncomfortable.

"My goose is already cooked," Wade said with angry regret in his tone. "I shoulda been more of a man and stood my ground. If my business is hurt, I got nobody to blame but myself." He looked at his wife, and it was in his eyes but he didn't add, "and her."

Meriel got tears in her eyes and quickly sat on a bench in the front row.

Mayor Gibbs moved to the front of the gathering, and Nate took a seat.

"I'm hearing that the general consensus is that we may have been a little swift in our decisions regarding the saloons," he said. "Nothing to be done about the new livery now, except see how it pans out."

It was a subdued group that left the building. The businessmen looked a little more confident in their decisions, but the women from the Women's Temperance Prayer League were positively scarlet with anger.

Nate found Evangeline in the dooryard, where she stood waving a fan under her chin. Her expression was one of mortification.

"Something wrong, Miss Gibbs?"

She glanced over his shoulder as though checking to make sure no one would hear her. "I hope my mother's stand doesn't reflect poorly on me in your opinion, Sheriff."

"Not at all. You told me you don't share her cause."

"It's almost an embarrassment to be a woman in this town."

Nate glanced at the couples and families leaving the churchyard. "I'll bet there's going to be some heat in the kitchens in Thunder Canyon today." He looked back at her. "Your mother might not take a shine to me after today."

She shrugged. "My father likes you."

"I'll pick you up in half an hour."

"I'll be ready." She joined her parents.

He mounted his horse and rode straight to the Shady Lady. The front doors were locked, so he hurried to the house next door and rang the bell.

Wearing a plain lavender dress and an apron, Mollie answered the door. "Afternoon, Sheriff."

He removed his hat. "Mollie. Is Miss Lily available?"

"Sure. Come on in." She stepped back so he could enter the foyer. "I'll go get her."

He glanced at the papered walls and the chandelier.

A table he hadn't seen the last time he'd been inside Lily's house caught his attention, and he studied it without appreciation. The thing was hideous, with cast-iron legs that looked like an elephant's, ivory tusks as braces and a marble top. The fringed lamp it held wasn't much more attractive.

"Hello, Sheriff."

Lily approached, and he turned toward her voice. She wore a gray skirt and a long-sleeved white blouse with a high neck, like something any woman would wear. Her auburn hair was neatly gathered in a knot, and he immediately noticed her fresh feminine scent. For a moment he couldn't think about anything except the kiss they'd shared.

"Lily."

"Admiring my table?"

He took one more painful glance. "Yes. It's…unusual."

"What brings you here on a Sunday afternoon?"

"There was a meeting after church today. I wanted to let you know."

"After church?"

His ears felt hot. She was excluded from everything that happened at church. He shouldn't have mentioned that part. "Two things were talked about. One was a community fund-raiser for the Stoddard family."

"I heard that Charlie died. I'll do whatever I can to help."

"That's not what I came about. I wanted to tell you the reactions about the livery. Your livery."

She reached for his hat and looked at it for a moment

before hanging it on a hook by the door. "Come into the parlor." She headed toward the other room and he had no choice but to follow. "I'll get you something cold to drink."

"No thanks. I have…something I have to do."

"Okay. Well…sit down."

He perched on a comfortable chair. When he'd searched the house with Judge Adams's assistant that day, he'd noticed the sturdy furnishings. This was a room a person could live in.

"You look very nice today, by the way," she said.

Her comment caught him off guard. Was she teasing him about church? Should he return the compliment? He chose a safer conversation. "The businessmen took a stand against the Intolerants."

She sat up straighter. "They did?"

"Your new business venture made quite an impact."

"That was my hope."

"You have a lot of support from the ranchers and the business owners. I just thought you should know that."

"Okay. What about the women?"

"I don't see them slinking away after their husbands stood up to them. Especially not Meriel. She was in a snit for sure. I suggested to Wade that if he lost revenue, he'd have to cut back on fripperies. She wasn't happy."

"She should have thought about that before."

"All hell's gonna break loose in those homes today, you can bet on that."

They looked at each other and shared a slow grin.

Nate wished he could stay and have a cold drink

with her. It was a good thing he already had plans, or he'd be sorely tempted, and the two of them together wouldn't lead anywhere healthy. Their kiss had proven there was enough combustible heat between them to blow up his good intentions.

"I'd better go. I just wanted you to know."

"Thank you. I appreciate it."

She followed him to the door, and he grabbed his hat before stepping out into the sunshine.

"Have a nice afternoon, Sheriff."

"You, too."

He headed toward the livery. What did a woman of Lily's reputation do on a Sunday afternoon? She had no acquaintances except those who worked in her saloon. Did she wish for more?

He rented a buggy and guided the horse to the mayor's home.

Evangeline had changed into a yellow dress with ruffles at the hem and shoulders and an eyelet bodice. The pale color set off her coloring and her eyes, making her look very innocent and feminine. She carried a wide-brimmed straw hat.

He took the basket she handed him and put it in the boot before helping her up onto the seat.

She placed the hat on her head, tied the ribbons under her chin and angled the brim to keep the sun from her face.

"Do you know of a picnic spot?" she asked.

"I think I know a good place." He turned the buggy toward the stream, and found a shady spot a good distance from Lily's swimming area.

Evangeline set about spreading a checkered cloth and unwrapping chicken and coleslaw and pickles. She'd even brought two thick slices of chocolate cake and a jug of milk. She took off her hat and he did the same, sitting at the opposite edge of the cloth.

They ate with the restful sound of the stream close by.

"Did you fix all this yourself?"

"Cook helped with the chicken and she had canned the pickles, but I made the slaw and the cake myself. Does the menu suit you?"

"Never had better." Nate had enjoyed every bite of the lunch. Impressive, he thought, finishing his mug of milk. What man wouldn't want a beautiful wife who could cook and bake—and who aimed to please?

He watched her wrap and pack away the plates and utensils, wondering what to say next. With a full belly and an afternoon without his usual daily concerns, he really would have liked a nap right about now.

"That was a fine meal," he said.

"My pleasure."

She took a slim volume from the basket. "I brought a book."

He glanced at it and up at her.

"Shall I read from it?"

"Sure. What is it?"

"Sonnets by Elizabeth Barret Browning. Have you read her poetry?"

"Can't say as I have, no."

"They're lovely. I'll start with a few of my favorites." He nodded.

Evangeline situated herself with her knees to one

side and her skirt forming a halo, half on the tablecloth, half on the grass.

"'My own beloved, who hast lifted me from this drear flat of earth where I was thrown,'" she read.

In a sweet voice she read verses that Nate tried to find some order and meaning to in his head.

"'And in betwixt the languid ringlets, blown a life-breath, till the forehead hopefully shines out again, as all the angels see.'"

Thinking about that shiny forehead, Nate moved so that the exposed tree roots weren't under him and leaned back against the trunk of the oak.

She had a pleasant voice. Not shrill or loud. He could listen to a voice like hers without irritation. He looked at her, remembered her presence in his kitchen and on his porch and tried to imagine that as a way of life. Thought about coming home to her of an evening.

"'As one who stands in dewless asphodel…'" She glanced up at him and smiled. Surely she hadn't cursed and then smiled?

He returned the smile. She was pretty, no doubt about it. Pleasant, too. In a young, fresh, life-is-so-new sort of way. She'd gone to a girls' school, learned to dance with other girls, been sheltered from men and life experiences.

Evangeline turned the page and continued to read.

He'd bet Peyton Gibbs had provided all she'd ever needed or wanted and expected a husband to do the same.

"'As a strong tree should rustle thy boughs and set thy trunk all bare…'"

Nothing like Lily. Lily talked about washing clothing for miners and shoveling horse manure out of the streets—she hadn't used that word, though. Lily could turn a phrase like a man. She supported herself and even employed and took care of other people. Lily hadn't been sheltered from life or men. She made her living "experiencing" men.

Lily wasn't the kind of woman a man imagined coming home to. Try as he might, Nate couldn't picture her in his kitchen or on his porch. She was so right in her own surroundings.

He imagined Lily in her own room, the big bedroom with the dark-stained hickory bed and the blue-and-white quilt. He'd seen a lot of Lily. Bare naked in the painting over the bar. Firsthand in the dark by this very stream in garters and a corset.

He couldn't picture Lily reading sonnets, but he had no trouble picturing her beneath him, her wild auburn hair spread across the sheets, the scent of her skin an aphrodisiac. He could easily imagine the pleasure of her body. He already knew the pleasure of her heated kisses.

"Nathaniel?"

He opened his eyes and saw blond hair. Innocent blue eyes. "I'm awake. I was listening."

"I haven't been reading for five minutes."

"I know. I was listening to the stream."

"I like the sound of it, too."

What the hell was he doing thinking about Lily Divine when he had a sweet respectable young woman at his bidding?

"Did you like the sonnets?"

He moved from his position near the tree so he could sit closer to her. "I've never heard anything like them before. Especially the bare trunks and the rustling boughs."

She seemed disconcerted at his nearness and looked at her hands in her lap. "Are you going to kiss me?"

"Would it be all right?"

She nodded. "Yes."

She looked right at him then, expectancy and maybe a little fear in her expression.

Without hesitation, Nate leaned forward and kissed her.

She was young and pretty, and what man in his right mind wouldn't want to kiss her?

She didn't move, didn't even breathe.

He ended the contact and sat back.

"That's it, then?" she asked.

"That's it."

"That's not so bad."

He couldn't help thinking of another kiss. "Thanks."

After that, she seemed more at ease. They walked along the stream bank for a time, but the place held too many memories for Nate, so he led her back to the buggy. He gathered the tablecloth and basket and helped her onto the seat, then headed for home.

After leaving Evangeline at her parents' house, he returned the rig to the livery.

Wade was hanging freshly oiled harnesses on their hooks inside the door.

"Have a nice afternoon?" he asked.

Nate nodded. "How about you?"

"A mite rough, actually. Fixed my own dinner. Prob'ly be fixin' my own supper, too. League's planning a strategy meeting for tomorrow night."

"What strategy do they have left?"

"I dunno." Wade hung the last piece of tack and stood with his shoulders slumped. "I never liked this women's temperance thing from the start. But Meriel came west to marry me, like the other wives did. I figured she needed the company of other women like herself. This is a different life than what she was used to back east. Harsher. Women can get lonely. I didn't want to take that one small comfort from her."

"Innocent enough if they'd stick to makin' quilts, I reckon," Nate replied.

Wade brushed his hands together. "I got some coffee on in the back. Come have a cup with me."

Nate accompanied the stable owner to the rear of the building and accepted a dented tin cup filled with strong brew.

"Make it the way I like it out here," Wade said.

The interior of the building was surprisingly cool, and they sat on nail kegs.

"Must be some reason the women are so all-fired riled about the saloons," Nate commented.

"Jealous, I reckon. Who doesn't like to have a beer and play a hand of cards?"

"Jealous of the drinkin'—or the whores?"

"Both, probably."

Nate only looked at him.

"I ain't visited a whore since I was wet behind the ears," the other man said.

"Does your wife think you have?"

"I told her I never. Those woman're mostly old and either skinny or fat, and them places are too dirty."

Nate had thought the same about Zeke's and Bernie's places. "What about Lily's? It's clean and the women are pretty."

"In the old days Antoinette ran a clean house. But Lily's girls ain't whores," Wade said matter-of-factly, as though Nate should have known that all along.

"Lily denies it often enough. Why do you say so? You know for a fact?"

"I don't know anybody who ever got a poke at Lily's."

"At least nobody ever told you if they did."

Wade shrugged.

"You ever tried?"

He tilted his head. "Years ago. Got turned down flat."

"I'm not convinced."

"You and half the women in town."

At that Nate sat up straight.

"Didn't mean no offense, Sheriff. It's just that those of us who've been around a good many years know Lily. Newcomers think what they want."

"No offense taken," Nate replied. "I guess I'm gonna have to get it straight on my own. Wade, you ever heard of an asphodel?"

"Nope, some kind of machine or somethin'?"

"Don't know." He stood. "Thanks for the coffee. Keep me posted if you smell trouble brewing." He dug into his pocket for a coin. "The buggy was personal, so I'm paying."

Wade took the coin with a grin. "How personal was it?"

Nate cuffed him on the shoulder and left the livery.

MONDAY MORNING, dressed in her dark-blue skirt, a pink striped shirtwaist and a hat with an enormous sweeping pink ostrich feather, Lily headed down Main Street with money from the safe in her handbag.

Blythe Shaw paused in cleaning the inside of the mercantile windows to glare at her as she passed. Lily gave her an unconcerned wave and continued on.

She walked all the way to the west end of town and opened the gate that led to Reverend Bacon's parsonage. The man answered the door in his shirtsleeves, an oddity even on a hot summer day.

"Good morning, Miss Lily." He offered her a warm smile. His spectacles were perched on his forehead. "How nice to see you. Come in. Mrs. Bacon will make us a cup of tea."

"Thank you, Reverend." Lily gestured to the small shaded porch. "Can we sit outside?"

"Certainly. Just let me ask her to bring a tray."

Lily took a seat on a padded wicker chair and rested her handbag in her lap.

The reverend returned and sat across from her. "Thank you for the pheasant you sent over the other day. Saul said he shot half a dozen that morning. It was delicious."

She nodded and they shared light conversation until his wife brought a tray with tea, biscuits and jam.

"You came in time for my midmorning ritual," he said.

Lily sipped tea and helped herself to half a biscuit.

She got right to the point. "I've come to sponsor a team for the community fund-raiser."

The reverend seemed to take a moment to absorb her words. He set down his cup. "A team?"

"Yes. The fund-raiser for Charlie Stoddard. I want to sponsor a team." She took twenty dollars in gold coins from her bag and handed them to the reverend. "Our entry fee. And if there's another team you know of who's having trouble coming up with the fee, you let me know and I'll sponsor them. Anonymously of course. All of us at the Shady Lady want to help as much as we can. Charlie was a good man."

Reverend Bacon looked at the coins in his palm. His expression showed surprise and hesitation. "I don't know what to say, Lily."

"Well, don't say anything. Just sign us up. And let me know if I can be of more help."

Something like real pain glimmered in his eyes.

A terrible feeling rose in Lily's chest. "You're not going to deny us entry, are you?"

"Who's your team?"

"We are. Does it matter?"

"Do you know how to play base ball?"

"Does anyone else? How difficult can it be?"

"It takes a lot of practice."

"We'll practice. Reverend?"

"This will cause problems, Lily, you know it will."

"There isn't a good reason on God's green earth why the Shady Lady shouldn't have a team. We live in Thunder Canyon. We all knew Charlie. We're part of the community and we want to help."

"Maybe you could help by being silent sponsors."

"Invisible, you mean."

He closed his fingers around the coins. "You're right. There's no reason why you shouldn't have a team. Mind you, not everyone is going to be pleased about this."

"I'll try not to cry myself to sleep at night over the rejection."

"You joke, but I know it hurts to have people think badly of you and disapprove of every little move."

"Only some people."

He studied her for a long moment. "I wish everyone knew your heart the way I do, Lily. You've given so much to the community, in ways they don't even know about."

"Ways they don't want to know about," she replied.

"Like the new pews you paid for. Should be about another month until they're finished and installed."

"You can't know what pleasure I'll get from knowing the good people of Thunder Canyon are sitting on those pews every Sunday morning." Lily smiled.

He studied her and finally laughed.

"I'll deposit this entry fee in the bank and enter your team in the competition."

"And?"

"And if someone expresses a desire to have a team but can't afford the entry fee, I will let you know."

"Thank you." She brushed a few crumbs from her skirt and stood. "I'd best be about the rest of my errands now."

The reverend wished her a good day and she left his

house with a determined spring in her step. Nothing like a fair challenge to get her blood going.

They opened the saloon midday as usual, and the local miners gathered to share news. Lily noticed a female miner she'd met on several occasions, a woman who dressed and spoke and drank like a man. She'd already been to the bath house and the barber and had her hair shorn like any of the others.

"Hey, Lily." Her voice was as rough as her chapped hands. She was taller than most of the men in the place.

"Hello, Charlotte. How's your claim panning out?"

"A little silver dust here and there. Enough to keep me in vittles and whiskey. I'm gonna hit it big one of these days, though." She settled on a stool at the bar. "'Tween you an' me, I'm gettin' too old for winters in the mountains."

"You could winter in town."

"Don't know what I'd do. Cain't afford a room."

"You could probably get work for a few months."

"Cain't cook. Too old and ugly for whorin'."

Lily laughed. "I'd give you a job."

Charlotte looked wide-eyed at Helena and Rosemary, who stood near a table talking with a group of miners. "Doin' what?"

"I'll be outfitting a livery in a few weeks. You any good with horses?"

Her eyes brightened. "Matter of fact I ain't half-bad with horses. Groom 'em, feed 'em, clean their hooves. Simple. They ain't half as ornery to get along with as people."

"Want me to save a job for you come fall?"

Charlotte's gaze left Lily's face and seemed unfocused for a moment as she thought. With a twitch of her mouth, she made up her mind. "I'll winter here."

"What are you drinking?"

"Whiskey."

"Old Jess, set up a whiskey and a sarsaparilla, please. To seal the deal."

They raised glasses and drank.

"You won't forget?" Charlotte asked.

"I won't forget."

IT WAS A PARTICULARLY hot evening. Miners had crowded the Shady Lady since afternoon. Lily had looked forward to the sun going down and the evening cooling off, but so far no cool breeze was forthcoming from the mountains.

She stood on the boardwalk for a breath of air.

Running footsteps alerted her, and she glanced up the street. The runner came into view. It was Mitch Early.

"What's the hurry?" she asked.

"It's the women," he panted. "They're in a fit. I heard from George and Joel that they heard you were signed up for the base ball tournament."

"That the Intolerants heard?"

"Yeah. That on top of yesterday's meetin' at the church has 'em fired up."

"They're just gonna have to get used to it. I'm not going anywhere."

"Celeste inside?"

"Yep. Go on in and tell her I said your dance is on the house tonight."

"Thanks, Miss Lily." He pushed through the bat wing doors.

Lily thought about a swim. The water sure would feel good tonight. Maybe she could get someone to lend her a horse. She looked at the mounts tethered along the hitching post and glanced at the level of water in the trough.

In the darkness, she made her way around back and pumped the well. After four trips, there was sufficient water for the warm night. She used the last of the water in the pail to dip her hands and pat her neck, face and chest.

The sound of women's voices nearby surprised her because she hadn't heard them coming. No singing tonight?

"The wages of sin is serious business," someone was saying.

"We're not going to just stand by and let this woman sully our town and lead our husbands astray!"

The Women's Temperance Prayer League was a slim gathering that evening. Beatrice wasn't with them, nor were a few of the other regulars, but what they lacked in numbers they made up for in zeal.

Lily moved to the top of the stairs as they approached.

"This is it, Lily Divine!" Blythe shouted. "This is the last time we're going to let you throw your sordid ways and your tainted money in our faces."

"You think you're so much better than the rest of us," Meriel called. "You might have money and clothes and friends, but you came by them in a sinful manner."

"I never thought I'd miss the singing," Lily replied.

"We're done singing. We're taking God's work into our own hands."

"That's a big job," she replied. "Hope you're up to it."

"Oh, we're up to it. We're filled with righteous fervor."

Lily thought it was more like self-righteous fever, but she bit her tongue.

"This is it," Dinah Sadler said. "Let's go."

With a combined shout, the women rushed onto the boardwalk and passed Lily.

She didn't have a good feeling about this. They meant trouble, and she knew it. But she couldn't hold them back single-handedly. "Be glad to serve you a drink, ladies," she said as they passed. "But don't bother the other customers."

She hurried in behind them and caught the sleeve of the first man she recognized, a miner.

"Rory, go get the sheriff. This doesn't look good."

The man got up and loped out the door.

Meriel was shouting above the sound of the piano. "This wickedness must stop! Men, go home to your wives and families! Addiction to liquor and these women is blinding you to the truth about your behavior. This is evil disguised as fleshly pleasure!"

Wade had been inside earlier, and Lily looked for him now to see his reaction to his wife's tirade. Sure enough, he got up from a table where he'd been playing cards with Doc Umber and Thomas and hiked up the waist of his trousers before walking toward the irate women.

"Meriel, you're makin' a spectacle of yourself. You'd best get on back home."

"Oooh!" Dinah screeched. "Oh, the shame!"

The women turned to look at her, then followed the line of her horrified stare. One by one their heads turned toward the painting of Lily behind the bar.

CHAPTER TEN

BLYTHE'S HANDS came up to her cheeks.

Dinah's face blazed with embarrassment and shock.

Meriel fumed.

A collective intake of breath sucked the air from the room, and for a minute Lily could hear the beat of her own heart.

Then Meriel turned in a blur of skirts and grabbed the six-shooter out of the holster of the nearest miner—Charlotte.

Charlotte was so surprised she dropped the glass of whiskey she'd been holding and took a step back with her hands up.

But Meriel turned toward the bar and aimed the gun at the painting with both hands.

Everyone within the semicircle of her range ducked. Old Jess scurried to the end of the bar and Lily's heart skipped half a dozen beats.

Meriel leveled the barrel and her hands shook with fury.

"Woman, hand me that gun right now," Wade ordered.

"You've been coming in here looking at that naked

harlot," she said. "Drinking and gambling and God only knows what all else."

"Hand me the gun," he said again.

Instead she squeezed the trigger.

Lily's ears rang with the silence that followed.

A click followed by nothing.

Meriel stared at the gun in her hand as though it had just betrayed her. With impotent rage, she threw it as hard and as far as she could toward the painting.

It hit the mirror instead. Lily's fifteen-hundred-dollar pride and joy shattered in a burst of flying glass, littering the floor and the bar, breaking glassware and toppling bottles of liquor. It was a deafening sound, and a potent smell rose from the bottles that chugged whiskey and rye onto the floor.

Meriel stared at the scene, her expression as shocked as anyone else's. She wrapped her arms around herself and pressed her forearms into her stomach as though her belly ached.

"Is anybody hurt?"

The voice came from the doorway. Heads turned to find the sheriff just inside the saloon.

Miners and townspeople looked at each other and shook their heads. Nate walked through the crowd of now-silent women, past Meriel to the bar. "You okay, old man?"

From the end of the bar, Old Jess nodded.

Lily realized what might have happened if Jess had still been standing back there when the glass splintered in all directions. Angry now, she walked forward and looked at the devastation behind her bar. Looked at the pieces of mirror and the spreading pool of alcohol on the floor.

The painting still hung in its spot, untouched.

She turned to Meriel. "You missed."

The woman started to lunge forward, but her husband grabbed her and held her with both arms pinned to her sides.

"Someone want to give me an account of what just happened?"

A dozen voices fought to be heard, but Nate held up a hand and asked for one person's story at a time.

"That how it happened?" he asked Lily. "They came in here yelling. Mrs. Reed grabbed a gun and threw it at the mirror."

"That's it," she replied.

"You want to press charges?"

"Damn straight! Can't let my place get busted up and not press charges." She looked at Wade. "Sorry. Don't take it personal."

His expression blanched. "Aw, hell, Lily."

"You can't arrest her," Blythe objected. "She's the leader of the Women's Temperance Prayer League!"

"She'll have plenty of time to pray, I reckon," Nate replied. "So will the lot of you. Will a few of you gentlemen please help me escort the ladies to the jail? We'll discuss bail in the morning."

"Don't touch me," Blythe said to the miner who came up beside her. "I can walk there on my own."

"Fine. Walk along beside just in case she gets lost on the way," Nate said to the man.

The women were escorted from the dance hall, leaving the customers and employees to stand and give each other long looks of speculation and regret.

"Let's get the place cleaned up," Lily said. "Jess, you and Saul round up some crates and a wheelbarrow. Molly, get the mop and pail, will you?" She stepped carefully behind the bar to grab several unopened bottles of whiskey and set them on the cherrywood bar. "Drinks are on the house for helpin' with the cleanup. I want everyone wearing a pair of gloves. We don't want to give Doc any business tonight."

"I was wonderin' there for a while," Doc said, and a few chuckles lightened the mood.

Lily stared at the wall where a splinter of mirror remained. Only part of her face was reflected in the jagged slice. She refused to see this as a symbol or a premonition of any sort; she was far too practical for that. But it was a discouragement all the same. The mirror had been a sign of her achievements, a visual affirmation of how far she'd come. She'd always looked into it with pride and seen an independent, hardworking woman who wasn't ashamed of her life.

She looked down at the hundreds of reflecting shards on the bar, the shelves and the floor. Nothing had changed. She'd been determined that it wouldn't. In fact, her triumphs over the women's cause had been the catalyst for this.

"Sorry about this." Charlotte plucked her Colt from the wreckage and gave Lily a sheepish look.

"Not your fault."

"My gun."

"Could have been a lot worse. Someone could have been shot."

"I never keep a bullet in the first chamber," she said.

"My way of not shootin' my own foot off. Seen a fella do that once."

Lily nodded.

Charlotte holstered her gun.

The cleanup took hours, but everyone was of like mind that they didn't want to see the mess again in the morning.

"Where are you staying tonight?" Lily asked Charlotte sometime before closing.

"I'll camp outside town."

"I'd be glad to give you a bed for the night if you'd let me use your horse for an hour or so."

"Fine trade in my opinion. He's the black with the turquoise bridle. Sam's his name. Talk nice to him. His feelin's get hurt easy."

"Use the room in the northeast corner upstairs. It's not big, but the bed is comfortable. And long." She grinned. "Come on, I'll unlock the door. You'll have to come down and stable your horse when I'm done, though. Reed doesn't do business with me."

Charlotte gave her a curious look at that comment, but agreed without hesitation.

Lily rode past Reed's livery atop Charlotte's black. All she had to do was ride on out and she'd be at her place. She'd be in that cool water. Swimming. Forgetting the day. But she couldn't do it. Not just yet.

With a sigh of resignation, she turned the horse's head and rode back along the darkened street toward the jail.

It was after midnight. Would the sheriff still be in there? Light showed from behind the windows that bracketed the door.

She slid from the horse, tethered it to the rail and stepped onto the wood platform that served as a porch. The door was unlocked, so she walked inside.

The sheriff was sitting at his desk, his head in his hands. The other two chairs were occupied by Wade and Howard. Dinah Sadler's husband and a couple other men sat on the floor along the wall opposite the cells. The iron cages were occupied by the six women who'd stormed into Lily's dance hall that evening. Half of them were lying on cots, the other half sitting, but they all roused themselves to look at her as she entered.

Nate looked up, too.

Lily walked directly to his desk. "Let them go."

"What?" He stood and frowned at her.

"Let the women go. I'm not going to press charges."

"You're perfectly within your rights. They broke the law."

"I expect restitution. If I have the Reeds' word that they'll pay for the damages, I don't want Meriel to face any charges."

Wade got up from where he sat. "You have my word, Lily. Give me the list of damages and I'll pay. It might take me a while, but I'm good for it. I'll help you, too, if there's work to be done."

"Most of the work is done," she said. "I'll have to order glasses, whiskey to replace what was lost and— a mirror."

"Came from Philadelphia, didn't it?" Wade asked. "Me 'n Howard was just talkin' about that. We remembered when it came on the railcar, all packed and padded, and we all stood in the Shady Lady and admired it."

Lily nodded.

"Sorry about your mirror, Lily," he added.

"You didn't break it. You can help hang the new one."

An awkward silence stretched, and one by one heads turned until everyone was looking at Meriel.

She looked pretty dignified for a jailbird, Lily thought. Her hair wasn't mussed, and her dress was tidy. But she'd obviously been crying, because her eyes were puffy and her nose was red.

She inched her chin up a tad. "Is an apology required by your offer to not press charges?"

Lily didn't hesitate. "Nope. You can't expect somebody to do something they don't feel. It was wrong what you did, but you can probably still justify it in that Lily-hatin' head of yours. I'm just not going to return the bad feelings. Pay up and we're even."

"We'll pay up," Wade assured her.

Meriel didn't say any more.

"There isn't going to be any more Women's Temperance Prayer League," Howard told her. "The whole thing got out of hand."

At his announcement, Lily looked at the men. "I feel bad about that. It isn't right for men to decree what their wives do and don't do. Everyone's entitled to work for something they truly believe in."

The women looked at her with raised eyebrows, then at each other.

"I have some pretty strong beliefs of my own," Lily said. She turned back to the sheriff. "Let them go."

He took the keys and walked toward the cells.

"Thank you, Lily," Wade said.

She nodded once and left to mount the horse and ride out of town.

LILY DIDN'T TAKE quite as much pleasure as usual from her ride or from the cool stream that night. Tonight she felt as if the fight had gone out of her, and she didn't like the feeling. She didn't feel quite whole without that battle light inside her.

She'd brought her shampoo paste, and she lathered her hair and tossed the tube up onto the bank. She dunked repeatedly to rinse, and ran her fingers through her tresses to get out the tangles.

"Why'd you do it?"

Startled, she turned toward the voice.

Her heart eased back into an easy pace. She lowered herself so her breasts were covered by the water. The sheriff had followed her. Or guessed her whereabouts.

"She's not a criminal, she's a woman threatened about her security."

"What are you talking about?"

"Wade does spend a lot of evenings in the saloon."

"She spends a lot of evenin's with the Intolerants. What's he supposed to do?"

"I can't believe I'm defending her to you."

"Me, neither. You hit your head on a rock in that water?"

"The water's perfect. You getting in?"

"Wouldn't waste the ride." He unfastened his holster and lowered it to the ground, then he sat on the bank and removed his boots. He stood and his shirt came off next.

The kiss they'd shared had changed all her thoughts toward this man—narrowed them in a direction that was new and frightening.

Lily turned aside as he finished undressing and splashed his way into the stream. He groaned with pleasure. "This feels good."

He stood a good twenty feet away from her, but she could see the muscles in his chest and shoulders defined in the moonlight.

"You're always surprising me, Lily."

"How's that, Sheriff?"

"You turn my thinkin' on end."

"Because of Meriel?"

"You could have made her sweat it out in that jail until Judge Adams came. She could have paid fines besides paying for the damages. She pulled a gun on you."

"Not on me. On the painting of me."

"It could have been worse."

"I don't think she meant to hurt anybody."

"Lily, you're excusing what she did."

"Sheriff, that's my prerogative."

He dipped down in the water and came up a minute later.

"I don't think she'll do anything like that again," she added.

He swam to where she was and stood beside her. Somewhere deep inside, had she been hoping he'd follow her? Had she come here with deliberate intent?

His warm gaze started her blood singing. "Not many people would have done what you did."

"Probably not."

"You like surprising people, don't you?"

"I just like making my own decisions. If they surprise people…" She shrugged.

"The men talked about the mirror as though it meant something special to you."

"I'll be ordering a new one tomorrow. It will have even more meaning."

"Tell me how."

"It'll be proof that no one can take away what I've worked for."

"Always lookin' at the shiny side of the penny, aren't you?"

"I just don't waste time feeling sorry for myself."

"Or seeking revenge."

"What's the point?"

He got a strange look on his face. "Satisfaction. Justice."

"Is everything black-and-white to you? Right or wrong? Some things just are."

"I'm a lawman. I get paid to separate right from wrong."

"What if the rules get changed?"

He reached up and slicked water from his hair, and the sight of his muscled biceps made Lily feel like her feet were slipping on the smooth stones of the streambed, though she stood perfectly still. Each time her reaction to this man came so unexpectedly and with such energy, she frightened herself.

"You once told me you'd been married," he said.

She regretted revealing that information. "Yes."

"And that your husband got what he deserved."

"Yes," she said again.

"Is he dead?"

The sheriff was standing too close now. She didn't want him to see too much. "What does it matter to you?"

"I'm just curious. Thinking of you as a widow seems so…unfitting. How did he die?"

Thinking of the man, her throat felt as though someone had both fists around her neck. "He beat someone. They stabbed him."

"Self-defense?"

She nodded. "I don't much like to talk about it. It was a terrible time in my life."

The sheriff tipped his head back to gaze at the sky. "I understand."

He was so close, she could have reached out and touched his throat where water ran in a trickle…or his chest, which looked smooth and solid.

He lowered his gaze to the distant bank. "I had a wife once."

His words stopped her meandering thoughts. She riveted her attention on his next words.

"I didn't always hunt men. I had a regular job in a foundry. A little house. A wife." With what appeared to be a breath dredged from his soul, his chest expanded. "A child," he said on a hoarse exhalation.

Lily's heart stopped. *Don't say any more. Don't tell me! I can't hear this.*

"In fifteen years, I've never said those words."

Her insides were quaking like the ground beneath a stampede. Against her better judgment, she opened her mouth and asked on a terrified whisper, "What happened to them?"

"Sarah took our son to visit her parents. Coming back, their stage was attacked and robbed. They were murdered."

Her name had been Sarah. Lily pictured the young, beautiful woman and her child. In her mind Sarah looked like Evangeline Gibbs, with blond hair and a fresh innocence. She pictured the sheriff as a young man, filled with love for his family, hopes for their future…and all that ending in a violent, senseless crime of greed.

"My son would be nearly a man."

She heard years of silent pain in that statement.

"What was his name?"

"Jonathon."

Lily's chest ached now. "That's a good name."

He brought his hands up out of the water and looked at them. "Those were the first men I ever killed."

"You tracked them down?"

"It took almost a year. And when it was done I didn't feel anything. Not satisfaction. Not relief. Just nothing. By then my life had changed. The house I'd built was on land that belonged to my wife's family, so I gave it to her brother and moved on. I'd discovered I was good at finding wanted men, so that's what I did."

The water felt suddenly chilly and Lily's limbs trembled.

"You're crying."

She raised her fingers to find tears on her cheek.

He wrapped his arms around her and she pressed

against his warm slick body, the water lapping against her back. Their naked bodies touched from breasts to thighs, a silky erotic sensation—warm skin, cool water…unthreatening. *Incredible.*

No one had ever touched her in tenderness before—no one except this man. Before Nathaniel Harding, no one had ever held her or kissed her or made her feel as though she was a desirable woman. Their first kiss had shown her a whole new world, one she'd never anticipated. It had changed the way she looked at him, the way she thought about him. And the way she thought about herself.

He bracketed her face between large, strong hands and wiped at her tears with his thumbs. "Don't cry for me."

He couldn't know how many of the tears were for both of them. For pain they shared.

He lowered his head and pressed his lips to hers. The salt of her tears combined with the heady taste of this man.

She shouldn't be here. She was inviting trouble. But she couldn't let go, wouldn't miss the mind-drugging experience for anything.

Lily wrapped her arms around his back and held him tightly, drawing every last measure of pleasure from the contact. His tongue sought hers and she allowed him entry and enjoyed the dance of heat and mounting anticipation.

Lily's fiery kisses were more potent than whiskey, warming Nate and going straight to his head—as well as every other part of his body.

She was trembling in his arms and he feared she was cold, so he urged her toward the bank without releasing her. He found where she'd dropped the toweling and quickly used the length of cotton to dry her, brusquely rubbing the curvaceous contours of her body with only the flimsy material between her skin and his hands. He pressed kisses across her collarbone and along her shoulder, then knelt to dry her hips and legs, pausing in discovery to kiss the indentation at her waist and the sleek curve of her hip.

She was more beautiful than the painting above the bar. More beautiful than anything he'd known or imagined, long and slim and full-breasted, and the sight and feel of her set him on fire.

He dried himself quickly, then spread the damp toweling on the ground and took her hand to urge her down beside him. She looked up at him as though she couldn't quite believe they were here and that this was happening. He felt the same.

"You're the prettiest thing I've ever seen, Lily." He lay alongside her and looked at her body in the moonlight. Unbidden came thoughts of other men who'd seen her body and enjoyed her kisses, but he banished those to the back of his mind and concentrated on this moment, on the feelings she inspired.

"I've got a fire inside for you like nothin' I've ever felt before. You feel it, too, don't you?"

She nodded.

He'd thought himself a strong man, hardened by life and living, but Lily exposed his weaknesses. All the willpower he'd thought he possessed was like dandelion seed scattered in the wind when he looked at her, thought of her, touched her.

He skimmed his thumb along her smooth cheek, the fine line of her jaw, and touched her lower lip. Her breath warmed his fingers.

He stroked the back of her thigh, up but not as far as her bottom, then back down. The back of her knee was silken and sensitive, because she caught her breath. Oh, to be touching Lily Divine was the most exquisite pleasure, to hear her responsive sighs the most rapturous torture on earth. Pure bliss to skim his palm along her flesh, to bring his fingers to the delicate skin on the inside of her thigh and feel her body tremble.

He wanted to move his hand higher, touch her intimately and make her shudder against him, but he waited, listened to her breathing even out, and kissed her.

She was the one who opened her mouth this time, tilting her head and taking his tongue in her mouth as though she was making love to his body. She had to feel him hard and aching against her, had to know how desperate he was for her. The pleasure he sought was so close his stomach knotted with anticipation. But he took his time kissing her, caressing her thigh, then brought his hand up to cup her breast.

Her breasts were even more luscious than the artist had portrayed them. And he had the privilege of them in his hands, against his cheek. He lowered his head and indulged himself in the sheer gratification of tasting her. She clutched his head to her breast, digging her fingers into his hair.

He flicked his tongue against her nipple, and she arched herself toward him with a soft groan. His desire for her wasn't satisfied, and he crawled upward to take her mouth, deep and hungrily this time. Why he should feel honored to make love to a woman who sold herself to every miner who came down the pike, he couldn't fathom. But here he was, deluded into feeling as though he was the man she'd been waiting for.

Nate grasped behind her knee and pulled her leg up around his hip, and she crushed into him. He splayed his hand across her lush bottom, stroking, kneading, as the need he'd stored up for years spiraled upward and spread like wildfire.

He rolled so that she was on top of him, her cold wet hair draping his cheek and shoulder, and she took control of the kiss while he caressed her backside with both hands.

She ran her hand over his face and down his shoulder to his chest, then along their sides to his hip.

He rolled them again, and they were on the bed of long soft grass now. Nate wedged his knee between her thighs, and she gasped and pressed into his thigh. Against his leg she was slick molten heat. Everything about Lily was more intense, more vibrant, more exciting than any woman he had ever known. Everything from her colorful speech to her sometimes flamboyant manner of dress. *This* was more splendid, as well.

He separated their mouths and stared into her lovely face in the moonlight. "You said you weren't sorry for the kiss that night."

"I wasn't."

"What about this? Will you be sorry for this?"

"Will you?" she returned.

"No."

She lay with one hand on his back, the other at his hip, her hair drying in ringlets around her face.

Their bodies strained to join. Heat pounded where Nate nudged between her thighs.

"Answer," he demanded. "Will you be sorry?"

"No."

Focused on her face, he reached between them and touched her. She was so still, he feared his touch didn't please her, but then she made a sound like a hiccup and he knew just where to focus his attention.

She turned her head aside and closed her eyes. Her hips arched convulsively into him.

"Look at me." He said it more gruffly than he'd intended.

She did and he poised himself.

She caught her lower lip between her teeth and grasped both of his upper arms.

Nate slid into her tight heat with a groan of pleasure and a shiver that spread from where they were joined all the way to his scalp. "You are divine, Miss Lily, no doubt about it."

He remained raised on his arms to watch her expression as he moved and took up a rhythm that was almost too much, too strong, too blissful to sustain. This woman carried him to the edge of reason and dangled him from the precipice, and he'd never loved anything more. He wanted to lose control, but he wanted to take her with him, so he kissed her, touched her, grasped her hips and angled himself to give her the most pleasure.

She encouraged him with breathless sounds and a tightening of her fingers on his shoulders. His senses were so full of her, his body so lost in her, he didn't want to miss a moment or return to reason, ever.

But he had to, of course.

Her body tensed and pulsed around him, and she pulled him down to hold him close. He buried his face in the delicious scent of her neck, held her tightly and took his own release in a blinding rush of sensation.

Neither of them moved for long seconds as their breathing slowed and their bodies cooled. Nate slid to her side and cradled her in his arms.

Lily would never let him know how deeply she'd been touched by his gentleness and unselfish concern. She'd never known a man's tender caress before, never taken pleasure in this act she'd only feared and dreaded. Just as she'd learned what she'd been missing in his kisses, she now knew the vast extent of what had been stolen from her.

Her pride. Her self-respect. Her dignity and worth. Her pleasure in being a woman. All the things her father had sold so cheaply and that her husband had crushed with his abuse.

Lily knew them now. She felt a newly awakened sense of power and a burgeoning confidence. This man found her worthy of respect and had honored her body with his. He had taken nothing against her will, but accepted what she willingly gave him with reverence. She'd felt admired. Revered. She felt it still in the way he held her in his arms and threaded his fingers into the tangle of hair at her neck.

She looked up at him, and he took it as an invitation to kiss her. Lily felt tears welling in her eyes and a tightening in her throat. Even now he kissed her. Even now he showed tenderness.

He was a strong man. A man who'd killed. A man she doubted feared much of anything. A man who wore a gun like another arm.

The first man she'd ever trusted.

She ended the kiss to say, "I'm not sorry, Sheriff."

"I should hope not. But I do hope we know each other well enough that you can call me by my name."

She smiled and he brought a finger up to run it over her lips. "I'll have to try it out. Nathaniel."

"It's Nate."

"You don't seem like a Nate to me."

"What do I seem like to you?"

"Sheriff comes natural."

He sighed. "Just plain Nate will do."

The breeze touched their skin, and she became aware that the evening had finally cooled down. She didn't want this time to end, but it was growing late.

"I have some shampoo paste on the bank. Want to wash quickly before we head back?"

He rose to find the shampoo, and she admired the beauty of his body in the moonlight.

"You gonna help me?"

"No."

Finally he found the tube and they bathed quickly. The towel was still damp, so Nate gave her his shirt to dry with. She used it and so did he, and they dressed.

Lily stuffed her corset, stockings and garters in

Charlotte's saddlebag and wore only her satin drawers and dress.

He stepped close behind her as she prepared to mount the horse. Lily felt his breath on her shoulder and turned her cheek into his.

"I've never known a woman like you," he said.

She brought her palm up and stroked his jaw, felt the prickle of his evening beard. "And I've never known a man like you."

He was the kind of man women dreamed of having notice them, the kind of man a woman wanted to have court her, to love her.

He had loved a woman once. Sarah had been her name. A woman with family and land. A woman who'd no doubt been a virgin when he'd bedded her the first time. A woman who'd given him a child...

Lily turned away and stepped into the stirrup. Nate aided her with both hands on her rump and a healthy push.

"The pleasure was all mine," he said.

She picked up the reins and nudged the horse forward. Behind her he mounted his roan and followed.

They rode slowly, as though neither of them was eager for the night to end. As they reached the outskirts of town, an orange glow on the horizon caught their attention. Dark smoke curled into the sky.

Dread clenched in Lily's stomach. "Fire!"

They kicked their horses into a run, heading toward the site of the blaze. Lily noted in relief that the flames were coming from too far away to be her place, and as they thundered past the darkened Shady Lady, she shouted, "Fire! Grab buckets and hurry!"

Celeste stuck her head out an open front window, then ducked back in, presumably to alert the others.

At the end of Main Street flames shot from the back of the Big Nugget. "Bernie's place!" she called to Nate.

But as they dismounted and tethered the horses to a post a safe distance away, Nate said, "I don't think so."

Lily looked again.

The flames could be seen over the top of the Nugget, but there was no activity at the saloon, and the sounds of shouting came from behind.

Her new livery was burning.

CHAPTER ELEVEN

SHE MET NATE'S hard unreadable eyes for the briefest of moments before they both took off at a run around the side of the Nugget.

The entire back of the new livery structure was in flames. The waves of heat reached them where they stood, and the stench burned Lily's nostrils. Bernie and Zeke were among half a dozen men who were flapping scorched blankets at the blaze and carrying dripping buckets of water. Among them were Howard and George, and even Amos Douglas had shown up to help.

There weren't enough people or enough buckets, and the men were losing ground fast, even though the new wood burned slowly. Lily could see that if they lost this battle, the flames could easily jump to the Nugget.

She grabbed a stack of blankets from a pile on the ground and ran to the trough out front to soak them. As she was returning, a dozen more volunteers came to help, all of them her employees. They carried kettles and pails and all manner of containers.

The sheriff organized a line of people from the front of the building to the rear.

"The water's going to run out," Lily called to him.

"We can get water from my trough system at the garden plot."

He called to Big Saul and Howard, and they lugged barrels to the back of a wagon and began the process of filling and transporting them. Lily's back ached by the third trip, and her eyes burned from the smoke, but she didn't slow down.

A crowd gathered on the street to watch and speculate, and she noticed a few from the Women's Temperance Prayer League, as well as Catherine Douglas and Evangeline Gibbs.

Violet dropped onto a step at the front of the saloon. She wore a dressing gown and a pair of boots. Water had soaked the front of her robe.

Celeste fell into place beside her.

Lily made another trip with the men before she did the same, catching her breath and resting her back. Violet and Celeste joined the bucket line this time.

After a moment Lily stood.

"Take a rest, Lily." With a hand on her shoulder, Nate gently pushed her back down on the step. "Sit for a few minutes."

She looked up at him and agreed with a nod.

He loped back to his task.

Her gaze moved across the bystanders to observe the women. Most had taken time to dress and hastily pin up their hair. She glanced down at the stained and torn satin dress she wore, one with a low-cut bodice and a hem that showed her ankles. She hadn't put on her corset or stockings after she and the sheriff had…gone swimming. Her hair had dried to a nimbus of wild ringlets after that swim and consequent tumble. She must look like a wild woman.

"Nathaniel?" Evangeline Gibbs, ever the proper young lady, waved a white hankie at the sheriff as he passed on the wagon.

He motioned Saul to drive forward and jumped down to see what she wanted.

She handed him a bandanna and a jar of something Lily couldn't see in the darkness. She imagined lemonade.

Nate drank the contents thirstily and wiped his face with the cloth. A moment later he tucked the bandanna in his pocket and chased after the wagon.

The incident left Lily with a disturbed feeling. Evangeline had certainly seemed *familiar* with the sheriff. Bold and confident enough to seek his attention and offer him a drink.

Thirty people were running and sweating to fight this fire and she'd singled out and catered to the sheriff?

Lily stood.

Evangeline looked her way.

She might have seen Nate instruct Lily to take a break. Perhaps that had reeked of familiarity, as well.

Lily joined the bucket line with her friends.

An hour later, the fire was out. An exhausted community gathered in the street in front of the Big Nugget.

"Somebody set that fire," Bernie said, wiping sweat and soot from his forehead. "Somebody set on destroying our livery."

The sheriff agreed. "There's no other explanation. It was an empty structure. No cooking fire."

Lily felt sick at the loss. She'd sunk a fair investment into that building. So had Bernie and Zeke—at her urging. She felt responsible now.

An uncomfortable shift of attention brought sets of eyes to Wade Reed. He stared from one person to the next with his mouth agape. "You don't think it was me! Hellfire! Bernie's a friend of mine. Zeke, too. And Lily."

Lily spoke up. "I don't think you did it."

"What about your wife?" Clive Callahan asked. "Where was she after you took her home from jail?"

"She was in bed with me when we heard the commotion. She never left my side. She was pretty shook up and grateful to go home." His gaze skittered to Lily's and away.

She didn't believe Wade would destroy property, but she wasn't sure he wouldn't lie to protect his wife.

A heated discussion broke out between several of the business owners.

"Let's all get some rest," Mayor Gibbs said. "It's too late to solve anything tonight. Not that we're going to with any certainty. But at least we can look at things fresh in the morning. Go home, people."

Charlotte came to Lily's side. "Sorry 'bout yer place. Guess I don't have a job no more."

"I'm not letting some underhanded firebug get the best of me," Lily told her with conviction. A dozen people heard her reply, including the sheriff. "You'll have a job come winter, don't doubt it."

"Hell, Lily," Bernie said, scratching his neck. "I ain't sinkin' any more money into this thing. Most ever'body said they'd do business with us as usual, and the women been set on their ear. What're we fightin' for now?"

"For our right to run any business we damned well please," she replied. "And not to be run off. Nobody's taking away something I worked for!"

Bernie headed for his place. "You'll be workin' twice for it."

"Nobody said things come easy," she called to his back.

The crowd broke up, walking toward their various homes.

Harold looked at the piles of buckets and blankets. "I guess we'll sort through this mess in the morning, huh?"

"I'll help you, Miss Lily," Dutch Hulbert said.

"Me, too," Wesley Clark added.

A couple of the miners who'd been staying in town and had come to help spoke up, as well.

"All right," Lily said. "We'll start cleaning up bright and early tomorrow. See how bad it looks and what needs to be replaced. Thanks, all of you."

The men said their good-nights and the street was soon silent. The stench of burnt wood pervaded the air. Lily could smell it in her hair.

"Guess another bath is called for," she said aloud.

The sheriff was standing a few feet away. They were on a public street. "Shame I'll miss this one."

She grinned. "The girls are probably heating water now."

"Get some rest. I was gonna walk your horse to the livery, but it's gone."

"Charlotte took him. Sam's hers."

"Get up. Ride mine to your place."

He didn't help her up this time, but he walked alongside.

In front of her house, she slid to the boardwalk.

"Shame about your building," he said.

"Do you think Wade would lie if Meriel had anything to do with it?"

"I wouldn't've thought so, but people always surprise you."

"Disappoint you, you mean."

"That, too. I plan to look around inside the livery while I'm there."

Lily stifled a yawn. "It's almost morning."

"See you tomorrow." He turned to go.

"Nate?"

He stopped at the use of his name and came back. "Yeah?"

"Nothin'. Just trying it out."

He grinned and led the horse away.

LILY'S MUSCLES ACHED as soon as she sat up in bed the following morning. Not only did she have an unfamiliar ache between her thighs, but her back and arms felt as though she'd carried a horse up a hill.

Mollie and Violet had breakfast ready, and Thomas, Saul and Old Jess joined the women as usual. Charlotte had joined their gathering today. Somber faces lined the kitchen table until Lily threw a biscuit at Celeste and the girl's eyes widened in surprise. Lily laughed, and Celeste threw the biscuit back but missed and hit Helena in the chest.

In her dramatic accent, the Polish woman said, "I will have crumbs in my cleavage all day," and fished for the remainder with a frown.

They all laughed.

"This fire is just one of those things we move past," Lily said. "I'm not discouraged and I don't want any of you to be. Whatever it takes to repair and replace, I plan to do it. Charlotte, you're still going to have a job come fall. I already had a mirror and glassware and whiskey to order today. Now I'll be adding lumber to the list."

"No one was hurt," Rosemary said.

"And there were no animals inside yet," Mollie added.

"You see, it's not as bad as it could have been." Lily smiled. "And we have something to look forward to. We're going to start practicing our base ball. George is going to explain the game and the rules, and I want to practice every morning. We're going to have a winning team."

Mollie got up and moved around the table to give Lily a hug. "We should be the ones cheering you up, but you're always the one to do it for us."

Big Saul got up to hug Lily then, and by the time they finished cheering each other up and hugging and eating, the morning was burning bright.

"Work clothes today," Lily suggested. "I'm going to find a pair of trousers, 'cause we'll be shoveling and hauling ashes."

They kept a stack of cast-off clothing in the storeroom at the saloon and gave it to anyone who needed it. Today she had need of something practical.

THE SMELL OF SMOKE and ashes hung over the town that morning. It wasn't a hurdy-gurdy dress that had neighbors looking twice at Lily Divine, it was the pair of men's trousers she wore with a faded shirtwaist tucked into the waistband. She'd tied a bandanna around her hair and wore a felt hat with a string that tied under her chin. A sturdy pair of boots completed the ensemble.

Nate grinned at her long-legged approach and the reactions of the bystanders.

"What are you looking at?" Lily asked. "Never seen anybody dressed for work?"

"Not anybody who looked like that in a pair of pants," he replied. "You just love to cause a stir, don't you?"

"It'd be foolish to wear a skirt to wade through ankle-deep ashes and mud, now wouldn't it?"

"That it would."

"Well, stop yappin' and let's get to work."

Most of the business owners left their wives and children running the stores and came to offer a hand. George closed the barbershop and said he and Joel would reopen late in the afternoon to serve up baths before suppertime.

Several of the miners returned, and Spooner sent Mitch to pitch in. With so many hands, most of the work was accomplished by the end of the morning. Catherine Douglas showed up with her son, John, and they spread out a feast on the tailgate of a wagon.

"This lunch is a kind thing to do for us," Lily told her.

"It was the least I could do," the woman replied.

They shared a secret look. "You don't owe me a thing," Lily said.

Celeste and Mitch prepared plates and carried them to a shaded boardwalk a few doors down, where they sat and shared their meal in private.

Lily ate a piece of chicken and went back for a sandwich.

A few of the men were gathered at the tailgate. "So what does the mayor's daughter serve up for lunch?" Wade was asking.

"How in tarnation would I know?" Harvey Munger replied.

"I wasn't askin' you, I was askin' the sheriff."

The men all turned toward Nate.

He looked at Wade with a warning message in his eyes.

"You had lunch with Evangeline?" Harvey asked.

"A Sunday picnic," Clive clarified.

Lily placed the sandwich on her plate and walked on past, to the boardwalk in front of the saloon, and sat. A dirty yellow cat padded close and sat observing her with its tail flicking.

A Sunday picnic. He'd come by Lily's house after church to tell her about the meeting and he'd said he had something to do. He'd been on his way to meet Evangeline Gibbs. On his way to a picnic.

And Wade and Clive knew about it, so it was public knowledge. The sheriff was seeing Evangeline.

Lily took a bite of the sandwich, and it tasted like the ashes she'd scooped all morning.

Evangeline. Sweet looking. No, damned pretty, actually. Blond hair in smooth curls, blue eyes, fair skin. Delicate manners and sensibilities. A lady. A young lady. An innocent young lady. The kind men married. And respected. And protected.

A pain so deep and so severe she couldn't bear it pressed in on Lily's chest and crushed her breath and stifled her heartbeat.

The mayor's daughter had been to school in the East, had been tutored in manners and etiquette and all sorts of charming parlor skills. She'd been groomed to make some man a fine wife. Lily glanced at Catherine, standing near the wagon and making sure people had enough to eat and pouring them glasses of buttermilk and cold water.

Catherine had been a woman like that, but she'd been unfortunate enough to be wed to an abusive and degrading man.

Sheriff Harding would be a good husband. Dutiful, respectful, loving. A good lover.

Evangeline wouldn't have to worry about surly moods or flying fists.

The cat meowed and studied Lily with narrow slits of green eyes.

Why had Nate come to Lily last night, sought her out, made love to her, when his intentions were plainly focused on another woman?

He thought she was a whore. He'd never believed her denials.

The realization brought burning tears to her eyes.

Perhaps he'd become overtaxed in his efforts to restrain himself from his innocent and nubile young woman and had sought relief from those frustrations elsewhere.

He'd been attracted to Lily, and she was, after all, the kind of woman a man didn't have to play games with. She'd been a physical outlet. A means to ease his needs.

It hurt like no physical beating she'd ever received to know she wasn't his choice. His type. Her heart was a throbbing bruise, and she hadn't even known how involved her heart had been until this moment.

She'd even pictured his Sarah looking like Evangeline. He'd told her when they'd first met that he was starting over. He'd come to Thunder Canyon for a second chance. A new young wife. A bright new future. He was leaving his ugly past behind.

Lily didn't begrudge Evangeline. The young woman didn't know about Lily. And for the first time since she'd known Nate, shame swept over Lily in a hot flush. If Evangeline knew, she'd be crushed. Heartbroken.

She must never know. No one must ever know. And it could never happen again. Lily wouldn't do that to another woman.

She tossed her sandwich to the cat and stood.

Catherine took her plate. "Did you have enough to eat, Lily?"

"The lunch was so thoughtful," Lily told her.

"I didn't know what else to do, but I wanted to help."

Lily got tears in her eyes.

"It's going to be all right," Catherine said, and Lily could tell she wanted to move forward and comfort her, but they were in the public street, so she remained where she was.

Wouldn't do to be seen hugging the town whore.

Lily immediately regretted the unkind thought. Catherine would befriend her openly in the blink of an eye if she didn't fear her husband's retribution.

"I'm just tired." Lily wiped her sleeve across her face. A lady would have had a hankie. A lady wouldn't have had dirt and soot on her face in the first place. A lady wouldn't have been the target of an arsonist. A lady wouldn't have enemies or build a livery or run a saloon or be called a whore or sleep with another woman's intended husband.

Lily hadn't thrown up since she was ten years old, but her lunch was threatening to come back up.

The possibility jerked her thoughts in another direction and a moment of panic seized her. What if she'd gotten herself in a family way?

Lily stared at Catherine.

The woman placed her hand on Lily's shoulder. "You're white as a sheet. Are you ill?"

Lily nodded, then shook her head. "Yes. No. I'm fine. Really. Just tired."

"You'd better go home and lie down then before you faint. I'll walk you."

"No, you stay here." She moved away from her. She unerringly zeroed her attention in on the sheriff.

The sheriff. She'd only just started to think of him as Nate.

He'd finished eating and was talking to George over a cup of coffee. Nate looked up and met her eyes. He must have recognized her distress, because he sent a silent question with his eyes.

Lily looked away.

The work was done. She had only to thank those who'd shown up and volunteered and she could escape to her home. She methodically made it around to each person and thanked them, avoiding the one person she didn't want to speak to.

It wasn't going to happen that easily, though. He caught up with her as she turned away from Clive.

"It was a good morning's work, wasn't it?"

"It was. Thanks for your help."

"Glad to do it."

She didn't look up past his shoulder. Half a dozen people were within six feet of them, and all she wanted to do was slip away.

She caught sight of Rosemary heading toward the Shady Lady.

"I'm coming with you." She joined her and didn't look back.

She wasn't going to look back again, ever.

Ever was a long time.

LILY THREW HERSELF into the repairs to the saloon and the livery, ordering supplies and auditing finances. She didn't see the sheriff for three days, and made sure she wasn't in the Shady Lady during the usual times he dropped by.

Celeste asked for an evening off, and Lily simply told her to trade with one of the other girls.

The following morning at breakfast, Celeste burst into the kitchen with a smile as wide as the Montana sky.

"Mitch asked me to marry him!" she announced in breathless excitement.

A stunned silence was followed by cheers and congratulations and quite a few tears.

"You said yes?" Helena asked.

"Of course I said yes! I'm head over heels for him, and he's just as wild about me. He has a steady job, and he's already got a little place that was his grandpa's. It's not fancy, but it's a start. We can fix it up some. I can still take in laundry."

Lily absorbed the news with a combination of joy and sadness. Seeing Celeste and Mitch's burgeoning love had been heartwarming and reassuring. So many of her friends bore the scars of past hurts and abuse, and it pleased her immeasurably to know that some of those wounds could be healed.

But thinking of Celeste leaving their tightly knit circle of safety and Lily's protective eye felt like letting go of a child.

"Will he let you come see us?" Molly asked. "After you're married?"

"Well, of course he will, silly. Mitch thinks all of you are like family. Just like I do."

Mollie glanced at Helena and then at Lily. They were all probably thinking that once Celeste moved out and became a part of the community, it would be better for her if she didn't look back here. She would be more accepted if she cut her ties.

"Ten minutes and we'll meet for base ball practice!" Lily called.

"I'm real pleased for you," Lily told Celeste when they had a few minutes alone on their way to the section of land Saul had mown for their practice field.

"You deserve this, remember that. Any man who is smart enough to love and appreciate you is one hell of a man in my book."

Celeste hugged her, and Lily closed her eyes and held back tears. "I told him, of course. That I'm not a virgin." Celeste moved back and Lily noted the young woman had tears of her own in her eyes when she met Lily's gaze. "He said it didn't matter. That we're starting our lives together and the past doesn't count."

Lily nodded. "I always did like Mitch."

"I didn't think I'd ever be able to trust again," Celeste told her. "But I feel safe with him. Loved."

Lily's throat was too tight to speak, so she just squeezed her friend's hands and gave her a watery smile. Few women had come and gone in the years Lily had operated the Shady Lady, and none of them had been with her as long, nor been as dear to her, as Celeste.

This was what it was all about, she realized: seeing the girls gain confidence, helping them develop into women who could make good decisions and be in charge of their own lives.

"No more tears." Lily took a deep breath and exhaled. "We have a game to learn."

George joined them later that morning to go over the rules for the game and to help them measure their diamond-shaped field.

"This is like town ball," George explained, "but some of the rules are different. We use bats instead of paddles—Lily already bought those—and there are four flat bases instead of posts." He held up a book for them to read: *Beadles Dime Base Ball Player.* "Every team gets a copy of this."

"I've played this," Thomas called. The man had stayed with them all summer and never mentioned moving on. "There are base ball clubs in all the big cities back east."

"What's the first thing we have to learn to do?" Mollie asked.

"To hit the ball with the bat when it's pitched. That's the whole point."

"Okay, let's practice that. We can read the book at home."

"I'll explain as we go," George said. "Let's see who can pitch the ball."

Turned out Old Jess was the best pitcher. His wiry upper-body strength lent what he needed, and his aim was right on.

Lily laughed time after time as she watched the women swing the bat, miss the ball and spin in a corkscrew. But when it was her turn, she discovered it wasn't so easy. Big Saul took right to it, though, hitting that ball and sending it flying.

George whooped and waved his hat when the ball sailed across the field into tall grass. "*That's* what you're supposed to do!"

"He's our secret weapon!" Thomas shouted.

Determined now, the women lined up for their turns. Mollie hit the ball twice and Celeste managed to strike it once, too. Lily made up her mind that she wasn't going to let them show her up. When her turn came, she hammered the ball on the third try. The impact jolted her arm and shoulder and the ball flew into the sky.

Everyone cheered for her.

By then it was midmorning, and their arms were tired and sore. "Let's call it a day and practice again tomorrow," she suggested.

"None of the other teams have started practicing yet," George said with a grin.

"Who's our competition?" Lily asked.

"Bernie and Zeke formed a team of men from their places with a couple of miners. Howard got together a bunch with Wade and some ranchers. Peyton Gibbs asked the sheriff to be on his team, and they've recruited Amos's son, John, plus Spooner and Clive. I think there's a team entirely made up of miners, too."

Of course, the sheriff was playing on the mayor's team. He was courting the man's daughter.

Lily followed the others back to the Shady Lady, where they washed up and changed clothing and resumed their daily tasks.

Lily took paper and pencil to the bar and worked on a list to plan Celeste's wedding. There was a quiet card game underway in the far corner, and Old Jess was napping on a chair near the stove.

It was difficult to imagine Celeste leaving. Lily's was a home where the members were free to come and go as they pleased, but rarely did anyone leave. Lily was glad to offer refuge and work and support. It was only natural that some would grow and leave the nest. Celeste was making a good choice for herself. She deserved to be a wife. Maybe someday a mother.

Lily only hoped that if she and Mitch chose to stay in Thunder Canyon, the town would be accepting.

"Penny for your thoughts."

The familiar voice caught her unaware. She turned to find the sheriff moving to sit beside her.

She'd been able to avoid him most of the week. He never came by the Shady Lady in the afternoon.

"I was just thinking about Celeste and Mitch."

"Something's going on there, isn't it?"

"They're getting married."

"Well. Something's *really* going on there." He eyed her. "Are you unhappy about it?"

"Not at all. I'm very happy for them."

He stood up. "Mind if I help myself to a draw?"

"Go ahead."

He flipped over a mug and tipped it under the tap on the barrel. He flicked foam off into a pail by the keg and came back to sit. "You've been keepin' yourself scarce lately."

"I've been busy."

"Too busy for a swim?"

Had he looked for her? Waited for her? "Yes."

"Shame. Let me know if you want to borrow a horse."

"Wade told me he'd give me a horse anytime I wanted. No charge."

"You taking him up on it?"

"If I need one."

He studied the wall behind the bar where the portrait hung beside a huge bare expanse. "Looks mighty strange not to see that mirror up there, doesn't it?"

She agreed. She tried not to think about it.

"Did you make some kind of deal to get the damages paid for?"

"We did. He was able to pay half. The rest comes in installments over the next year. Meriel is earning part of it."

His eyebrows shot up. "How?"

"Turns out she was a seamstress before she came here and married Wade. She's taking in sewing."

"I'll be hanged." He sipped his beer. "I still don't have a good idea who started the fire. One of the women would seem most logical—Meriel especially, since the livery will cut into their business—but Wade swears she was home with him from the time they left the jail until he heard the shouts about the fire."

"You don't think he'd lie to protect her?"

"I don't know. He's sympathetic to her feelings and the fact that she feels like a fish out of water here, but I can't see him lying."

"Me, neither. And I've known him a long time."

"He has a lot of respect for you, Lily."

She didn't even understand words like respect or honor anymore.

"How much did the fire set you back?"

"Lumber, nails and shingles. Hiring the men. The supplies and stock hadn't arrived yet, so we got off easy there."

"Are Zeke and Bernie sharing the loss?"

"I'm paying for it. I think they'd have backed out if I'd let them, so this way everybody's happy."

"You ever read sonnets, Lily?"

She gave him a curious look. "You mean like poems?"

"Uh-huh."

"I read the catalogs at Howard's, the ledgers on my desk and the labels on the cans of coffee. Oh, and the stock invoices. Poems don't have much to do with my life, Sheriff."

He looked to be thinking.

"What made you ask that?"

"Just wonderin'."

Wondering how she compared to Evangeline, she'd bet. She gathered her papers in a stack and glanced to make sure nobody was within earshot. She met his eyes and took a breath.

"We're not going to be meeting for midnight swims anymore."

CHAPTER TWELVE

"WEATHER'LL BE TURNING cooler," he agreed.

"The weather has nothing to do with it. We're not going to—to *see* each other anymore. Not in private."

A muscle ticked in his jaw. "If you say what happened was a mistake, I'm going to hit somethin'."

"I'm not saying that."

His quiet voice was angry when he said, "You told me you wouldn't be sorry. I asked ahead to make sure. I didn't want you to be sorry."

Lily could hardly speak around the lump that had formed in her throat. She lay awake every night thinking of the way he'd made her feel. She wasn't sorry that she'd experienced something beautiful with a man so considerate and unselfish.

What she regretted was being the means to satisfy his sexual appetites while sparing the lady he wanted to marry. What she hated was not being that woman.

She set down the papers. "Come with me, please."

He got up and followed her along the back hall into the house. Violet was seated at the kitchen table with a slate and a book. She glanced up, saw who'd entered and looked right back down at her studies.

Lily led him into the bathing chamber behind the kitchen where she closed the door, cocooning them in privacy. Violet would no doubt wonder what she was up to, but she wouldn't say anything.

Nate glanced around the room, his gaze taking in the tub, the stacks of white towels, the shelf of bath salts and various boxes and bottles.

"We've been honest with each other," Lily said straight-out.

"I've told you things I never told anyone," he said.

"I don't want to damage that. I don't want to take away from what we had together."

"What're you gettin' to?"

"I know about Evangeline," she said.

He blinked once, but he held her gaze. "What about her?"

"You've thought about marrying her, haven't you?"

"I thought about it. Yes."

"I won't take anything more away from her," Lily said. "You and I are not going to do again what we did. Ever. She is the marrying kind of lady, I'm not. She deserves your loyalty and devotion. You felt you were sparing her, but you weren't." Lily wanted to reach across the space between them and touch his face. Her palm burned with the desire, but she kept her hand clenched at her side. "Trust me, I know she'll appreciate you. And if she doesn't, she's crazy."

"What about *us?*" he asked.

"There is no us, Sheriff. There can't be."

"Why not?"

Because I run a dance hall and drink rye and wear

trousers and have my naked picture hanging over a bar.
"Because I'm Lily Divine," she said simply.

"You're saying we'll never be together again?" he
asked.

"That's right."

"And that you want me to be with someone else?"

She nodded.

Nate absorbed her words with as much dignity as he
could muster. He'd suspected she didn't have any feelings for him beyond those of physical desire, but apparently her curiosity had been satisfied or her goal met,
and she had no further need of him.

"All right, Lily. You're an independent, self-sufficient woman. You know your own mind. I admire that."

"I know you do."

"I'm still not sorry."

Something in her expression flickered. "Neither am
I."

Did something about him threaten her independence
or her confidence? He would never have asked her to
change. Maybe she *wanted* him and her rejection was
simply because she didn't *need* him. She took care of herself, she'd known every sort of man there was, and she
didn't care to have any of them. He was just another
man.

He'd been sorting things through in his head ever
since the night at the stream and he didn't know if he
could be attracted to another woman after Lily. He'd
been trying with Evangeline, but everything about her
paled in comparison.

He hadn't felt anything particularly movin' about

kissing Evangeline. Just *looking* at Lily's mouth sent his blood pumping.

Impulsively he hooked one arm around Lily's back and pulled her flush against him where he could feel the crush of her breasts against the front of his shirt. Her eyes opened wide, and he kissed her before she could protest.

Lily's mouth was heaven, the taste of her a craving he'd never kick. He wanted to leave part of himself with her. He wanted to take part of her as his own.

He wanted Lily.

But she didn't need him. She didn't need any man.

This was what he got for sticking his neck out like a fool.

He released her and looked at her one last time before turning on his heel. He made his way past the girl they called Francesca. She didn't look up and he continued on until he was out of Lily's house.

She was Lily Divine. As if that should be enough of an explanation for anyone. *Was it?*

She had the best of all worlds right there in her carefully built and stocked and populated home and dance hall. She didn't have to depend on anyone. She didn't have to conform to society or any rigid structure of rules because no one expected her to. She had her choice of men—if she chose to have one—and she was pretty much adored by everyone who knew her.

She was Lily Divine all right. And she'd told him to direct his interests toward another woman. No other woman could ever compare. And he suspected Lily knew that, too.

IT TOOK NEARLY A WEEK of rolling it around in his head and avoiding women of any ilk before Nate told himself he'd blown his attraction to Lily out of proportion. She was a larger-than-life figure in this town, and he'd let the romance of her legendary popularity influence his judgment.

He'd made up his mind to effect a change and he was determined that it would still happen.

Beatrice had once again invited him to dinner, and he accepted the invitation, intent on taking up where he'd left off with Evangeline before he'd become sidetracked.

Over Evangeline's peach torte, they drank tea from delicate china cups.

"The mayor and I have another engagement this evening," Beatrice announced. "You young people enjoy your after-dinner tea and conversation while we go prepare."

Nate stood as Beatrice got up, and she and her husband took their leave.

Evangeline poured hot tea into his cup and offered him the sugar bowl. "Father says your team is shaping up quite nicely."

Nate stirred a spoonful into his cup.

John Douglas's youth was one of the positives about their team. Spooner and Clive were pretty fair, but the mayor was hopeless. He had yet to hit the ball during practice, and his pitching was worse. Nate had seen the teams from the Shady Lady and the other saloons practicing in the mornings. Their business hours afforded them daytime to practice, while the rest of them were putting it off or meeting in the twilight after work.

"I can hardly believe how seriously everyone is taking this competition," she added.

"If you're gonna do something, do it right," he replied.

"That's an admirable philosophy."

"Been meaning to ask you something."

"What's that?"

"What's an asphodel?"

"Asphodel is an herb. Why do you ask?"

"It was in the poem. Did you learn about herbs at finishing school?"

"I believe I just read about it somewhere. I can't recall, actually."

"What did you learn at finishing school?"

"We were trained in deportment. Manners. Skills a wife needs, such as baking and embroidery."

"You learned the baking part well."

Her cheeks turned pink. "Thank you."

Classes for being a wife. He pondered the mystery of that for a moment. Kind of reminded him of training a horse to do its master's bidding.

"So, what do you do during the day?"

"I bake and sew, and Mother's been showing me how the household is run. We go visiting and have ladies over for tea. The women still hold meetings at one another's homes and Mother insists on dragging me along."

"I thought the Prayer League had been disbanded."

"The women still meet for prayer, but Mrs. Reed

isn't among them any longer. The focus has shifted for the better."

"That's promisin'."

"Do you play cribbage, Nathaniel?"

"I'm pretty rusty, but I could probably hold my own."

"Let's retire to the parlor with our tea, and we'll play."

Evangeline was just setting out the cards when her mother paused in the doorway. "We'll be leaving now. Oh, Evangeline dear, do set those dreadful cards aside and play the pianoforte for Mr. Harding. Good evening."

"Thank you for dinner, Mrs. Gibbs," he called as she left.

Her daughter met Nate's eyes. "Mother doesn't approve of card games. She believes they're vulgar."

"What do you think?"

"I don't understand her distaste. I rather enjoy the strategy." She looked at the cards in her hand for another moment, then laid them down. "I shall play something for you first."

Nate took a wing chair beside the fireplace and settled in.

An oil lamp burned on the top of the pianoforte, and a gas light on the wall, bathing Evangeline in a glow that softened her pale complexion and shone on the golden waves of her hair.

With its dulcet tones and lilting melodies, the music she played was nothing he was accustomed to hearing. It was pretty, but a little stiff and formal.

"Do you read the notes?" he asked.

"Yes, but I've memorized several drawing-room pieces. It's fashionable for people in the city to gather in someone's home for an evening of culture. I played for all of my aunt's friends when I was visiting her."

"I haven't known much culture," he said. "But I can tell you're good."

At his compliment, she sat up even straighter and finished the piece.

"Do you know anything with words?" he asked.

She played and sang "Beautiful Dreamer" in a voice as sweet as her temperament. The words made a little more sense than those of her sonnets, but still wrapped his thinking in a knot. As she finished and played another song, his thoughts wandered to the town outside this house and his duty of checking on the saloons. No one ever mentioned anything to him if he took some time for himself, but he knew his responsibilities and held himself accountable. Time spent here seemed at odds with his purpose, though he knew he wasn't single-handedly in charge of overseeing Thunder Canyon.

Evangeline finished.

"That was real nice," he said.

"Shall we play cribbage now?"

He was getting a headache and wanted some fresh air. "Tell you what. I need to make rounds. How about if I come back tomorrow evening—after dinner—and we'll play cribbage?"

Her smile indicated he'd pleased her with his suggestion.

"Please tell your mother again that I thank her for dinner."

She stood to walk him to the door.

He faced her as they lingered inside the front hall, and she glanced at his shoulder and barely met his eyes.

From a place in his mind he didn't want to visit, a nagging concern reared its head. Could he do this for the rest of his life?

She was pretty, he assured himself. *Lily is exquisite,* his internal demon wheedled.

She had dignified manners, she spoke in a soft unassuming tone, and she'd been tutored to please a husband. *Lily got what she wanted, would never back off if she held an opinion and took her pleasure in any man she chose,* the voice beguiled.

She wore soft pastels and yards of crisp pleated ruffles and flounces. No man had ever seen her feminine assets. *Lily struck a pose in a red satin dress and knew how fine her breasts were spilling over the top of a corset.*

The comparisons had to stop or he'd never move on and get the life he wanted.

Nate stepped forward and kissed Evangeline, wrapping an arm around her shoulder and urging her toward him. She held herself stiffly and brought a fist up to his chest to keep their bodies from touching. He moved his mouth on hers, and her body relaxed somewhat. Her lips softened under his, and she opened her fist to spread her palm on his shirtfront.

Nate released her.

Evangeline pressed her fingertips to her lips and studied him with wide, uncertain eyes.

Nate stepped out into the night, disappointment whispering a taunt in his head.

The night air felt good on his skin and his long, determined strides swallowed up the distance to Main Street.

He made his rounds, visiting the other dance halls first and leaving the Shady Lady for last. Lily had stopped avoiding him.

She stood at the end of the cherrywood bar deep in conversation with Wesley Clark. There were three cowboys Nate hadn't seen in town before standing with them, mugs of beer in hand. Lily walked to the side with one of them, tilting her head as she listened to something he said.

The cowboy jerked a thumb over his shoulder, and with a grin, she joined him for a dance.

Nate couldn't take his eyes away. He moved to the bar and asked Old Jess for a beer. Helena sat down beside him. "Good evening, Sheriff."

"Miss Helena."

Lily was wearing a purple dress he hadn't seen before. He glanced down at the bar and spotted her black lace fan with the fringed tassels.

He wouldn't let the woman tie him in knots. She wasn't going to change, and she'd told him so in no uncertain terms.

He raised his gaze to the portrait. He'd known every silken inch of that body. He'd held those breasts and kissed those lips.

So had a hundred other men, he told himself. Didn't make him special. So would that cowboy tonight, probably.

Nate drank his beer, put down the mug with a whack and left.

"Goodnight, Sheriff," Helena called to his departing back.

THE SATURDAY of the elimination tournament arrived cooler than all the days that had preceded it. Fall was in the air, and the reprieve was a welcome one to the residents of Thunder Canyon.

Nate showed up with his team, all of them dressed in dungarees and chambray shirts with the sleeves rolled back. The mayor had said they'd needed a uniform of some sort, and this was what they'd come up with.

The miners wore any old thing they'd washed that month, and Zeke and Bernie's team all had new red bandannas tied around their necks.

The Shady Lady's players were unmistakable and right in character in their colorful low-cut satin dresses and ankle-high boots. Lily never missed an opportunity to flaunt or shine, and she was shining this morning.

She wore the red dress she'd had on the day Judge Adams had inspected her employees and searched her business and home for the Brand girl. Black lace trimmed the bodice, and she wore a black straw hat to keep the sun from her eyes.

Nate scanned the crowd for reactions and noted that Lily had drawn attention exactly as he knew she'd planned. "Costumes don't make a good team," he told his teammates.

George gathered the team leaders and went over the rules. They drew straws to determine who would play each other first.

Everyone got a look at the competition this way, and the weaker teams were defeated quickly.

The miners were tough competition, lasting to the finals. By the time they broke for lunch, everyone needed a second wind.

Mitch sat with the Gibbs family, the Douglases, Spooner, and Clive and Suzanna.

The Callahans had prepared and packed baskets full of food and drinks. "Don't overeat," Clive warned his team members.

The employees from the dance hall were lounging on the back of a wagon and in the surrounding grass. They had unpacked a crate of sandwiches, fruit and cheese, and were obviously enjoying the outing and the nice day.

"Can you believe they wore those dresses?" Beatrice spoke to Evangeline and Catherine Douglas, but Nate overheard. "It's bad enough they were allowed to join this activity, but to flaunt their sordid occupations in our faces is rude beyond extreme."

"Clothes don't make the person," Nate said.

Beatrice gave him a disapproving look, and Evangeline studied him.

"It's for a good cause," Catherine said. "Their entry fee is going the same place ours is."

Amos frowned at his wife, and she looked sorry she'd spoken. She studied her sandwich in her lap.

Evangeline observed the gathering from beneath the brim of her wide hat. "I think I'd have been disappointed if they'd come attired in any other fashion."

The comment surprised Nate.

It apparently shocked her mother. She stared at the young woman as though she'd spoken heresy and her hand went to her bosom.

"Well, they're sure colorful," Spooner pointed out. "And they whupped all the other teams so far, no matter what they got on. Guess we'd best be thinkin' less about their dresses and more about hittin' the balls."

Howard and Wade's team lost that afternoon, as did Bernie and Zeke's. At the end, the miners competed against the mayor's team to see who would play the Shady Lady after church the next day.

Nate remained frustrated with Peyton's lack of performance. Now that Lily's team had done so well, he didn't want to lose.

One of the miners got struck in the head with a fly ball. Doc Umber treated him and he was hauled off the field.

Nate took his turn at bat with determination. When the ball was pitched, he swung and hit it with a thwack that splintered his bat and sent the ball sailing beyond the field. His home run brought in the players on the bases and won the match.

So it would be his team against Lily's.

They glanced at each other as congratulations and good-natured ribbing went on all around them. Lily loved a good fight, and he had no doubt that she'd give the game her all the following day.

"Will you stop by this evening for a game of cribbage?" Evangeline asked.

She'd beat him three games out of five the last few times they played. "I probably do need to salvage my dignity."

She laughed. "Mother says if I insist on occupying myself with such a vulgar pastime, I should at least let you win."

"I appreciate that you don't," he replied. "I wouldn't want to wonder. This way, the fact that you're more clever than I isn't a secret."

She seemed inordinately pleased by his statement, smiling and tucking her arm through his.

"I'll see you early this evening," he told her. "I won't be able to stay long. It's Saturday night."

He bathed at home, dressed in fresh clothing and buckled on his holster. At the livery, he saddled his horse and rode the perimeter of town, observing tracks and studying the landscape.

Smoke he'd noticed earlier in the day caught his attention and he rode out to investigate. The smoke curled from a campfire near the Little Deer Creek, as he'd suspected.

Instead of the miner he thought he'd see, however, he found a woman and several children camped beside a wagon. Roasting on a spit over the fire was a squirrel.

Nate climbed down and walked toward the campfire.

The woman looked nervously toward the oldest boy, who appeared about twelve. He wore pants that showed the tops of his boots and bore patches in both knees.

She said something to him, and he picked up a rifle that had been leaning against the wagon and handed it to his mother. She kept the barrel lowered, but the message was plain.

Nate swept off his hat. "How do, ma'am. Sheriff Nathaniel Harding's the name."

"We haven't broken any laws, have we?" she asked.

Two little girls sat on the ground and nearby another held a baby.

"No, ma'am. I saw your fire and came to have a look. Been mighty dry in these parts."

"I'm very careful," she told him. "We're not bothering anybody out here."

"No, no," he agreed easily. "Just doin' my job."

"We're preparing our supper. Would you care to join us?"

That squirrel would barely feed the lot of them, let alone another mouth, but the woman had her pride. "Thank you, ma'am, that's generous, but I had my supper. You travelin' alone?"

He didn't even see a coffeepot. A jug that probably held water sat on the ground.

"No. My husband is hunting."

"He a miner?"

She nodded.

"Where are you headed?"

"East," she said simply, then looked away.

"Good luck to you. Maybe I'll see you in town."

Nate got on his horse, paused to look over the woman and five children, then rode out.

There was no man, he'd bet a dollar to a plug nickel. She'd either been too afraid or too embarrassed to say so.

Later as he played cards with Evangeline, he had trouble focusing on the game. Making rounds of the streets and businesses in the dark, his thoughts strayed back to that mother and her children alone out there in the night. He'd camped out a thousand nights alone, but he was a man. He'd even be uncomfortable knowing

Lily was alone at a camp, and she was the most self-sufficient woman he knew.

He couldn't imagine how they'd make it any farther east with those tired-looking horses and no food or supplies. Maybe there'd been provisions under the tarp on the wagon, but he doubted it.

Later in the evening, Nate visited each of the saloons and eventually made his way to the Shady Lady. Lily and her girls were celebrating their base ball skills with an evening of red beer and red dresses. He perched on a stool at the bar and smiled at their frivolity. Thomas played his banjo and made up a ribald song about Lily and the balls she'd sent flying that day.

Lily called an end to his composition and asked the musicians to play a song Helena could sing to.

The Polish woman stood on a chair in the midst of the gathering and sang a song in her native language. It was haunting, the simple notes and the longing in her voice conveying a universal message of love. When she sang it through once more in English, there wasn't a dry eye in the dance hall. Love lost. Love longed for. The applause was slow in coming as listeners came out of the spell she'd woven.

"I didn't tell you to make us all blubber like babies," Lily chided her, swiping at her eyes. "Get on with something cheerful."

As the music resumed behind her, Lily picked up a few empty bottles and made her way to the bar.

"Evening, Sheriff."

"Miss Lily."

He was nursing a now-warm beer.

"Want a fresh drink?"

"I'm good."

"That was an impressive hit today."

He shrugged. "Your whole team is impressive."

Her grin brought a sparkle to her eyes. "We are, aren't we?"

"Sheriff?" one of the miners called to Nate from the doorway. "There's somebody out here wants to talk to ya."

Nate got up and crossed to the bat wing doors. In the glow of the gas lamp stood a boy. Recognition dawned immediately. The boy who was camped outside town with his mother and siblings.

CHAPTER THIRTEEN

Nate led him away from the noisy saloon, and they stood at the corner of the street. "What's on your mind, son?"

"You're really the sheriff, ain't ya?"

"I am."

"I don't think my ma trusted you right off."

"That's understandable. And wise."

"We don't have a place to live anymore."

"What happened?"

"My pa sold all the furniture and the stock and took off. The house and land didn't belong to us. The mortgage came due and we couldn't live there no more."

"So you've been living out of your wagon since then?"

The lad nodded.

"How long has it been?"

"Weeks, I think. Not sure how many. Even I know fall's comin', and that means winter. We might be doin' all right for now, but soon it'll be cold and there won't be blankets or food. My ma's doin' the best she can."

"Sure she is. Do you have any family? Grandparents?"

"My grandma back in Nebraska is old. My mom's pa won't have nothin' to do with us."

"What's your name?"

"Boone, sir. Boone Waldrop."

Nate extended a hand. "Pleased to meet you, Boone. You're a fine man for looking out for your ma and your sisters."

The boy's hand was small, the bones in his fingers delicate in Nate's enormous paw. "Brother, too," he added. "He's just one."

"It's a good thing you came to me. You and me can get some help."

"Like what?"

Nate glanced down the street. "I'm not sure what just yet. But don't you worry. We'll take care of things. Does your ma have bullets for that rifle?"

Boone nodded.

"Good." He propped his hands on his hips. "What about food? You got supplies in that wagon?"

Boone shook his head.

"Okay. Come back to the saloon with me." He guided the boy to a bench. "Sit right here. Don't move. I'll be right back."

Inside, he found Lily. "You have any dinner left?"

"Sure," she said, drying a glass. "I can make you a plate."

He took several coins from his pocket and placed them on the shiny wood surface of the bar. "Not for me. Could you make up several sandwiches with cheese and maybe a couple jars of milk?"

"You planning a late-night ball practice?" She leaned across the bar. "You're gonna need it."

He chuckled and then explained the situation, knowing Lily would understand and maybe even have an idea of how to help.

She pushed the coins back toward him.

Nate covered her hand with his. "You're not the only one who can lend a hand. I'm paying for the food."

Lily took the money and placed it in the box under the bar. Then she went to the kitchen and returned with a gunny sack. Nate suspected it held more than a few sandwiches.

"Come meet him."

Lily followed Nate out the door.

"Boone, this is Miss Lily. She made some sand-wiches for your family."

"Thank you, miss," the boy said solemnly.

"You're welcome."

"My ma'll likely be mad I came into town," he said.

"That's because she'd be worried about you." Nate looked him over. "Did you walk all the way here?"

"Nah. Rode Nelly. Couldn't get lost 'cause I could see the lights and hear the music."

"Well, I'll ride back with you. It's a little harder to find a campfire than a whole town."

"Thanks, Sheriff."

Lily stood on the boardwalk behind them as they headed out.

Nate rode within a shout of the campfire and handed the boy the gunny sack. "Tell your ma I said she wasn't to be mad at you. And I'm the law in these parts."

Boone grinned and shifted the weight over his shoul-der. "I'll tell her."

"There's no shame in needin' a little help now and

then, Boone. You remember that. And remember, you did the right thing."

"Yessir."

Nate watched from the cover of night as the boy approached the camp and his mother caught sight of him. He slid from the horse and showed her what he'd brought.

His mother's gaze lifted and she scanned the darkness. Nate knew she couldn't see beyond the ring of light thrown by the fire. He turned the roan's head and started back toward town.

NATE RAPPED on Lily's kitchen door the following morning, and Mollie opened the door to him. "Sheriff Nate! Come in. Helena made cinnamon rolls, and I'm cooking up some eggs and sausage. You're just in time."

Nate glanced around and took a seat. "Does Miss Lily cook?"

"Some," Mollie replied. "She has a knack for game. You want me to get her?"

"If she'll be along for breakfast, I can wait."

Within twenty minutes the household had gathered around the long table, and Mollie and Helena served up heaping platters of food.

"You're not in church this morning," Lily said to Nate. "Backsliding already?"

He took a cinnamon roll from the plate that was passed and refused to be goaded by her teasing.

"I've been trying to come up with something to help the Waldrop woman," he said.

Lily explained the situation to those gathered around the table.

Helena clucked in distaste. "Someone should find the husband and introduce him to the end of a rope."

"Probably didn't even do anything illegal," Nate replied.

"Not since all the property was his in the eyes of the law and she has no legal claim to any of it. Think on it," Lily said angrily. "If I married, all that I own would become the property of a man who could sell it and leave me destitute. And the law wouldn't blink an eye!"

"Well, we're not changin' any laws today," Nate said.

Lily ate her breakfast in a thoughtful manner.

"I've thought and thought how to supply more jobs for women," she said. "I can't buy enough butter or soap or find any more room here."

"My room will be available soon."

All eyes focused on Celeste, a few of them clouded with tears.

"That will be one room open," Celeste said with a shrug. "And one less hand around here."

"You are not replaceable," Helena told her.

"And even so," Lily went on. "That's just one room. I'm thinking *bigger.* The livery will employ only men, with the exception of Charlotte. What other occupations are there for women?"

"Schoolteachers," Rosemary said.

"Laundry," Mollie added, "which me 'n' Helena already do."

"Cooks," Thomas added.

"What kind of business employs a lot of people? You've been in plenty of cities, Sheriff. Where have you seen women employed? Besides dance halls."

"Restaurants," he replied. "Bakeries. Hotels."

"Hotels." Lily's attention had been arrested. She laid down her fork. "Beds to change, laundry to do, meals to prepare. That'd take a lot of workers, wouldn't it?"

"I'd say so."

"What are you thinking, Lily?" Celeste asked.

"I'm thinking the sheriff really came to practice with us this morning. Did you, Sheriff? Because we can't let you in on our secrets for winning the ball game today."

"Your tactics are no secret," he said. "Distract the other team with those—" he gestured with his fork "—dresses."

Everyone laughed, and Lily pretended to take offense. "You're underestimating our talent!"

Nate threw up his hands.

One by one they finished eating and went about their tasks.

"I'll let you know if I have any ideas," Lily said to him.

They studied each other, and Nate couldn't help thinking how fleeting and elusive the best moments in his life had been. What he and Lily had shared so briefly were among the times he most regretted losing.

He grabbed his hat and left.

THE PEOPLE OF THUNDER CANYON stood beneath an overcast sky that afternoon. The rain would be much welcomed, but what a day for it to announce its arrival.

"We could postpone the game," George said.

"Those dark clouds are on the other side of the mountains," Howard replied. "The rain might blow on over."

By an overwhelming vote, the players chose to go ahead with the match.

They tossed a coin, and Lily's team was up to bat first, a discouraging predicament in Nate's opinion, because they started tallying points immediately. Each time Rosemary ran, she hiked up her dress with both fists and ran to the bases with her red drawers on display.

Saul was a powerhouse behind that wooden bat, and Lily could send the ball sailing herself. Once, she hit it low and it bounced up at first base where Nate was standing, striking him in the knee. He hit the ground in pain.

As the ball rolled away, Lily ran past in a blur of skirts and petticoats. Scowling, Nate got up and rubbed his knee. By the time they changed positions, her team already had six runs.

Old Jess pitched the ball fast and low and struck out a good many of Nate's team. Nate hit the ball and hobbled to a base. They only had two runs by the time Nate got his second turn. Ignoring his throbbing knee, he remedied the score, and by the time the first drops of rain hit the dirt, they were tied.

Most of the women bystanders headed home, but Evangeline remained. She held a black umbrella over her head and called encouragement to Nate and his team.

Lily and her girls had the energy, physical agility and drive it took to compete and win. They won the game and received good-natured congratulations from the other teams and most of those who'd come to watch. The fact that the other women had already left helped keep the atmosphere friendly.

As Lily headed for home, she crossed Evangeline's path.

"You played very well," the young woman told her.

Surprised to be addressed in public, Lily said, "Thanks."

"It's a shame it had to rain and spoil the afternoon."

"Yes." Lily was getting soaked, and she had mud caked to her boots. Evangeline still looked pretty as a picture under her umbrella.

As an awkward silence stretched, Mayor Gibbs joined them. "You showed us all how the game is played, Lily. Well done. Let's get home, Evangeline."

Father and daughter hurried to a covered buggy.

Lily ran through the rain toward home.

MONDAY MORNING Lily sat in Amos Douglas's office at the bank and announced, "I want to buy the vacant hotel building."

No reaction showed on his face, but his hands paused on the papers he'd been shuffling on his desk. He released them and sat back. "Well. This is a surprise."

"You keep telling me I should invest and vary my holdings. You said you'd support me."

"That's right, and I do. I just wasn't expecting this particular request."

"Does the building belong to you?"

"It does."

The previous owner had unloaded it in a hurry, so it had probably been a bargain, but Lily knew Amos would never pass that good fortune along. He was in the money-making business.

"How much?"

He probably knew to the penny how much he had invested, but she could see the wheels turning in his head as he calculated how much he could get. He named a figure.

Lily didn't have that much ready money, not after rebuilding the livery, and she would never use the savings that cushioned the Shady Lady from hard times.

"What can I do?"

"Do you have any property to put up against bank notes?"

"I won't put up the Shady Lady. I have too many people depending on it."

He shrugged. "What about the other lots you own?"

"I could use those."

"Of course, they're not worth much without buildings on them."

"I have some jewelry that was Antoinette's."

"That might take care of part of it."

She thought about the rest of her holdings, and something occurred to her. "I have the deed to a mine."

"Indeed."

"The Queen of Hearts. It was—my father's." It bore the whole of her worth to her father. It was what he'd traded her for a share in.

"It has sentimental value, then?" Amos asked.

It had a whole lot of bad memories tied to it, and she didn't know why she hadn't gotten rid of it before, except for the fact that she owned free and clear what her father had so badly wanted. "It's a good piece of land."

"You can sign an interest-bearing note," Amos suggested. "Are you sure you want to do this? If for any reason you can't pay the installments, the collateral and the property will default back to me."

"One lot, the jewelry and the mine deed," she said. "Three things, three separate bank notes. That way I could only default on one at a time, not all at once."

"You make a hard bargain," he told her. "Bring the jewelry and the deeds in this afternoon so I can have a look at them. Once you sign, I'll hold the deeds. You can hold the jewelry."

Lily stood and shook his hand across the desktop.

"By the way, what are you going to do with the building?"

"Run a hotel," she replied. "When do I get the keys?"

THAT NIGHT LILY SHARED suggestions for Celeste and Mitch's wedding and asked Celeste for her ideas. "I really don't have any idea how to go about a wedding," Celeste told her.

"Neither do I," Lily confided. "But I know of someone I can ask." She could send a letter to Catherine Douglas. The woman would know the proper order and form for a ceremony. Lily wanted something other than just a quick pronouncement by a judge for her friend.

She sat at the end of the bar with her stationery and an ink pen and wrote a letter requesting help and suggestions, then asked Big Saul to deliver it to Catherine in the morning. It wouldn't do for him to show up at the Douglas home while Amos was there.

"HOW IN SAM HILL did you manage that?" Nate asked the next morning.

After the deeds and jewelry met Amos's satisfaction

and Lily had signed the bank notes and received the keys, her first stop had been the sheriff's office.

"I put a few things up as collateral and signed bank notes."

"Not your dance hall," he said, his expression one of alarm.

"Of course not. I'm going to go over there now and see what needs to be done to make a few rooms livable. And then we'll work on shaping it into a hotel. I need you to go find the Waldrop woman and tell her she has a job if she wants it. How's your knee?"

"It's black and blue, but I'll survive. Lily, she has five children."

"It's a big place. I'm sure there's room for them."

"Woman, what are you doing?"

"I'm expanding my interests."

"Not everybody is your responsibility. You can't take care of the whole damn world."

"No, but I can take care of those in my little corner of it."

"I would have gone in with you on this," he told her. "We could have been partners and you wouldn't have had to owe Douglas."

"I don't think we could be partners," she answered.

"I can get along."

"It wouldn't have been a wise decision for you."

"Why not? No, wait. Is this another because-I'm-Lily-Divine reason?"

"Are you going to see Mrs. Waldrop or not? I can probably find her on my own."

"I'll go."

"Thank you." She spun on her heel and walked out of the jail house.

Half an hour later, Lily and her entourage stepped into the building with considerable curiosity and excitement. Lily had watched the structure being built years back, of course, but once the walls were up and the doors and windows in, she'd never seen the inside.

The front door opened into a grand room with a tile floor and a dark-walnut counter that divided an office area from the foyer.

There was a dining room with a tin ceiling, crown moldings and glass chandeliers. Lily pictured it filled with tables set with white cloths and people bustling about, carrying trays and pitchers to paying customers.

The kitchen was three times the size of the one at the Shady Lady. Mollie and Helena made appreciative comments about the stoves and ovens. There was no icebox, and the amount of dishes, cookware and supplies needed staggered Lily's thinking for a moment. What had she been imagining? That the place would come fully stocked and furnished and ready to open? Hardly.

There was a suite of rooms on the main floor, as well as a parlor and storage rooms. On the second and third floors were two bathing chambers and eighteen bedrooms, six of them with adjoining dressing rooms.

Not a single bed, mattress, sheet, curtain or any other stick of furnishing was to be seen, of course.

Lily thought about the three bank notes she'd signed, the huge scale of this project and the overwhelming cost of getting it underway, and she experienced her first stabs of doubt.

She would not touch the savings that protected the Shady Lady. That was her first priority, always. Right now what she had available to spend was the money coming into the dance hall one day at a time. It added up, certainly, but not fast enough to get this place running anytime soon.

"Are we going to start cleaning today?" Mollie asked.

Lily looked at the dust-streaked and rain-spattered windows of the room she stood in. Here and there on the bare wood floors were traces of plaster and sawdust the builders had left behind. Eighteen bedrooms and the downstairs would take some elbow grease, so they might as well get started.

"We are. Some of us will go get buckets and rags, while others stay and get the windows opened. We'll sweep first and then clean the windows and floors."

"This is beautiful woodwork," Thomas commented. "But it all needs to be oiled and polished."

"That will be your task," she told him with a grin. "There's a ladder in the shed. Somebody has to run the saloon this afternoon. Jess and a couple of the girls can handle that without us until suppertime."

Everyone set about their assigned tasks, and Lily was standing behind the desk in the foyer, thinking about ordering ledger books, when the door opened and Nate entered.

On his heels was a petite woman and a small crowd of children.

"Lily, this is Mrs. Waldrop."

The woman came forward with a baby on her hip. "I'm Naomi. This is little Ben. I guess you've met Boone. My girls are Rachel, Prudence and Mary. Thank you for the job, Miss Divine. You can't know what a godsend this is."

"Call me Lily. It's going to be hard work, don't think it won't. There's room for you back here." She gestured and led the way to the rear of the building. "We've only just seen all this for the first time. The girls have gone to get cleaning supplies."

Lily glanced around, realizing there were no beds or anything for this family to stay here.

"We have pallets in our wagon," Naomi told her as if she'd been thinking the same thing.

Nate had followed and stood back from the women as they made plans for the sleeping arrangements.

"We'll clean our own rooms," Naomi said. "And then we'll bring our things in."

Mollie and Helena returned, and Lily made introductions. Helena took the baby and held him. He looked at her shyly but didn't object.

Nate showed Lily the laundry chutes he'd discovered while browsing the upstairs rooms. "The bedding falls right down into the big room behind the kitchen. You'll need wash tubs and wringers. I could string some clothesline out back."

Overwhelmed, Lily simply nodded and opened the nearest window. They were alone in the room.

"You all right?" he asked her.

"What have I done?" She turned and stared at him.

"When I asked that, you said you were expanding your interests."

"I never do impulsive things, especially not with my money. I always plan and save and invest."

"Well, you invested."

Panic was rising inside her, and she pressed her palms over her heart as though she could keep it still. "With money I didn't have!"

"A little over an hour ago, you didn't have a qualm."

"There are five children involved now."

"I mentioned that, and you said it was a big place."

She put a hand to her head. "Stop telling me what I said." With an outstretched arm, she gestured to the empty room. "Look at this. An entire empty building— no rugs or beds, no sheets or dishes, not a lick of furniture or a crumb of food."

"That's what *empty* means."

Letting the doubts assail her, Lily raised her gaze to Nate's. "I don't have anything left to risk."

"Sure you do."

"What?"

"Our friendship."

"What do you mean?"

"You said we couldn't be partners. But there's no good reason for that. I have money to invest. You have this place. I could pay for the furnishings and supplies and get a percent of profit."

"You have money like that?"

"Men's lives don't come cheap," he told her. "But living on the hunt does. I made a lot of money over the past fifteen years and spent very little. It's there. It's yours if you want it."

Lily moved back to the window and studied the street

below. Rosemary and Celeste were walking along the boardwalk where two women in calico dresses and bonnets turned to look at their backs.

"What would Mayor Gibbs think about you investing in one of my projects?"

"Does it matter? My personal life isn't under his authority."

She turned to meet his gaze. "What would Evangeline think?"

His mouth drew into a line. "Why are you bringing her into this?"

"It's a fact that interacting with me would be a strike against you, plain and simple. Those temperance women are here to stay. They may have been subdued for the time being, but I have no doubt they'll gather reinforcements eventually and come back stronger than ever.

"I'll never be seen as a respectable business owner, not even if I pay for the hotel and run a first-class establishment. Buying into my project could hurt your standing in some people's eyes."

"Evangeline's, you mean?"

She nodded. "Among others."

"You know what? I could say we won't tell them, but that stinks of cowardice to me. If I was ashamed to make the offer, I wouldn't have done it. I'm not ashamed. I'm not ashamed to call you my friend and I wouldn't be ashamed to call you my business partner. Anyone who doesn't like it doesn't know me and, frankly, doesn't hold my respect."

Lily's emotions were already running a little close

to the surface. She attributed that to Celeste's announcement and this overwhelming task she'd taken on, and she swallowed any sense of gratification his words unleashed to remember the stand she'd already taken for Evangeline's sake.

Nate looked her in the eye. "You work so hard at being defiant and carving out your own pattern in life," he said, "but when it comes right down to it, *you're* the one who doesn't think you're as good as other people. I know what that red dress means now, don't think I don't. It's your fortress between you and the rest of society. It might not be made up of much material and it might show an abundance of your assets, but it's like one of those suits of armor you see in history books and museums. It keeps you from letting anyone close, so you won't be hurt."

His words opened too many wounds and revealed more of Lily than any dress ever could. The fact that he saw right into her soul and scraped those truths from inside her protective shell was more than she wanted to admit. She turned toward the window so he couldn't see the effect he was having on her.

"I'm not aimin' to hurt you, Lily. Think on it. You don't have to say right now. The offer isn't going away. I told Boone last night that there's no shame in needing a little help now and then. No shame in needing another person. You might want to remember that."

Lily couldn't answer. She didn't want him to expose anything more.

The receding sound of his boot heels echoing in the room and the hallway told her she was alone.

Lily was so stunned and confused she felt as though she was walking through a nightmare. No one had ever spoken to her like that before. No one else's words would have touched her the same way, in any case.

She went downstairs and told Thomas that she was going home to change and would be back shortly. As she walked along the boardwalk, the things Nate had said resounded in her head.

Blythe was rearranging a display in the window of the mercantile and glanced up. Lily saw her own reflection in the glass, as well as Blythe's haughty expression. Having to fight for every shred of dignity hurt. Knowing that people always thought the worst of her twisted a knife in her heart. Pretending not to care, she'd even fooled herself.

Lily Divine would have waved and smiled at Blythe and marched past as though she owned the street. Today's Lily turned away from the scornful look and walked toward home.

She cared about her standing in the community. If she didn't, she wouldn't have gone to such great lengths to prove herself. She cared what people thought about her and her girls. If she didn't, she wouldn't have taken pains to teach them they were as good as anybody.

Caring had served her well. Hiding it had done one better.

Needing someone had always been the most degrading point she could imagine slipping to. But each of her girls had needed her once. Mollie, Helena, Rosemary and Celeste had needed homes and jobs and security. They'd thrived and grown, and now any one of them could make it on her own without Lily. Violet still needed her, but one day she'd be ready to move on as well.

There were the Waldrop children. She had great expectations for them.

Lily had needed someone once. Antoinette had been there for her then. What about Nate? Had he ever needed anyone?

Maybe needing another person's help wasn't such a shameful thing. Wasn't a sign of helplessness or weakness. It was simply proof of being human.

In her room Lily changed into a skirt and shirtwaist for cleaning. She paused to study the red dress hanging on her wardrobe door. Mollie had just cleaned and pressed it. Nate had likened it to a suit of armor.

She shook her head at the comparison. The dress did make her feel defiant and lent her confidence. Was it truly as scandalous as the women in town seemed to think? Or did it threaten them in a way she'd yet to understand? Did they see her as a threat?

Of course they did. But she couldn't see any way to change that. And—being honest with herself—she didn't know if she wanted to change that right now.

Lily placed the dress in her armoire and closed the doors.

CHAPTER FOURTEEN

BY SUPPERTIME they had the bottom floor clean, and the Waldrops had taken care of the suite of rooms they would occupy. Lily asked Naomi, Helena, Mollie and a few others to gather at the building after they'd eaten.

She outlined a few plans for getting the hotel up and running, and they made lists of things they would need.

"Are you okay like this for a few nights?" Lily asked Naomi. "We do have rooms at the Shady Lady."

"We'll be fine here. It's not cold, and we have our own things."

"All right. I'm going to make arrangements for the supplies, then. Hopefully, we can buy some of the furniture and items locally. A lot will have to be ordered."

Lily walked to the jail and sheriff's office and found the door locked. She peeked in the front window. She hadn't seen Nate on Main Street, but he could be anywhere. She checked the restaurants to see if he was eating a late supper.

Suzanna Callahan came out on the boardwalk to stand beside her. "Could be he went home for his supper. He hasn't been in, and he does that sometimes."

Lily thanked her and stood at the corner of the block

in indecision. She could wait until she saw him some-time that evening, but they wouldn't have an opportu-nity to speak alone. Or she could shrug off her hesitation and go to his house.

It was an impressive structure from the outside. Lily admired the two-story home with its red shutters and wide, shaded front porch.

On the front door was a knob to turn that rang a bell on the inside.

The door opened. Nate looked at her through the screen with surprise, then held it open. "Come in."

Lily stepped inside and glanced around. "You need some more furniture."

The side of his mouth quirked up. "Maybe some-thing with tusks?"

She shrugged. "Were you eating?"

"I was done. Washing dishes, actually."

She noted then that his sleeves were rolled back and the dark hair on his forearms was wet. "I'll help you finish and we can talk. You'll probably need to get back to work."

"I take a few hours here and there. But come on back."

He led the way to the kitchen, where he handed her a towel and buried his hands in a pan of suds.

He rinsed a few plates in a basin of clear water and stood them beside the pail.

Lily picked one up and dried it as she glanced around.

The room held a table and chairs, a stove and an old china hutch, which was empty.

"I'll show you the rest of the house if you want to see it. I've ordered furniture."

She nodded, trying to find the correct words now that she was here.

Nate washed and rinsed the last fork and then dumped the basin outside the back door. "Sorry if I was out of line earlier," he said, drying the basin and hanging it on a nail on the wall.

"No." She dried a plate and found the shelf where it went. She played with a loose thread on the towel. "You were pretty much right."

Nate's eyebrows lifted in surprise. He hung his towel and propped his hands on his hips.

"That's all I'm going to say. You were right about me not being willing to let anybody help me."

"Okay."

"And I want to take you up on the partnership and let you pay for everything we need to get the hotel running."

He smiled then. "All right. We'll get started tomorrow."

She dried the forks and handed him the towel she held, and he hung it behind him. "Show me the rest of your house."

He led the way through the downstairs, then gestured for her to go upstairs first. His room was the only one with furniture, and it held a bureau and a bed covered only by a wool blanket. His washstand was a stack of crates with a bucket on top.

"You said I was right," he began.

Lily looked at a comb on the bureau instead of at him.

"Does that mean you might've been wrong about a few things?"

"A few," she admitted. There were half a dozen pennies lying beside the comb. She touched one with her fingertip.

"Think you might've been wrong about us?"

Lily looked over her shoulder. "No, I don't."

When her gaze traveled to the doorway, he backed away so she could make her escape. At the bottom of the stairs she paused. "We can go through the catalogs in the morning, if that suits you. I've already started lists."

"I'm sure you have."

"I'll probably see you tonight."

"Probably."

Lily let herself out onto the porch and hurried down the steps and toward the street.

It was full dark and the saloon was filled with patrons when Celeste came to get Lily.

"There's a woman out back. She won't talk to me. She wants you."

"I'll go, thank you."

Lily hurried to the back door and opened it to find Catherine Douglas with her face hidden behind the folds of a scarf.

"Are you hurt?"

Catherine lowered the green silk to reveal a swollen and bloody lip.

When Lily took her arm, Catherine gasped in pain.

"I'll get ice and some water. Go on up to my room."

A minute later she found Catherine sitting on the end of her bed, sobbing.

Lily dipped a cloth in warm water and knelt in front of her. "What happened?"

Catherine took the cloth from her and dabbed at her own mouth. "I burned the letter you sent, but there was a scrap of it remaining in the ashes."

"He saw my letter?"

Catherine shook her head. "No, only a few words remained, nothing readable."

"What was the harm?"

"He accused me of having a lover. Of carrying on a tryst behind his back. I told him it was only a letter from a woman friend."

"He didn't believe you?"

"He's not rational when he gets like that."

"And you couldn't tell him it was from me."

"He would have beaten me regardless of who it was from."

"Not if it had been from another woman and not me, Catherine. It's all my fault this happened this time. I'm so sorry."

"It's not your fault. It's because he's unreasonable and doesn't allow me to have friends."

Lily took the cloth from Catherine's hand and rinsed it. This time she insisted on washing the cuts on her face.

"Would it make any difference if I told him I wrote the letter?"

"I don't think so. And then he'd know where I went on these nights, Lily, and I don't want him to know. This is where I am safe. You are my place of refuge from him and his outbursts of rage."

"Of course. You're right." Angrily she wrung out the rag and draped it over the washbowl. She then brought the wrapped ice for Catherine to hold against her lip. "Let me see your arm."

Catherine allowed her to roll back her sleeve, and they both looked at the bruises. "We'll put ice on that, too." She backed away and sat on an overstuffed chair. "I despise that I had to do business with him to get the hotel."

"I wish you hadn't done it, either."

"Why?"

"I just don't have a good feeling about it. He doesn't talk about his work to me, but I've heard him mention your holdings and properties several times. I've looked at papers on his desk at home, and he makes lists of things. He even had documents from the assayers about your properties."

"He probably did that for the loan I just got."

She shook her head. "It was months ago. I should have told you, but I didn't know what it meant. I still don't."

Lily didn't, either, but she knew she didn't like Amos Douglas looking into her affairs.

"It's going to be all right," Lily told her. "You're going to stay here and get a good night's sleep. We'll think on it again in the morning."

"Thank you, Lily."

"You're welcome. And Catherine, that son John of yours is a fine young man. I watched him during the ball games."

"Thank you, Lily."

Lily laid out bedclothes and a wrapper for Catherine, then brought her a cup of tea.

By the time she returned to the dance hall, she'd missed the sheriff's round.

SHE SLEPT in her sitting area that night. The chaise longue that had been Antoinette's was every bit as comfortable as her bed. Her dreams were elusive images of lost and hungry women, and Lily didn't have enough soup to feed them all. She woke with a start to the muffled sound of a rifle shot.

Not all that unfamiliar in this town, but unsettling all the same. Someone could have been shooting at a fox getting to their chickens.

"Did you hear that, Lily?" Catherine called from the other room.

Lily got up. "I did."

She opened the front window and looked down onto the empty street.

Another shot sounded just then, the sound echoing hollowly.

An upstairs window at the saloon opened and Old Jess stuck his head out.

"I'm thinking we should go look," Lily called.

Jess's head ducked back in.

Lily pulled on her dressing gown and slipped her feet into her shoes. "Stay put," she told Catherine and took a derringer from a drawer.

Saul and Jess met her on the boardwalk. They stepped into the silent street and looked up and down.

"It came from that way," Lily said.

They started down the street, and Wade Reed opened his door and stepped out carrying a rifle and pulling up his suspenders.

"Look, Miss Lily!" Saul pointed to a finger of flame

reaching up from the other side of the street and behind the row of buildings.

"Damned if it ain't the hotel!" Wade stopped in his tracks, raised his rifle and fired three rapid shots into the air.

Heart hammering, Lily ran toward the building where Naomi Waldrop and her five children were staying.

CHAPTER FIFTEEN

SHE DIDN'T HAVE THE KEY, LILY realized. They couldn't get in the front door. "Saul, go back. Run up to my room and get my key ring off my bureau. There's a woman in my bed, don't frighten her."

Saul turned and followed her orders.

She and Jess reached the hotel and she beat on the front door. "Check the windows," Wade called.

Old Jess ran to do that and Lily took off around the rear of the building.

Flames were shooting out a window, but the back door stood open. She was a good thirty feet away when she saw a man dash out the back door and stagger away toward the cover of the other buildings in the alley.

Lily took the derringer out of her pocket, but she couldn't hit anyone at this distance.

The Waldrop family was in danger, so she let him go and ran inside. "Naomi! Boone!" she screamed.

The kitchen window frame and the surrounding cabinets were on fire, and that appeared to be the extent of the threat so far.

Old Jess entered behind her.

"Jess, pump water. There's still pails beside the door there."

"Naomi!" Lily tore toward the other rooms and found the woman ushering her children toward the front door.

"Thank God!" Lily followed them outside, where Wade met them. "There's a fire in the kitchen," she told him.

He ran past her into the hotel.

"What happened?" Lily asked Naomi.

The woman took the crying baby from her oldest daughter and comforted him. "I shot him."

"Who?"

"The man who was setting the fire."

"You saw someone setting the fire?"

She nodded. "I heard sounds echoing from the kitchen, and I got my rifle and went to see what it was. He was making a fire along the back wall. He was surprised to see me, and he jumped up and pointed a gun at me. I did what came natural and shot first. Shot him twice."

"What did he look like?"

"It was dark and he had on dark clothing. He was just a man. But I think he's hurt bad. I didn't miss with either shot."

Several men came running then, among them Harold and George, and Lily directed them to the kitchen.

Nate showed up a few minutes later. "Everybody all right? What happened?"

"Naomi surprised someone starting a fire," Lily told him.

"Where is he?"

"He held his belly and ran out the rear door," Naomi told him.

"You're sure it was a man?"

"Pretty sure. It was dark, but it looked like a man."

Several women stood in the street, and Evangeline broke away from them to approach. "Is there anything I can do to help?"

Naomi looked from the young woman to Lily.

"The children are pretty frightened," Lily said. "You could comfort them. You could take them to my place so they can go back to sleep. One of the women will show you a room."

The women standing a few feet away murmured, but Evangeline ignored them and took the baby from Naomi. "I'd be glad to do that. Come along, sweet-lings, we're going to find you a nice cozy bed for the night."

Lily covered her surprise by nodding her approval.

"Can I stay here, Ma?" Boone asked.

Naomi looked from her son to the young woman. "Just the girls and little Ben. Boone will stay with me for now."

Evangeline smiled and herded the children toward the Shady Lady.

George came around the side of the hotel. "Fire's out. Probably need to keep an eye on it overnight, though, just in case."

"Thank you, George," Lily called. The other men who'd helped soon followed him on their way toward their homes. The women dispersed.

"Me 'n' Saul will stay to keep an eye on things," Old Jess offered.

"I need to have a look around," Nate told Lily and Naomi.

Whoever had set the fire hadn't been expecting a woman and children on the premises. He'd felt perfectly safe breaking into an empty hotel to set a fire. It was too dark to see much tonight, but the door looked just fine to Nate. The only window broken was the one where the fire'd burned, so it was possible the man had broken it to gain entrance.

Nate peered at the smelly, soggy mess on the floor, the gaping black opening where the wall had burned around the window, and then inspected the back door. There had been only a few people out after the shots were fired, but tomorrow he'd ask everyone if they'd seen someone running from the hotel.

First person he'd go check with was Doc Umber. If the man'd been shot badly, he couldn't get too far.

LILY AND NAOMI WASHED their faces and hands in the bathing chamber, then Lily led her up the stairs and into a small bedroom that held two beds and a cot. A lamp burned low on the bureau, and Evangeline was sitting in a rocking chair, holding the sleeping baby.

"I've never known people as kind as those in this town," Naomi said. "Thank you, both of you."

"I didn't do much," Evangeline told her. "Your children are very sweet and well behaved."

"I feel responsible for what happened tonight," Lily said. "I don't even want to think about what could have happened if you hadn't heard that man and caught the fire before it spread. I've had way too much experience with the damages of fire recently, but at least it's all been property lost and not lives."

"You're not responsible," Naomi assured her. "And God was watching out for us."

"You sleep here with the children," Lily told her. "I should have insisted you didn't stay alone."

They left the Waldrops in their room, and Lily accompanied Evangeline downstairs. "I could use a cup of tea," Lily said. "How about you?"

As usual, Lily was dressed inappropriately and her hair was flying askew while Evangeline wore a proper dress and had her hair neatly plaited.

"I'd love a cup," she replied, and took a seat at the kitchen table. "Your home is very warm and inviting."

"I've always felt safe here." Someone had recently stoked the fire in the stove, so it only took a few minutes for the water to heat. Lily steeped the tea and poured.

"You're not what I expected," Evangeline said.

Lily looked into the clear-blue eyes of the woman she'd urged Nate to court. "Neither are you."

"I admire you, Miss Divine."

"You do?"

She nodded. "You don't live your life by what others expect of you."

"Sadly enough, in a way I do."

"How's that?"

"I know you're thinking I don't bend to society's mores or conform to what people think is proper and acceptable."

"Isn't that so?"

"It is so. But people do expect particular dress and behavior from me because of the mistaken conclusions they've drawn. Not only do I live up to those expectations, I go above and beyond."

"Like wearing your red dress to the base ball game."

"Like that."

"It was a sight to behold," Evangeline told her. "I can see why Nathaniel admires you so."

Lily paused with her cup halfway to her lips. "Nathaniel?"

She nodded. "I've heard the sheriff when he speaks of you." She kept her hands in her lap. "I've seen the way he looks at you."

"I assure you I don't have any claim or designs on the man," Lily told her. "My hope was for him to endear himself to you and for you to return his devotion."

"When we're together, I sense the guarded reactions of a trapped animal," Evangeline told her. "And to be quite frank, he makes me feel the same way."

"You don't have feelings for him?" Lily couldn't bear it if this girl broke Nate's heart.

"I have affection for him," she answered. "But not the kind of feelings that make me want to sacrifice. Not the kind of feelings that the great poets write about when they pen sonnets of enduring love. I could love him…" She paused and seemed to be gathering her thoughts. "But I would never hold the passion for a marriage that I hold for discovering what other avenues await me."

"I underestimated you," Lily said. "I did something I abhor others doing. I assumed. Because you're a young lady of privilege and you're pretty and bright and just so…feminine and perfect, I assumed you were looking for a husband. He would make a fine one."

"My doubt isn't regarding Nathaniel's suitability as

a husband. It's about my own fulfillment. I've been confused. My parents want exactly what you've assumed. I've been tutored and trained and taught until my head swims with the knowledge of what society demands I should be and do.

"I've never spoken about this to another soul, Miss Lily. It's just that I know you're a free-thinking woman and you inspire me to follow my own drummer."

Lily listened with growing trepidation and hard-won understanding. "I'm a big phony."

"I doubt that."

"It's true. I've exhausted my energies making sure I'm independent and owing nothing to any man. But when the smoke has cleared, when I dare to look into that secret corner of my heart—I want the same thing that everyone wants. I want to love and be loved." A tear dropped from Lily's cheek to her hand on the cup.

"That's not fake," Evangeline said. "That's real. It doesn't mean you have to give up anything, any bit of your independence. A love like that shouldn't mean taking away from who you are, but rather adding to. I want that one day, too. One day when I know I'm all I want to be before I let someone make me something else."

"I'm sorry I underestimated you," Lily said.

Evangeline smiled. "I'm sorry I never had the courage to speak to you like this before. Or to befriend you openly."

"We're quite a pair, aren't we? What will your parents say when they know you don't want to marry the sheriff?"

Evangeline spread her fingers on the tabletop. "I'm sure I'll find out soon enough." She stood. "It's quite late—or early, I'm not sure which anymore. I'd better get a few hours' sleep before morning."

"Thanks for your help."

Lily walked her to the front of the house and stood on the boardwalk to watch Evangeline make her way home. She locked up the house and made her way upstairs.

She entered her room to find that Catherine was not in her bed. Nor was she anywhere else in the room or the house. Lily thought sadly that Nate had been right about more than one thing. She couldn't take in and care for the whole world. She couldn't even help all of those who came to her. All she could do was give it her best.

She climbed into her own bed and fell into an exhausted sleep.

LILY HADN'T BEEN ASLEEP more than an hour when a rap on her door wakened her. It was still dark. Would this night ever end?

She got up and stumbled to the door to find Rosemary. "Sorry, Lily, but there's someone at the kitchen door for you. She wouldn't come in."

Lily grabbed her dressing gown and ran. Catherine. She'd gone back home too soon.

Indeed, Catherine Douglas stood outside the door.

"Why did you leave?" Lily pulled her into the kitchen, studying her face for additional bruising and cuts.

Catherine glanced around. "Get dressed quickly, Lily. I need you to come with me."

"What is it?"

"I don't have time to tell you—just hurry!"

Lily ran back up and pulled on clothing and shoes and tied her hair back with a scarf. She joined Catherine, and the woman led her along the back alley to the corner, then across the street.

"Where are we going?"

"To my house."

"Are the children all right?"

"They're fine." Catherine guided her to the Douglas house and in through the rear door. A lamp burned in the kitchen.

"Isn't your husband going to be angry if he finds me here with you?" she whispered.

"He won't be objecting."

"Catherine, I insist you tell me why you brought me here."

Catherine pushed her into a room and closed the door behind them. It was a small bedroom, like a servant's quarters, and it held a narrow bed and a few furnishings.

Amos Douglas lay on the bed, eerily still. His eyes were closed.

"Is he sleeping?" Lily whispered.

"No. He's dead."

"What?" Her heart threatened to stop. "What's happened to him?"

"He was gone when I returned from your place. I went up to our bedroom and later I heard him down here. I came down and found him on the kitchen floor."

"Dead?"

"No. Holding his stomach and moaning something terrible. His face was white. He told me to help him get in here to lie down, so I did. He wouldn't let me go get help. I was going to go for the doctor, but he grabbed my wrist and told me not to leave the house. I got rags and tried to stop the bleeding, but I couldn't. He got weaker and weaker. I was afraid to leave and afraid to stay. Then—" she pressed her fingers to her mouth and a tearful sob escaped "—it didn't take very long. He sort of gasped and then he stopped breathing."

Lily stared in horror, absorbing Catherine's description of the recent events.

The woman clutched at Lily's arm. "What if someone thinks I did this to him?"

"Of course they won't."

"Look at me, Lily. I could have shot him for what he did to me."

"He's shot?" At those words, everything became crystal clear. "In the belly?"

"And he has burns on his hands. Look."

Lily didn't want to look, but she did. She knew without a doubt. "He set fire to the hotel tonight."

"What?"

"The sheriff brought a mother and her children to the hotel," she explained. "They were staying there when someone came in and set a fire. Naomi surprised him, and he pulled a gun on her. She shot him. Twice."

Catherine's eyes widened. "There are two bullet holes. And he's wearing a revolver." Her grasp on Lily's arm trembled. "Why would Amos do such a thing?"

"He'd been making me loan offers for the past couple of years," Lily told her.

"And those papers I saw on his desk had something to do with it. He wanted you to lose your property to him."

"If the hotel burned, I'd have to default on the loans in order to keep all my irons in the fire."

Catherine gave Lily a long look, then she picked up a ring of keys on a table and brushed past. Lily followed her to another room. The woman went directly to a set of walnut doors and turned a key in the lock. Inside, she lit a lamp and began a methodical search of the desk.

"Here," she said, taking a deed from a ledger book. "Ownership of the hotel. As his widow it belongs to me now, and I'm giving it to you."

"Catherine, you might need—"

"No. I own it all now. It's mine to do with as I see fit."

"You might need it for your children. I'll pay you a fair price for the hotel."

"Whatever he held of yours, you'll take it back."

"All right, Catherine." She took the piece of paper and placed it in her skirt pocket. "I'd better go get the sheriff now."

"No!"

Lily stared at her. "Why not? He's not going to think you killed your husband."

"If word gets out about what he did, it will destroy my family. My children are already without a father. But a father with a bad name will haunt them their whole lives."

Lily understood Catherine's fear, but she didn't know

what choice they had. "What are you going to do? You have to do *something*. He'll have to have a burial."

"I don't want John and the girls to know the kind of man he was. He's dead now, what does it matter, truly?"

"Catherine, what do you suggest?"

She thought a moment. "We can make it look as though he died some other way. Place him at the bottom of the stairs as though he fell."

"The undertaker would notice the bullet holes."

"What if we changed him ourselves and laid him out?"

"Wouldn't that look pretty suspicious? The first thing we should have done was to go for the sheriff."

"Then let's do that. And we'll tell him a story to make it look as though Amos died some other way."

"How?"

"What kind of description did the woman at the hotel give?"

"She just said it was a man. That's all she could make out in the dark."

"Then I'll say a man tried to force his way inside our house." She ran from the den and Lily followed.

"What are you doing?"

Catherine took a hammer from the pantry and struck the knob on the back door.

Lily stopped her. "You'll wake your children."

Catherine glanced at the ceiling. "We'll say a man was breaking in and he had a gun. He shot Amos and then he ran away. I only caught a glimpse of him. Who's to know?"

Lily took Catherine by the shoulders and turned her to face her. "And you could live with that lie?"

Catherine let the hand holding the hammer drop to her side. "For my children's sake—yes."

Lily leaned back against a counter, weary and confused. She didn't have a problem with lying to protect Catherine's children. But there was another problem that kept her from agreeing. An insurmountable one. "I won't lie to the sheriff," she told Catherine.

The other woman's lip was swollen and scabbed. Lily's heart went out to her. Amos Douglas didn't deserve protecting. But his children did.

"What, then?" Catherine asked, hopelessness in her eyes now.

"Let's tell him the truth. All of it. And let's trust him to protect your children."

"He's a lawman, Lily."

Lily nodded. "But he's a good man. I trust him."

"All right. I don't have a choice, do I? I'm putting the future of my children in his hands."

Lily nodded. "I'll go get him."

She walked the dark street, nearly numb after the shocking events of the night, wishing she could turn back the clock and fix things. Wishing there was some other way.

His house was dark when she reached it. She turned the bell knob, pounded a few times and waited.

She heard movement inside, saw a light behind the curtain on the glass, and then Nate opened the door.

"Lily? What're you doing out this time of night?"

He was bare-chested and barefoot, but he'd strapped on his holster over his trousers.

"Something has happened. I need your help."

"What is it?"

Just like Catherine had with her, Lily preferred to show him before saying anything. "Come with me."

"Let me get my boots and a shirt."

A few minutes later they were hurrying along Main Street in the dark of night.

"Where are we goin'?"

"To the Douglas house. Many times over the past few years, Catherine Douglas has come to me for help. She's often been beaten pretty badly."

"That son of a bitch," Nate replied.

"You're not getting an argument from me on that one."

"Is she hurt badly?"

"No. Well, he hit her earlier this evening, and she came to me then, but she's all right. It's not her I'm taking you to see. Well, not entirely."

They reached the house, and Lily led him through the back door to where Catherine waited in the kitchen. Catherine led Nate into the small room where the body of her husband lay.

Nate looked at him, then at the two women. Finally he stepped forward and touched Amos's neck, then raised the blanket to look at the wounds. He turned back to the women. "What happened here?"

"It didn't happen here," Catherine explained. She went on to tell him the story of how Amos had arrived home and wouldn't allow her to go for help. "Then I got Lily and she filled in the rest, so we figured out what happened."

"He started both fires," Nate said. "The livery and the one tonight."

"That would be my guess, too," Lily replied.

"Do you know why?"

"He was obsessed with getting his hands on Lily's property," Catherine said. "He spoke very strangely about her, and he had papers from the assayers about her real estate."

"Burning your property was sure to put you in debt to him eventually," he said to Lily.

"Sheriff Harding, I'm pleading with you as a mother," Catherine said. "Please keep this knowledge from the townspeople and the authorities."

"What?"

"I don't want my children to know what their father did. I don't want them to grow up with everyone looking down on them because of him. John will be going to university in a year or so. I can't let his father's actions keep him from being accepted. Amos will not be hurting anyone anymore. What difference will it make that no one knows, as long as he's dead?"

Catherine explained the story she wanted to tell.

Nate met Lily's eyes. She remembered the talks they'd had, the side of him he'd revealed to her in private. "I asked you once if you always saw everything in black-and-white," she said. "Right or wrong. You told me you were a lawman and that you got paid to sort out the difference."

"That hasn't changed."

"Well, I'm asking you to change it right now. I'm asking you to be satisfied in knowing the man is dead and won't cause any more harm."

Lily sensed Nate's apprehension. The man who'd

stared death in the face a hundred times, the man who'd captured and killed wanted men for money, looked as though he was afraid of what she was asking of him.

Had the request come from anyone else, she knew he'd never even consider it. But she also knew she held an edge.

"You're holdin' an unfair advantage, Lily," he said finally.

"All's fair in love and war, isn't that what they say?"

"This isn't war."

"No, it isn't."

His jaw muscles bunched. He looked from her to Catherine. "From this moment forward, we will never speak another word regarding this except the story of how the man came to your door to rob you, Mrs. Douglas. The three of us—well, four actually—carry this to our graves. He's just already there."

Catherine stepped forward and flung herself into Nate's arms. She cried openly against his shirtfront. "Thank you, thank you. Lily said you were a man we could trust."

Lily met his eyes, and Nate patted Catherine's shoulder awkwardly.

"I'll go for the undertaker," he said. "Lily can stay with you."

Catherine told her story to a few people who gathered outside the house once the undertaker had been summoned and the news spread. It was dawn when John Douglas woke and came downstairs. Lily sat with them while Catherine told him the story of his father's death. The young man cried. "He was just trying to protect us! What if that man comes back?"

"He won't," Lily told him. "Men like that are cowards and move on when someone stands up to them."

Lily left the family and headed home. She asked Mollie to let her sleep for a few hours and wake her mid-morning. Her bed had never felt so good.

WITHIN TWO DAYS the story of the robber spread, and Amos Douglas was buried in the cemetery north of town. After the funeral, Catherine spoke to Lily. "I've found your property deeds and have set them aside to bring to you."

"You hang on to them until the hotel loan is paid," Lily told her. "I'll feel better about that."

Catherine reluctantly agreed.

Nate sought out Lily that afternoon as she worked in her garden. She was at the end of a section of melons, a distance from Rosemary and Violet, who were tearing out the last of the bean plants.

"What did you say to Evangeline?"

Lily straightened at the sheriff's question and shaded her eyes with one hand. "What do you mean?"

"I lay awake for two nights planning how I'd approach her and talk to her, and when I got up the nerve I could tell she was relieved. She said the two of you had talked about a lot of things and that not being willing to conform meant she was being true to herself."

Lily smiled. "She said that?"

"Yes. She packed and she's heading for Denver, where she plans to find work and learn photography. Her mother's fit to be tied."

"Photography. Fascinating."

"So you don't think she's making a mistake?"

"I think she's doing what's right for her."

"She's wise, you'd say?"

"I would say that."

"Well, she also said you love me. How much wisdom can be found in that statement?"

Lily's ears rang for a moment. The sun felt hot, and a trickle of perspiration slid down her back.

"Cat got your tongue, Lily?"

"I…um…." Finally she shrugged.

"You always have something to say," he prodded. "I'm not always sure if it's the whole truth, but you're never at a loss."

"I've never lied to you. I didn't lie to you about Amos, did I? I could have kept the secret myself."

"I appreciate that. It's the other things, the more *personal* things, where you hold back."

She'd only held back two things from him ever. The truth of her husband's death…and the fact that she'd fallen in love with him.

"I saw gray for you, Lily. Remember?"

She nodded. He'd done something he'd never done before, because she'd asked him to. He'd looked past right and wrong to the connotation of justice. If he'd been able to see it once, he would again.

"Let's meet this evening," she suggested, glancing at the other two women and the sun overhead.

"Name the spot."

"Pick me up when the Shady Lady closes."

He grinned and walked away. Lily watched him for a few minutes, then turned back to her task.

THAT EVENING she looked at the red dress, then at the green one and an entire armoire full of other costumes, and chose not to hide. She wore the most sensible gray skirt she owned with a pink-and-white-striped blouse.

Her attire didn't raise any eyebrows with her staff, and she worked through the evening, waiting for the time when Nate would come for her.

He'd shown up once during that time, and with a lift of one curious brow had surveyed her clothing. She'd made him a Buffalo Bill special and seated herself beside him until he moved on.

Now she stood on the front steps, watching the street.

A horse came into view and Lily watched Nate approach. He slid his foot from the stirrup and reached for her. They were comfortable with this routine.

Neither spoke until they'd reached the stream. Lily slid from the horse and Nate untied a roll of blankets and carried them to the bank. "It's getting cooler, and I didn't know if you'd want to swim."

"For now, let's just talk."

He spread the blankets and she took a seat. Nate's knee popped as he sat beside her. "Where were we?"

"Which time?"

He chuckled. "Today, I reckon. We were talkin' about honesty. I told you that Evangeline said—"

"Okay. I remember."

He draped both wrists over his bent knees as though he had all night to listen.

"You told me about your wife," she said softly, her voice not as strong as she would have liked. She'd had most of the day to think about this and how she'd say it, but her good intentions and pretty words fled. "It was a terrible thing. But you shared it with me. I can't tell you how much that meant to me."

"It wasn't easy to get the words out."

"My words won't come easy, either." She took a deep breath. "My father was a miner. My ma and I followed him from camp to camp, living out of a tent all those years. We panned for gold, cooked, did laundry and lived a mean existence. He always had a big dream that someday he'd find a vein and he'd be rich."

"That's what keeps 'em all in these hills, isn't it?"

She nodded. "I thought about running away all the time, but I couldn't leave my mother. She was never strong, and as time passed she got thinner and weaker. Finally she died."

"That must have been hard."

She nodded. "No sooner was she buried than my father met up with a man who owned a deed to a mine. One night Pa came and told me I was getting married so to pack my things. Like I had anything worth taking. I cried and told him I didn't want to get married. Too late, he said. He'd traded me for a half share of the man's mine."

Nate was looking at her in the moonlight. She was telling this story as though it had happened to someone else, but her insides were quaking as though it was taking place all over again.

"What happened?" he asked.

"We packed up and moved again. My father came, too. He lived in the tent we'd always shared and I lived in my—in Harm's."

"That was his name?"

She nodded. She hadn't said it in all these years. "Harm Augusta."

"You never called yourself by that name, though."

She shook her head.

"He mistreated you?"

"Whenever it struck his mean-hearted fancy. I only knew sex as a debasing, hurtful thing men did to women. A way to wield their power and strength. Some of the girls told me it could be good with a man, but I didn't believe them. I couldn't imagine *giving* that to a man. Ever."

"What are you saying?"

"When you and I—that night right here—that was the first time I ever let a man kiss me. The first time I let a man touch me and touched him back. That was— the first time for me. Like that. Without getting hit or slapped or bitten."

Nate made a sound like he was strangling and laid his hand on her arm. The warmth of his touch burned through the fabric of her sleeve. "Lily, God, Lily, I'm sorry. I'm sorry I thought you were sellin' yourself to every man who paid your price. I'm sorry I didn't believe you when you told me the truth."

"How could you believe me? I showed you what I wanted you to see. Just like I showed everyone. If I didn't care about what people thought—if respecting myself wasn't an issue—none of what happened in the past would matter. None of the future insult would hurt."

"I'm honored that you shared yourself with me," he said in a hoarse whisper. "I understand how submitting your will and offering your body in any way is a diffi-cult thing for you to do."

"That's not all."

There was more? Nate didn't know if he could bear to hear it. But she'd lived it. Borne it inside her all these years, and he'd asked her to tell him the whole truth. Now he had to listen.

"My father's tent was close by. He had to have heard the—beatings. But he never did anything to stop them. He had his share of the mine.

"After almost a year, I learned I was going to have a baby."

A child? She had a child? His mind rolled over which of the girls at the Shady Lady could be young enough to be her daughter and couldn't think of a one.

"I tried to keep him away from me after that. I pre-tended sickness and I even stole some laudanum and put it in his food to make him go to sleep at night. One night I was feeling poorly. He came to the tent in one of his tempers and started after me. I fought him—like I'd never done before. I don't know why it was different that time. Some protective instinct just came over me and I was more afraid for my baby than for myself."

Nate listened with his breath caught in his throat.

"He beat me pretty bad. He was insane with anger and he came at me with this look in his eyes. I grabbed a knife that was lying by the cook fire. Next thing I knew, he was lying on it. I was covered with his blood because he was on top of me. I pushed him off and I ran.

"I stole a horse from another miner and rode as far

and fast as I could. When I got to this town, the only place with a light on was the bordello. I didn't know what it was, I didn't care. I was bleeding and weak. I went to the door and rang the bell.

"Antoinette Powell answered the door. She was wearing a fancy red dress and a dozen strands of pearls around her neck. She took one look at me and pulled me inside."

"What happened to your baby?"

Lily paused before continuing. "She did her very best. She called a midwife and they sat with me for two days and nights straight. But I lost my baby."

He pulled her into his arms then and she didn't resist. "You knew how it felt," he said. "When I told you about losin' my son."

"I never got to hold my baby," she said. "Or hear him cry or laugh. I only got to see a little grave."

"If that man wasn't dead, I'd kill him myself," he said, his voice low and filled with passion.

"But I killed him, Nate. Antoinette hid me until we knew no one was going to come looking. He was a no-account miner, and my father was glad to get his hands on the mine. He used to come into town."

"Your father? He came to Thunder Canyon?"

She nodded against the comfortingly hard plane of his chest. "For years. A couple of times he asked me to grubstake him for another season."

"Did you?"

"Yes. I used to give him food and buy him socks and shirts. He died one winter, all alone at that godforsaken mine. His belongings were turned over to Sheriff Parson, and I got the deed to the Queen of Hearts. I hated that worthless mine and everything it stood for."

"So you own a played-out mine?"

"Actually, Catherine is holding the deed while I pay back the bank notes. She wanted to give me the hotel, but I insisted."

Nate lowered her back on the blankets and kissed her tenderly. "There's no way to change the past. I've learned that the hard way. No amount of revenge will bring back what you had."

"And runnin' and pretending to be tough as nails doesn't make it go away," she added.

"You're the strongest woman I've ever known, Lily."

"Something to be said about being delicate and well mannered, too. Smooth hair and pretty talk must appeal to a man."

"Don't ever compare yourself to another woman."

"Pretty hopeless?"

"I've never met a woman as beautiful or one who got my blood pumpin' the way you do."

"You do want me, don't you, Sheriff?"

"I've wanted you since the first day I clapped eyes on you. You're the one who spouted all that 'I'm Lily Divine' stuff and made me think you didn't need me."

"It was easier to believe I didn't need you and to point out how wrong I was for you before someone else did it," she said softly.

"Nobody's gonna tell me you're wrong for me," he said. "Even if they did, I'd know better. We're alike, you know."

She skimmed his jaw and framed his face in one palm. "How?"

"Both livin' in our own safe little worlds where we weren't going to let anyone in. Both of us afraid to feel."

"I couldn't admit that I'd ever want a man in my life. I couldn't let myself love," she told him.

"This isn't a risk," he promised her. "I don't want any of your property. I don't ever want you to feel like you're not in charge of your life. If you'll just give me your love, I'll treasure it. And you. For all my days. I can't make up for what happened in your past. But I can promise you love in your future. I love you, Lily. Marry me and let me show you every day."

Lily's heart swelled with joy. "You sure you don't want a delicate little wife who sews and cooks and waits on you hand and foot?"

"Positive."

"'Cause you still have a chance at finding one. Once I say yes, you're stuck with me. And I won't be giving up the Shady Lady or my friends there." She stroked his jaw. "I might be persuaded to give up the red dress."

"How about if you wear it just for me?"

Lily kissed him with every bit of love she'd been holding back. She held him close and felt the beat of his heart against hers.

"You'll marry me, then?" he asked.

"I'll marry you. I love you, Sheriff."

They made love on the bank of the stream with the frogs chirping a love song and the stars winking approval. Nate told her all the ways he was going to make her his and proceeded to make good on his promises.

Lily gave herself body and soul to a man for the first time in her life, speaking his name in the stillness of the night, whispering words of love and trembling with the tide of emotion that crested over her.

Much later, Nate helped her dress and ran his fingers through her wild mane of hair. "I love your hair, Lily. It's wild and untamed, like your spirit."

She laughed and wrapped her arms around him. "And here I just thought it was difficult and unmanageable."

He helped her up and swung into the saddle behind her. "I wouldn't change anything about you."

They rode back to town and dismounted in front of her door. "Can we go into the Shady Lady?" he asked.

She dug into her skirt pocket for the key and opened the front door.

Nate lit two lanterns and set them both on the bar. "There is one change I'd like to make."

She gave him a skeptical glance. "What's that?"

He pointed. "That portrait. From now on, I think I should be the only man who appreciates the delights of your lovely form."

She relaxed her guard. "Edward Mulvaney would probably appreciate knowing how fond you are of that painting."

"Who is Edward Mulvaney?"

"He's a painter studying in the east. Someday when my portrait is long forgotten, people will still remember him."

"I know I want to hear all about him."

Lily laughed. "He's a man with a vivid imagination."

"And a fairly accurate one, too," he replied, studying the alluring curves of the body in the painting.

Lily pulled a stool behind the bar and took down the painting. "Here you go, Sheriff. Lock it up. From here on out, Lily Divine is yours alone."

AMERICAN *Romance*®

A three-book series by
Kaitlyn Rice

Heartland Sisters

To the folks in Augusta, Kansas, the three sisters are
the Blume girls—a little pitiable, a bit mysterious and
different enough to be feared.

THE LATE BLOOMER'S BABY
(Callie's story)

Callie's infertility treatments paid off more than a year
after she and her husband split up. Now she's racked
by guilt. She's led her ex-husband to believe the toddler
she's caring for is her nephew, not Ethan's son!

Available October 2005

Also look for:
The Runaway Bridesmaid (Isabel's story)
Available February 2006

The Third Daughter's Wish (Josie's story)
Available June 2006

American Romance
Heart, Home and Happiness

Available wherever Harlequin books are sold.

SPECIAL EDITION™

Go on an emotional journey in the next
book in

Marie Ferrarella's

miniseries

THE CAMEO

Don't miss:

SHE'S HAVING A BABY

**Available October 2005
Silhouette Special Edition #1713**

Left heartbroken and pregnant,
MacKenzie Ryan scoffed at her best friend's
suggestion she wear the legendary cameo
that paired the wearer with her true love in
one day's time...until she slipped it on and
Dr. Quade Preston moved in next door!
Could the legend of love be real?

Available at your favorite retail outlet.

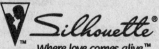

Where love comes alive™

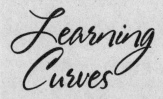
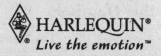

If you enjoyed what you just read,
then we've got an offer you can't resist!

Take 2 bestselling love stories FREE!

Plus get a FREE surprise gift!

Clip this page and mail it to Harlequin Reader Service®

IN U.S.A.	IN CANADA
3010 Walden Ave.	P.O. Box 609
P.O. Box 1867	Fort Erie, Ontario
Buffalo, N.Y. 14240-1867	L2A 5X3

YES! Please send me 2 free Harlequin Historicals® novels and my free surprise gift. After receiving them, if I don't wish to receive anymore, I can return the shipping statement marked cancel. If I don't cancel, I will receive 6 brand-new novels every month, before they're available in stores! In the U.S.A., bill me at the bargain price of $4.69 plus 25¢ shipping and handling per book and applicable sales tax, if any*. In Canada, bill me at the bargain price of $5.24 plus 25¢ shipping and handling per book and applicable taxes**. That's the complete price and a savings of over 10% off the cover prices—what a great deal! I understand that accepting the 2 free books and gift places me under no obligation ever to buy any books. I can always return a shipment and cancel at any time. Even if I never buy another book from Harlequin, the 2 free books and gift are mine to keep forever.

246 HDN DZ7Q
349 HDN DZ7R

Name	(PLEASE PRINT)	
Address	Apt.#	
City	State/Prov.	Zip/Postal Code

Not valid to current Harlequin Historicals® subscribers.

Want to try two free books from another series?
Call 1-800-873-8635 or visit www.morefreebooks.com.

* Terms and prices subject to change without notice. Sales tax applicable in N.Y.
** Canadian residents will be charged applicable provincial taxes and GST.
All orders subject to approval. Offer limited to one per household.
® are registered trademarks owned and used by the trademark owner and or its licensee.

HIST04R   ©2004 Harlequin Enterprises Limited